I've travelled the world twice over,
Met the famous: saints and sinners,
Poets and artists, kings and queens,
Old stars and hopeful beginners,
I've been where no-one's been before,
Learned secrets from writers and
    cooks
All with one library ticket
To the wonderful world of books.

© JANICE JAMES.

A DAMNED SERIOUS BUSINESS

At first, the driver slumped over his BMW looked like another drunken driver come to grief, but when he turns out to be a diplomat, everything changes. Everyone is involved — the Foreign Office, MI5, MI6, the Germans and the Pakistani Secret Service. When Detective Chief Superintendent John Gaffney goes to Islamabad, the search for a solution discovers other startling information, until finally, the whole network of intrigue is laid bare.

GRAHAM ISON

A DAMNED
SERIOUS
BUSINESS

Complete and Unabridged

ULVERSCROFT
Leicester

First published in Great Britain in 1990 by
Macmillan London Limited
London

First Large Print Edition
published March 1992
by arrangement with
Macmillan London Limited
London

British Library CIP Data

Ison, Graham
A damned serious business.—Large print ed.—
Ulverscroft large print series: mystery
I. Title
823.914 [F]

ISBN 0–7089–2610–X

Published by
F. A. Thorpe (Publishing) Ltd.
Anstey, Leicestershire
Set by Words & Graphics Ltd.
Anstey, Leicestershire
Printed and bound in Great Britain by
T. J. Press (Padstow) Ltd., Padstow, Cornwall

1

THE light rain had started just after midnight. It had cooled the temperature enough to make the humid night a little more bearable, but had put a glistening sheen on the greasy surface of the road sufficient to make it treacherous. It also meant that the crew of the police area car had had to wind up the windows or get wet.

The BMW had skidded off the road on one of the few bends on the division that had a grass verge. The car, fortunately, had had nothing to hit, and had come to rest gently, its headlights staring blindly into a front garden that was a wide expanse of lawn sweeping upwards to one of the more expensive houses in the neighbourhood.

Inman grunted and braked to a standstill, but Oakley was already out and running. With a sigh at such youthful impetuosity, Inman switched on the blue beacon as a warning to any traffic there might be at that time in the morning, and sauntered across to join his colleague.

"By the smell of him, he's well pissed," said Oakley, who was vigorously shaking the figure slumped over the steering wheel.

Inman yawned. "So wake him up and breathalyse him."

"Yes, right." Oakley ran back to the police car, found the breath-testing meter and ran back again.

"I don't know what you're rushing about for," said Inman. "There's no bloody hurry. He's not going to escape."

The driver was roused, muttering incoherently, and tested.

"Positive," said Oakley triumphantly.

Inman just nodded, and taking the keys from the BMW's ignition walked round to the back of the car. He unlocked the boot and peered in. An expensive leather overnight case was all that it contained and Inman opened it, wondering if he would find any drugs.

"Anything?" asked Oakley, now supporting the driver who was out of the car but leaning heavily against it.

Inman chuckled. "Mostly sexy under-wear," he said. "Ladies' underwear." He held up a pair of skimpy black briefs that were little more than a triangle.

Oakley laughed. "One of those, are you?" he said, turning back to the driver of the BMW, but the man just stared blankly at him.

Inman closed the leather bag and slammed the boot shut. Then he rejoined his colleague and studied the driver of the car closely. He was probably about thirty and well dressed in a dark suit with a tie that looked as though it meant something. "This your car?" he asked.

The driver blinked. "Not exactly, officer." He was quite coherent now and had probably been overcome by sleep rather than alcohol despite being over the limit.

"What's that supposed to mean?"

"It belongs to a friend."

"Oh yes? And what's your friend's name?"

"Do you have to . . . I mean is it necessary . . . ?"

"Don't ponce about," said Inman. "I've just checked it on the computer."

While Oakley had been flapping around, Inman had done a check on the registration. He looked down at his pocket-book. "The registered keeper is a Mrs Gisela Hunter of Number Five Fancourt Mansions, Kensington. Is that the friend you're talking about?" The driver nodded and looked at the ground. "And who are you?" asked Inman.

The driver did not respond immediately and Inman reached into the man's inside pocket and took out his wallet.

"Here I say — "

Inman ignored the protest. "Roy Foster. Is that you?"

"Yes."

"Right, now we're getting somewhere." Inman kept hold of the wallet. "So, Mr Foster. Your friend is this Mrs Hunter, and she lent you her car, yes?"

"Well, I er . . . "

"We shall check, Mr Foster."

"Well, not exactly."

"I see. Anything you say will be given in evidence." Inman glanced at his watch, noted the time in his pocket-book and then wrote the word 'Caution' beside it. He looked up at Foster again and raised his eyebrows. It wasn't exactly a question, but Foster felt impelled to say something.

"I sort of borrowed it."

"In other words, you took the vehicle without the owner's consent?"

"Yes." Foster's answer came in a whisper.

"And the kinky underwear in the boot . . . is that yours?"

Foster looked genuinely puzzled. "I don't know what's in the boot," he said.

Inman nodded. "Roy Foster, I am arresting you for taking a conveyance without consent of the owner, and driving under the influence of alcohol. I've already told you that anything you say will be given in evidence." He shut his pocket-book with a decisive snap. "Well, put him in the car," he said to Oakley.

"Has this vehicle been reported lost or stolen?" asked the Custody Sergeant.

"No, skip, but the owner may not know it's gone, yet. Our friend only took it about thirty minutes before we found him." Inman leaned against a filing cabinet.

"From where?" The Custody Sergeant laid down his pen and stretched.

"Dunno. From outside her address presumably."

"What does he say?" The Sergeant glanced through the glass panel into the charge room where Foster sat on a bench, head bowed, hands linked loosely between his legs.

"Won't say anything, not since the Divisional Surgeon took the sample. I think he's sobered up a bit now, and realises he's in bother."

"Well, we'll need her to sign the charge-sheet, this . . . " He paused and shuffled through the papers on his desk. "Mrs Hunter. Got her phone number, have you?"

"Ex-directory."

"Doesn't matter. The operator'll put you through." The Sergeant paused. "It might be better to go and see her, I suppose. Where does she live?"

"Kensington." Inman handed a sheet of paper across the desk. "That's the computer print-out on the car."

"There's something a bit odd here, Sid. She's a friend, so he says, but he nicks her car. Now he clams up. Odd. And what about the kinky underwear?"

"Says he knows nothing about it. Quite frankly it looks like tom's stuff. Black and red. G-strings and suspender belts. All that sort of gear. There's a bit of make-up, too . . . hairbrush and a can of hairspray."

"Is she on the game, d'you reckon?"

Inman shrugged. "Could be. But we haven't seen her, skip."

"Could check the toms register at the Yard." The Sergeant was a worrier. "Is he her ponce, d'you reckon?"

"Shouldn't think so. He doesn't look the part. Could have been a customer, I suppose. Maybe she's one of those high-class call-girls. But does it matter?"

The Sergeant frowned. "He's not in the job, is he?" he asked, unhappy at having loose ends. He didn't think so, but he had known of policemen being found drunk at the wheel of a car and having kinky underwear in the boot, or even having it off with a prostitute. They usually clammed up at the station, as

Foster had done, and, more often than not, claimed to be a civil servant or a clerk.

"There's no warrant card among his property, skip. But there is a government pass. One of those for getting into official buildings."

"Where's it for?"

"No idea. They don't put it on them."

"What's he say he does?"

"Clerk." Inman smiled cynically. "But they all say that."

"Go and see her." The Sergeant stood up.

"What, at two in the morning?"

"What's wrong with that? Crime never stops." The Sergeant glanced across at another constable. "Where's the jailer?"

"He's at grub, sarge," said the PC. "I'm relieving."

"Right. Put Foster down until we've sorted this out. Oh, and Sid . . . "

"Yes, skip?"

"Take Oakley with you. If she is a tom, I don't want any nasty allegations."

Inman looked offended. "I was going to," he said. "Anyway, he's my wireless operator."

8

Number Five Fancourt Mansions was on the second floor of a century-old block of large flats in that labyrinth of streets that lies to the west of the Albert Hall. Most of the residents in the area were either retired people with money, or retired people without money trying to pretend, for the sake of appearances, that they still had money. Among them were to be found the last survivors of those who had served the Empire in India and Africa, many of whom still believed all people of dark hue to be subservient, and who constantly complained to the police about youthful Iranian or Arab neighbours whose late-night parties and booming stereos they could never — and would never — come to terms with. It was not the disturbance that irritated them so much as the fact that their swarthy neighbours were now richer than they.

Inman had to press the bell-push for some time before the intercom crackled and a voice answered irritably. "Yes, what is it?" There was a pause.

"The police madam," said Inman.

"How do I know that?"

"If you look out of the window you'll see us . . . and a bloody great police car," he added quietly as he turned away.

The two officers retraced their steps to the pavement and looked up expectantly. After a while a curtain twitched, followed a few moments later by a buzzing noise as the safety lock on the communal front door was released.

The two policemen made their way silently up the carpeted stairs and tapped lightly on the door of Number Five. There was a further pause while the occupant examined her callers through the spy-hole and then, finally, she admitted them.

The woman who opened the door looked to be about forty-two, was tall, and dressed in a floor-length black satin robe, from beneath which peeped bare feet with red painted toe-nails. She had short black hair flecked with grey and high cheekbones that gave her face a sculptured appearance and made her attractive without being beautiful. Inman had to acknowledge that she could be a prostitute.

"Mrs Gisela Hunter?"

"D'you know what time it is?" The woman had left the door open and was walking back down the hallway as she spoke.

"Nearly a quarter to three," said Inman, following her and leaving Oakley to shut the door.

"Exactly. I just hope this is sufficiently important for me to be woken up at this hour in the morning." Her English was good but Inman detected the slight trace of a foreign accent that he couldn't place.

Mrs Hunter led the way into an elegant sitting room, pausing to touch a switch which illuminated a solitary brass standard lamp. Inman, the older of the two policemen, felt uncomfortably out of place in his uniform, as though his very presence might sully the expensive decor. He was no expert but the carpet looked as though it had cost a fortune, and he was pretty sure that some of the furniture was genuine antique. As for the painting over the fireplace, that would probably buy him a new car . . . a top of the range car at that.

"You'd better sit down," said the

woman, carefully arranging herself in the centre of a sofa that was upholstered in tan velvet. "Well?" She looked imperiously at Inman.

"Do you know a Mr Roy Foster, Mrs Hunter?"

Gisela Hunter gazed at the policeman for some moments. "I might." Her response was cold, incisive.

"Only might?"

"It rather depends on what you're going to say next." She seemed unperturbed by the arrival of the police in the middle of the night, apart from her annoyance at having been woken, and Inman wondered if she had guessed why they were there.

"He was found in possession of your car."

"Oh, is that all?" She smiled and relaxed against the large cushions.

"Not quite, Mrs Hunter. He had been drinking and a breath-test showed him to be over the limit."

"Oh no! Oh, poor Roy."

"He also admitted, under caution, that he had taken the car without your permission."

"What nonsense. Of course he had my

permission." She forced a laugh. "You surely don't think he's a thief do you?"

Inman spread his hands. "He admitted to taking it, and taking a conveyance is an offence under the Theft Act, madam.

"Oh, how ridiculous. He must have had more to drink than I thought." She looked away, glancing at two glasses on the low table. Each contained a tired-looking slice of lemon.

"He had been here . . . drinking with you, then?"

Mrs Hunter probably realised that she had said too much. Thought perhaps she might get into trouble herself. In common with most people, she was unsure of what the law of aiding and abetting really meant. "Yes he had. But I went to bed. We only had the one drink and I was terribly tired. I left him here. He wanted to see the end of a television programme, so I left the car keys and asked him to lock up."

"I see." Inman nodded, apparently satisfied. "Well, that all seems to be all right," he said quickly. "So you're not willing to sign the charge-sheet?"

"Whatever for?" The woman raised her eyebrows.

"I mean you're not willing to say that he took your car without your permission."

"I've just said all that." Mrs Hunter looked despairingly at Inman, wondering why policemen were so dim at times, which was exactly what he wanted her to think. It may have been that she didn't want to get involved, and he didn't really blame her for that. Particularly if there was a Mr Hunter somewhere . . . or a Mrs Foster.

"There's just one other thing, Mrs Hunter . . . " Inman stood up.

"Yes?"

"We found a quantity of ladies' underwear in the boot of the car."

"Well, it is my car," she said curtly.

"It is your property, then?"

"Of course." She looked at the policeman coldly. "I suppose you've been through it?"

"We always search vehicles coming into police possession, madam."

"Well?"

"Nothing. I just wanted to be sure that

it was yours, that's all."

"Did you think that Roy was a transvestite, then? Or couldn't you bring yourself to believe that a woman in her forties would wear sexy bras and G-strings?" She lifted her chin provocatively, trying deliberately to embarrass Inman, but he was too old. He'd seen it all before.

"Is your car insured to be driven by Mr Foster, madam?" asked Oakley.

Gisela Hunter chewed briefly at her bottom lip. Oakley reckoned she must have put lipstick on to receive him and Inman. Either that or she hadn't bothered to take it off before retiring. "I think so. Yes, I'm sure."

"Perhaps we could see the certificate, madam?"

Mrs Hunter stood up with a toss of her head and strode haughtily from the room.

"What d'you reckon, Sid?" Oakley spoke in a whispered aside to his colleague.

Inman shook his head. "Don't know. Probably just that she's over the side with Foster."

Gisela Hunter returned and thrust a piece of paper under Oakley's nose. "That says 'any driver'. I presume it includes Mr Foster?" she added sarcastically.

Oakley laboriously wrote the details in his pocket-book before returning the certificate of insurance. "Thank you, madam," he said.

"What happens now?" Mrs Hunter stood facing the two PCs.

"We await the result of the blood-test," said Inman. "But you can collect your car from the police station whenever you like. And your other property."

"Thank you. Kensington, is it?"

"No madam. Barnes."

"Good God, but that's miles away."

Inman smiled. "Good night, madam."

"It seems a bit odd, I must say." The Custody Sergeant shook his head. "Why admit to nicking a car when he didn't? He must have known we'd check."

"P'raps she's lying," said Inman.

"D'you reckon she is a tom, Sid?" asked the Sergeant, still worrying.

Inman shrugged. "Could be, skip. She certainly looked the part. Black satin robe, barefooted, painted toe-nails. There again, she might be an actress . . . or just a woman who knows what it's all about." He grinned. "I reckon she does, too. But what the hell? She won't sign the charge-sheet, so taking a conveyance is a non-starter and her insurance covers him even if his own doesn't. That just leaves the breathalyser. So they're having it off! That's no offence."

"Okay. But we'll see what he says. Get him up, Sid, and I'll bail him."

"Sober enough is he?"

"Sober enough to hail a cab. He's not getting Mrs Hunter's car back, that's for sure."

A contrite and dishevelled Roy Foster was brought back into the charge room and seated on a chair in front of the Custody Sergeant's desk.

"Officers have been to see Mrs Hunter — " began the Sergeant.

Foster looked up in alarm and glanced at the charge-room clock. "What, in the middle of the night?"

"Yes," said the Sergeant mildly. "And she wasn't too happy. Not with you, anyway. However, she denies that you took her car without permission. Says, in fact, that she gave you the keys."

"But that's not true. You see, I — "

"Is she a prostitute, Mr Foster?" asked the Custody Sergeant, hoping to resolve his niggling doubt.

Foster looked startled at the suggestion, as though it was something he'd not considered. "No," he said, "she most certainly is not." There was anger in his voice, prompted more by the implication that he was the sort of man who would consort with such women, than because of the slur it cast on Gisela Hunter. "I think I need to talk to someone," he said slowly.

"Once you've signed this recognisance you're free to go," said the Sergeant. "Then you can talk to who you like."

Foster stood up and signed the several forms on the desk before pocketing the notice that the Sergeant gave him. "That's not quite what I meant," he said. "You see I work at the Foreign Office, and I think I'm in trouble."

The Sergeant frowned. "What sort of trouble?"

Foster glanced at the two constables.

"I'd rather talk to someone higher up if you wouldn't be offended."

"Not at all," said the Sergeant cheerfully. He was never offended when someone wanted to avoid giving him any work. "But I'll need to know something, otherwise I shan't know who to get in touch with! What are you talking about? Fraud, ringing motor cars, drugs, prostitutes?" He put emphasis on the last word.

Foster hesitated and the Sergeant looked over at the two PCs. "All right," he said. "You can get back on patrol. And don't be late booking off." It was a wry, policeman's way of telling them to look after themselves. He turned back to Foster. "Well, sir," he said, "and what is this problem of yours, exactly?"

"I think it's espionage," said Foster.

2

ROY FOSTER was a bit disappointed that his allegation had not been taken more seriously by the Custody Sergeant at Barnes Police Station. But then he was not to know that almost every day people walk into police stations all over London wishing to inform the authorities of the most bizarre matters. Sometimes they are people who have been taken there to be charged with an offence and mistakenly believe that the police will trade leniency for information. Others are playing out wild fantasies, although in all fairness some believe their own fears and suspicions. Probably less than ten per cent have something of substance to report.

Shortly before bailing Foster, the Custody Sergeant had telephoned Scotland Yard and spoken to an officer called the Night Reserve Special Branch Sergeant. This officer had listened to the Custody Sergeant's report of espionage with a measure of scepticism — people were always dropping in at the Yard to report the existence of spies — and suggested that Mr Foster call at Scotland Yard at some civilised time when he could be interviewed in the presence of a chief inspector, a necessary requirement when dealing with a person on bail. The Special Branch Sergeant then put down the phone and carried on playing chess with the Night Reserve Detective Constable.

Foster nearly didn't go to Scotland Yard. After his release from the police station he had gone home, made some excuse to his wife about having worked all night on an urgent Foreign Office telegram, and then secretly telephoned the office to report sick before going to bed and sleeping until half-past two in the afternoon.

As a consequence it was well past four o'clock before he reached the main entrance of New Scotland Yard, having nearly turned back on at least two occasions when he thought that he was making too much of it all. He pushed his way through the revolving doors and glanced around, at the eternal flame of the war memorial, at the Roll of Honour containing the names of those officers killed in the execution of their duty, and was mildly surprised to be confronted not by a policeman but by a rather attractive young lady seated at the reception desk.

Foster told the young lady that he had been asked to come there, and after a telephone call and a delay of fifteen minutes he was approached by a youthful-looking man wearing a light grey suit.

"Mr Foster?"

"Yes."

"I'm Detective Sergeant Simpson. I believe you gave some information to the police when you were arrested last night?"

"Yes, that's right."

"What about, sir? I've only got very brief details here." The Sergeant flourished a message flimsy.

Foster looked around the crowded entrance hall. There were several people sitting on the bench seats waiting to be seen, and a uniformed commander stared fretfully out at the roadway wondering why his car had not arrived.

"I'm a diplomat, at the Foreign Office, and I have reason to think that someone is trying to recruit me . . . as a spy." Foster spoke in low tones, fearful of being overheard. The Sergeant looked sceptical, and Foster produced his office pass.

Simpson glanced at the plastic card and shrugged; it could have been a pass to any government building, but it did tend to indicate that Foster was an official of some sort. "I think you'd better come into one of the interview rooms," said the Sergeant. "This way." He led Foster across the entrance hall to a room sparingly furnished with a table and a few chairs. "Just take a seat," he said. He turned to the telephone and tapped out a number. "I shan't keep you a moment, but I have to wait for another officer."

Some five minutes later the door opened and the Sergeant stood up. "This is Mr Foster, sir."

For a moment or two, the man stood in the doorway, his hand resting lightly on the doorknob as he surveyed the diplomat. Then he nodded. "I'm Detective Chief Inspector Tipper," he said. He slammed the door and walked across to the table. "Sit down," he growled, glancing at Simpson. He was not at all happy about having to sit in on an interview for no better reason than that the caller was on bail for drunken driving, and now doubtless had some cock-and-bull drivel to relate about spies. "My sergeant here says you work at the Foreign Office," said Tipper. "Got any proof of that?"

Foster produced his pass once more but the Chief Inspector waved it away. "Doesn't mean anything to me," he said. "Doesn't say anything on there about the Foreign Office."

"Well I'd hardly say I worked there if I didn't, would I?" Foster was beginning to think that giving information to the police was not an easy matter.

"You'd be surprised what people come in here and tell us," said Tipper. "Anyway, what have you got to say?"

"About two months ago, I went to a

reception at the Pakistani Embassy, and I . . . " Foster paused. "Perhaps I should explain that I work in a department at the FCO that interests itself in the Indian sub-continent."

"Really," said Tipper flatly. He was not yet prepared to believe anything this clown said; was firmly convinced that he was trying to get off the hook for drunken driving.

"Anyhow, I went to this reception. They're awfully tedious things really. Hordes of diplomats circulating, being polite to each other, and occasionally meeting someone interesting, usually businessmen, but even they're after something."

"Would you like to get to the point of all this?" said Tipper.

"Yes, well, I met this woman Gisela Hunter. She's German, I believe — perhaps Austrian — and we got talking — "

"Age?"

"I beg your pardon?"

"How old is this Gisela Hunter?"

"Oh, about . . . well, forty-ish, I should think. It's difficult to tell, really."

"Yes, go on."

"She was a very personable woman — "

"Sexually attractive, you mean?" asked Tipper coldly.

Foster frowned. This policeman seemed to have a knack of stripping away the diplomatic niceties that he was accustomed to using. "Yes, I suppose so."

Tipper sniffed. "And what did you talk about?"

"Oh, this and that."

"Would you care to elaborate on that?"

"People mainly. The people who were there. She was very critical. Called them parasites."

"Yes," said Tipper. It was a flat response, and Foster wasn't quite sure whether it was agreement with Gisela Hunter's views or an invitation to continue.

"Well, that was about all, actually."

"And is that it?" asked Tipper brutally.

"Oh no. I met her again, a few weeks later. At the Indian High Commission this time."

"And?"

"We got talking again, but this time she seemed more interested in me. Asked me what I did . . . "

"And did you tell her?"

"Well, I told her I was with the Foreign Office."

"Yes?"

"And she said something trite like how interesting it must be. You know the way people say these ingenuous things at cocktail parties. Anyhow, she asked if I ever went abroad, and of course I said that I did."

"Of course," murmured Tipper.

"But when I said that I was due to go to Pakistan she seemed to get very interested."

"In what way?"

"She asked if I had been before."

"And have you?"

"No. But I've been working in the Pakistan section at the Office. A sort of preparation, I suppose you'd call it."

"And when are you going?"

Foster thought about that. "In about seven or eight weeks' time."

"What form did this renewed interest take?"

"She told me that she knew the country well, had lived there, in Karachi. She went on to say that she had lots of photographs, and asked me if I'd like to see them."

"What did you say?"

"I said that I would. It's always useful to get as much information as you can about a country before going out there."

"So you went and looked at her pictures?"

"Yes."

"Well I suppose it's better than etchings," said Tipper.

"What?"

Tipper shook his head. "Doesn't matter. When did you go?"

"That evening," said Foster. "The reception was due to finish at eight anyway, so we got a cab out to Kensington — she lives near the Albert Hall — "

"Where, exactly?"

"Number Five Fancourt Mansions, which is in . . . " Foster put a finger pensively to his lips. "Isn't that silly? I could take you there, but I can't remember the name of the road."

"Doesn't matter. We'll find it." Foster looked alarmed. "If we have to," Tipper added with a smile, although he had already been told exactly where it was. The Night Reserve Sergeant hadn't just played chess, he'd made a few enquiries too. "So you went and looked at her photographs."

"Yes. She's got a very nice flat. Quite big. We had a couple of drinks and she got out some photograph albums. Expensive leather they were, typically Indian. And we talked."

"About Pakistan?"

"Yes. It was all quite innocuous. And then I went home."

"When?"

"I suppose it must have been about half-past ten, or eleven o'clock. It was certainly early enough for me to get the last tube."

"To where?"

"Richmond. I live in Richmond."

For a moment there was silence in the sterile interview room. "Well, is that it?" asked Tipper eventually.

Foster didn't answer immediately, but sat slumped in his chair, chin on his chest. Then he looked up. "No, it isn't," he said. "About a week later I got a telephone call at the office. It was her . . . "

"Had you given her your phone number, then?"

"No, but the Foreign Office is in the book, and she knew my name and the section I worked in. It wouldn't have been difficult to find me."

"What did she want?"

"She invited me to supper."

"To supper?"

"Yes. She made a point of distinguishing between supper and dinner. Her idea of dinner is when there are other people there and you dress."

Tipper laughed. "Sounds a bit old-hat. And did you go?"

"Yes, I did."

"Did she say why she'd asked you?"

"She said that she'd enjoyed our conversation, and was sorry that I'd had to go — to catch the tube — and anyway, she'd found some more photographs."

"Which you just couldn't wait to see, I suppose?"

Foster stared into space for a second or so. "As a matter of fact," he said slowly, "looking at other people's photographs is pretty boring. No, it was her. She's a very attractive woman, and I wanted to see her again."

"Ah!" Tipper let out a sigh. "And what happened?"

"Nothing really. As a matter of fact, she forgot about the photographs."

"And you didn't remind her. If there were any," Tipper added as an afterthought.

Foster smiled. "That did cross my mind," he said, "but not until later."

"So you just sat and chatted, did you?"

"Yes, we did. It was very pleasant. Supper and a few glasses of wine."

"Very cosy. And was there any mention of Mr Hunter — her husband?"

"Oh yes . . . "

"Was he there?"

"He's dead."

"I see." Tipper smiled.

"He was murdered apparently. In Karachi."

"Recently?"

"No. Some time ago. Nineteen seventy-one, I think she said."

Tipper scratched the side of his nose.

"What did your wife think of this little *tête-à-tête*? You are married, I presume?"

"Yes . . . " Foster looked down at the table. "Actually, she didn't know."

"How did you explain going out for the evening, then? Or didn't you bother?"

"I told her it was another diplomatic reception." Foster sounded guilty.

"Oh. Doesn't she usually go to these things?"

"She's invited, of course. But we've got two small children. We can't always get a baby-sitter."

"No, I suppose not." Tipper sighed deeply. "I'm afraid I can't see why you're apprehensive about this Mrs Hunter's motives, Mr Foster. Or did you see her again?"

"Yes. A week later."

"Further talks about Pakistan?"

"To start with, yes. She was telling me about her husband's business in Karachi."

"Which was?"

"Woollens and textiles. Export. He was a very rich man. Certainly if her life-style's anything to go by, he was."

"And then you finished up in bed with

her, I suppose?" Tipper's question was harsh, but wasn't exactly inspired.

Foster opened his eyes wide in amazement. "How did you know that?"

"I didn't, Mr Foster." Tipper smiled blandly. "I just guessed."

"She's a very attractive woman."

"And personable! Yes, you said all that before." Tipper reached across for the notes that Detective Sergeant Simpson had been making since the interview began. "Your writing's bloody awful, Simpson," he said. There was silence for a moment as Tipper laboured through the scrawl. "Well, Mr Foster," he continued, pushing the sheets of paper back across the table. "So far you've admitted to adultery — grounds for a civil action for divorce, if that worries you — but apart from that . . . " He looked at Foster and grinned. "Quite frankly, I don't know why you're here." He paused for a moment. "If you think that this" — he pointed at Simpson's notes — "is going to get you off the hook for last night's little fiasco, I'm afraid that — "

"Good heavens, no." Foster seemed genuinely shocked that Tipper should have said that. "That in itself was strange, but in any case, there's more to it . . . "

"Thought there might be." Tipper looked pointedly at his watch.

"She put a proposition to me."

Tipper raised an eyebrow. "So I gather."

Foster coloured slightly. "I didn't mean that. The next time I went to see her — "

"Oh, you went again, did you? That would be the third time — at her flat, I mean?"

"Yes. It was a week later."

"And did you go to bed with her again then?"

"Yes." Foster almost whispered it. "And then — when we were in bed — she started to question me about what I would be doing when I got to Islamabad. The sort of work I would be doing, I mean."

"And what did you say?"

"I just told her it was mundane stuff. Paperwork. The sort of thing I was doing here in London."

"And is it?"

34

"No, not quite. There are always diplomatic cables going to and fro, and reports about the state of the country. The political situation, trade, relations with other states, that sort of thing."

"But you didn't tell her that?"

"No. I sort of steered her off the subject. As a matter of fact, I made love to her again."

"A sort of self-sacrifice for the sake of state security, you mean?"

Foster had the good grace to smile. "It was the only thing I could think of."

Tipper smirked at that. "And afterwards?" he asked. "Did she start talking about your job again?"

"No. Not till the next time I went to see her."

"You went again?" Tipper sounded incredulous. "Did it not occur to you that this woman had got you into bed solely to pump you for information?"

"I suppose it did, but I didn't want to face up to that."

"So why did you go back?"

Foster hung his head like a naughty schoolboy. "It was the sex, I suppose," he said softly.

"Christ!" said Tipper. "The oldest trick in the game. And how many times did you go there?"

"Five."

"The fifth being last night?"

"Yes."

"Tell me about it."

"I went straight from the office. Told my wife I had to work late, and not to wait up."

"She accepted that? Your wife, I mean."

Foster nodded. "I often have to work late."

"Okay, but what happened?"

"Well, over the five visits, she had wheedled things out of me about my job." He had been talking with his head down slightly until then, but suddenly he looked up, staring straight at Tipper. "Nothing of any consequence, of course. I mean it wasn't secret, or anything like that."

"Then why were you reticent in the first place, on previous visits?"

"I don't know. I suppose that being at the Foreign Office you're naturally reserved about what you do."

"So what was different about last night?"

"She'd already told me that she had a lot of friends in the government — now that Benazir Bhutto was in power — and that she would put me in touch with them. Arrange for me to meet them, that sort of thing. She said it would help my career."

"So?" Tipper shrugged. "I should imagine that sort of thing goes on all the time. That's what being a diplomat's all about, surely?"

"Yes, it is . . . in a way. But then she said that I could probably be helpful to them, too."

"Ah! And that's when you saw the warning lights?"

"Yes."

"And? What happened then?"

"I said that I didn't think that that was a very good idea. That it could be risky, for me."

"Was she annoyed? Did you get the impression that she felt she'd been wasting her time?"

"No. Quite the reverse. She put her arms round me — we were sitting on the sofa — and then she started to . . . well, you know."

Tipper grinned, which didn't make Foster feel any more comfortable. "Yes, I know. So you went to bed with her . . . again."

"Yes." Foster mumbled his reply.

"If it's not a rude question, Mr Foster, what happened between then and your being arrested?"

Foster stood up, thrusting his hands into his trouser pockets, and walked towards the door. For a moment, Tipper thought that he was going to walk out, but he stopped and turned, leaning against the wall. Then he took a deep breath and looked up at the fluorescent light tube. "I'd had too much to drink," he said. "We'd been drinking all evening."

"Yes, we know."

Foster ignored that. "But afterwards, she went and got a bottle of champagne — Moët, I think — and we started drinking that." He looked reflectively at his feet. "Then she put it to me. She said that she had friends in Islamabad and Karachi who would be grateful for my help from time to time. So grateful, in fact, that they would be prepared to pay, quite handsomely." He paused thoughtfully for a moment. "She didn't actually say that . . . not in as many words. It was more something about making sure that I wouldn't be out of pocket, but the implication was there."

"What did you say to that?"

"I said it was out of the question."

"And what was Mrs Hunter's reaction?"

"She just smiled and took another sip of champagne. Then she asked what my wife would think about me doing what I was doing right then, except that she didn't say 'your wife', she said 'Daphne'."

"Which presumably is your wife's name?"

"Yes. But I'd never told her that."

Tipper shrugged. "Then what happened?"

"I panicked. I didn't know what the hell to do. I leaped out of bed and got dressed. Of course, the last train had gone, so I grabbed her car keys. In fact, I emptied her handbag on to the coffee table in the sitting room and took them. I wasn't thinking straight, otherwise I would have known that I'd had too much to drink . . . "

"Did she try to stop you?"

"No. She just called out from the bedroom. Something about making sure the front door was shut properly. Oh, and she shouted something about looking forward to our next meeting. It sounded rather sinister." He rested his head back against the wall. "I suppose you think I've been rather foolish," he said.

"Frankly, Mr Foster," said Tipper, "I think you've been a complete prat."

Foster walked across and sat down again. Then he leaned forward, a concerned and earnest expression on his face. "I know," he said, "but what do I do now?"

"At the moment, I've no idea," said Tipper. "D'you intend seeing Mrs Hunter again?"

Foster looked startled. "Do you think that's wise?"

"Well, what have we got?" Tipper spoke in matter-of-fact tones, and ran his finger along the edge of the table. "You're a diplomat and you've been having it off with some bird who's about ten years older than you. She has suggested — in very vague terms, from what you say — that you may be able to assist her and her friends in Pakistan, whatever that means. If you don't she'll make sure that your wife knows about your little bit of adultery. That's about the up-and-down of it, isn't it, if you'll excuse the expression? From what you say, she didn't actually ask you to become a spy, to betray Her Majesty's Government, to impart classified information."

"No, I suppose not." Foster looked miserable.

"I don't know what you expected by coming here," said Tipper. "Some sort of forgiveness, some absolution?"

"But I don't know what I should do. I can't very well go to my masters at the Foreign Office with that story. I'd probably get the sack."

Tipper laughed. It was a grating laugh that discomfited Foster. "It's too late to think about that. This isn't the Samaritans here, you know." He waved a hand round the room. "This is the police you've been talking to. I shall speak to my superiors about it and if they think the Foreign Office should be told, they'll tell them."

"Oh God!" Foster ran a hand through his hair. "What a bloody fool I've been."

"I think that's been established," said Tipper drily. He stood up. "Now listen. You did the right thing coming here. So far it would appear that you've done nothing very serious, not if you've told me the truth. You've done nothing you can go to prison for. Whether you get into trouble with your own bosses is between you and them. I shall talk to my guv'nor, and I'll be in touch with you . . . quite soon."

"Should I see Gisela again?"

"Matter for you," said Tipper. "If you can put her off without arousing her suspicions, then do so. But if not, keep your mouth shut . . . even if you can't keep your trousers on."

Foster flashed a hostile look at the Chief Inspector. "How long will it be before you get in touch with me?"

"Tomorrow, I should think. Maybe the day after."

"Thank you." Foster held out his hand.

"Goodbye, Mr Foster," said Tipper.

"Thank you for coming." He waited until Foster had reached the door. "Don't throw yourself off Westminster Bridge, will you? It's not worth it. Apart from anything else, it's unpleasant for the river police."

3

"**W**HAT is it, Harry?" Detective Chief Superintendent John Gaffney, head of the Special Branch International Squad, looked up from the report he was reading.

"Just had a caller, sir, here at CO." Tipper used the abbreviation for Commissioner's Office, the official title of New Scotland Yard.

"You saw a caller?" Gaffney smiled quizzically.

"Case of having to, guv'nor. He's on bail for driving with excess alcohol."

"Is that relevant?"

"Partly, yes." Tipper sat down and put the sheaf of Simpson's notes on the corner of Gaffney's desk.

"Well, let's have it."

Tipper summarised Foster's story as succinctly as possible and pushed the papers towards his chief.

Gaffney lit a cigar and sat thoughtfully for a moment or two. "Anything in it, d'you reckon?"

Tipper shrugged. "Dunno, frankly. Might be. But what's with Pakistan?"

"Daggers drawn with India. Despite Benazir Bhutto's summit with Rajiv Gandhi, despite all their fraternal exchanges of goodwill, et cetera, et cetera."

"D'you mean that this Mrs Hunter — a German or an Austrian, widow of a Brit — could be a Pakistani spy?"

Gaffney nodded slowly. "Every nation's got its spies, Harry, and a lot of them are here in London. It's where it all happens, after all."

"So what do we do? I've told this bloke Foster that I'll let him know. He's practically coming apart at the seams. He can see his marriage and his career going to pieces."

"Well, that's his problem," said Gaffney. "He's made his bed, and he's got to lie on it."

"I think he quite enjoyed that bit," said Tipper. "It's the rest of it that worries him."

"Two things," said Gaffney. "First we talk to Five, see if they know anything.

Then we talk to the FCO. After that — if Five are agreeable — we make some enquiries about the mysterious, and promiscuous, Mrs Hunter."

"Yeah, fine, but what do we tell Foster?"

"For the moment, to keep his head down."

"And other parts of his anatomy, too."

Hector Toogood always had a cold feeling of misgiving when a senior officer of Special Branch wanted to see him on an urgent matter. Toogood had been a Security Service officer for some years, long enough to have developed an ingrained caution. Normally he had time to ponder problems, and didn't like being forced into the corner of instant decisions.

"John, come in, come in. And Harry. Nice to see you both." He didn't mean it.

"I'll let Harry explain," said Gaffney, settling himself into one of Toogood's austere and uncomfortable government armchairs. "He got the story first-hand."

Harry Tipper made himself as

comfortable as possible and related Roy Foster's story.

Toogood listened in silence, tight-lipped and tense, and remained silent for some time after Tipper had finished. "Mmm . . . " he said eventually.

"I thought you'd be impressed," said Tipper. "But what do we tell Foster?"

"Nothing!"

"What? Tell him nothing, or tell him to do nothing?" Tipper smiled at the other's discomfort.

Toogood looked exasperated. "We can't guess at this," he said. "We don't know what we've got. We'll have to make some enquiries first."

"So let's do it," said Gaffney. "We've found out a little about Gisela Hunter."

"Oh?"

"Born Gisela Toller in Bad Salzuflen, West Germany, in nineteen forty-seven. Married Richard Hunter in London in nineteen sixty-seven. She was then twenty," he added unnecessarily. "Roy Foster, born Croydon nineteen fifty-eight. LSE and then Foreign Office. Married Daphne Rudd in nineteen eighty-four. They have two children. And that's it."

"What's her interest in Pakistan?"

"We only know what she told Foster. Her husband was in business in Karachi, exporting textiles, and was murdered there in nineteen seventy-one. He was British, born in India, and was quite a bit older than her. I think she told Foster that he was forty-one when he died, so that would make him born nineteen thirty." Gaffney looked at Tipper for confirmation.

Toogood shook his head slowly. "Well, I don't know . . . " he said.

"You mean if it's not KGB, you're knackered," said Tipper unkindly.

"Well it might be. KGB, I mean." Toogood was clearly at a loss.

"The first thing we've got to do, I should think," said Gaffney, realising that he wasn't going to get a quick decision out of Toogood, "is to investigate the Hunter woman's background thoroughly . . . and discreetly. Then we might know what we're dealing with. In the meantime, it might be useful to know if you've got anything on record about her." He dropped his cigar butt into an ashtray. "And to see if your sister service has anything as well."

"Yes, good idea," said Toogood, brightening a little. "But what about Foster?"

"What about him?"

"He'll have to be briefed."

"What a good idea," said Tipper. "And that gets us back to the original problem: what do we tell him?"

"I don't think he's too much of a problem," said Gaffney. "At least he's alert to what's happening. Or what he thinks is happening. His two concerns are what happens if his wife finds out . . . and the Foreign Office."

"Well he won't have to wait long to find out what the F and CO think about it," said Toogood, with an uncharacteristic earthiness. "We're going to have to speak to them fairly soon. I think we'd better have a conference."

"Ah!" said Gaffney with a sigh, "I wondered when we'd get around to that."

Detective Superintendent Terry Dobbs locked his car and glanced briefly around Horse Guards Parade before walking casually to the garden gate of Number

Ten Downing Street. The stands were still in place although it was now nearly two weeks since the Queen's Birthday Parade had been held. But there were still one or two other events to take place, like the Royal Marines beating retreat. It was an annual upheaval that he did not relish; it meant finding somewhere else to park his car on the occasions that the parade ground was used for its real purpose.

He walked slowly up the garden path, looking at the flowers so carefully tended by the Prime Minister, who managed to spend a few hours out there each week despite the pressing engagements of a full calendar. There was a sprinkling of moisture on the roses from the overnight air, and the flowers of the passiflora growing over the wall on the sunny side of the garden were beginning to open in the morning sunlight. Across to one side was what the Prime Minister called the patriotic bed: a mass of scarlet geraniums and blue cornflowers behind a border of white alyssum.

Dobbs waved at one of the girls who was standing at the Garden Room window before letting himself in the back door and making his way upstairs to the ground floor and his office, tucked away in the narrow corridor between Number Ten and the Chancellor of the Exchequer's residence next door at Number Eleven.

Bill Carson, the detective chief inspector who acted as Dobbs' deputy, was already in, sitting at the desk with a cup of coffee and going through the Prime Minister's definitive list of engagements that arrived in that and all the other offices at Number Ten early each morning.

"Morning, guv," said Carson. "Coffee's on."

"Anything changed?" Dobbs walked across to the coffee machine and poured himself a cup.

"They've poked in a lunch. The Anglo-Pakistan Society. George reckons it's been on the stocks for some time, but it's the first I've heard of it."

"I shall have to talk to that young man," said Dobbs. "It's not the first time he's slipped in something like that." George Perry was the assistant secretary who dealt with the Prime Minister's home engagements.

"He reckoned it wasn't his fault," said Carson. "Says the Foreign Office bloke put it in."

"Where is it?"

"Claridges."

"Bloody hell," said Dobbs. "They haven't just dreamed that up. They must have known for weeks."

"That's what I said, but apparently the PM's been dithering about whether to accept. Thought that something else might get in the way . . . "

"But it didn't presumably?"

"Well it did, but they moved it. Perry said something about the PM going to Pakistan and India in the near future, so suddenly it's become important."

"India and Pakistan? When was that decided?"

Carson shrugged. "Search me, sir. I can't keep up with it all." He grinned and poured himself another cup of coffee.

"What have you done about this Claridges thing, then?"

"Sent Peter up there to have a look round, get the lie of the land, and I've telephoned the Traffic Superintendent at

Area Headquarters, and the Diplomatic Protection Group. We shall have cones and policemen all over the place."

"Good." Dobbs hung his jacket behind the door, slipped his revolver out of its holster and unloaded it before laying it on the table. Then he sat down in an armchair. "There's been something in the wind about India for some time," he said. "I'd better see Charles Morris and get some details. Then we'll have to decide who's going out there to do the advance." He took a sip of coffee. "Been out there before, Bill?"

Carson shook his head. "No. Should make a nice change."

Dobbs frowned. "If you like that sort of thing," he said. "Frankly, the only thing that'll make a nice change for me will be to get off this bloody job altogether."

"How long will that be?"

"Another six months, if I'm lucky." Dobbs had been at Number Ten for nearly three years now, and had found that the initial glory — if ever there was any — of being the Principal Protection Officer to the Prime Minister very soon paled in the face of constantly living out of a suitcase, going to dinners that were both unpalatable and boring, and rarely getting home before eleven o'clock at night. And that didn't include late sittings at the House, or even the occasional all-night session.

Charles Morris was a diplomat. Seconded to Number Ten from the Foreign Office, with which he maintained a direct link, he acted as the Prime Minister's day-to-day adviser on foreign affairs and ranked equal to the Principal Private Secretary with whom he shared an office between the private office and the Cabinet Room.

"Got a minute, Charles?" Dobbs paused in the doorway.

"Morning, Terry. Of course. Come in." Morris was every bit the urbane official. "I suppose you've come to have a go at me about this wretched Anglo-Pakistani lunch thing, have you?"

"Not particularly, although we do appreciate more notice than that."

"Of course, of course. I can only apologise, but it wasn't firmed up until late last night."

Dobbs nodded. He didn't believe that for a moment, but there was no sense in making waves. He would mention it directly to the PM who had made it plain on more than one occasion that failure to keep the protection team fully informed of what was going on would not be tolerated. "As a matter of fact, Charles, I'm more concerned about rumours of a trip to Pakistan and India . . . "

"Ah, you know about that." Morris leaned back in his chair and balanced a government-issue paper-knife delicately between his two index fingers.

"Yes . . . but not much."

"Not been finalised yet, of course, but it looks very much as though the PM will be going in about four weeks' time. Two days in Islamabad, and two more in New Delhi seems to be the plan."

"Sudden, isn't it?" Overseas visits were generally planned well in advance, often as much as a year ahead.

Morris laid the paper-knife on his desk. "Well, Terry, you know how these things happen. All a case of fitting it into the calendar." He leaned forward suddenly, purposefully. "I'll let you have the provisional programme by the end of the week. Very much a business trip. Long sessions with heads of government, little bit of sightseeing, and meeting the expats at the embassy stroke high commission, as appropriate." He smiled. "But then you'll know the form only too well."

"Thanks," said Dobbs, rising from his chair. "Nothing sensational about it, then?"

"Good heavens no," said Morris. "Been in the wind for a long time, actually."

Dobbs nodded. "Thanks for letting me know," he said, leaving Morris uncertain whether that was a sarcastic comment or not. Dobbs could never understand why there were occasions when routine information of this sort had to be extracted like teeth.

"That's the report about our trip to Pakistan and India, sir," said Dobbs, laying the report on Detective Chief Superintendent George Winter's desk. "I've put myself down to do the advance."

Winter slid the report across and placed it squarely on his blotter. "Your typing's improving, Terry," he said.

Dobbs grinned. "Not me," he said. "Got one of the Garden Room girls to do it for me."

"Oh yeah, and what did that cost you?"

"Never you mind, guv," said Dobbs with a laugh. "When am I likely to get the okay for the advance?"

"Tomorrow or the next day, probably. Mr Scott's sitting on a discipline board but he reckons it'll be finished today."

Sir Brian Chester, the Chief Clerk at the Foreign Office, was much more important than his title implied. He was, in fact, the deputy head of the Diplomatic Service, and few, if any, outside the select band of the Whitehall mandarins out-ranked him. In view of that incontrovertible fact, and that the conference had been convened on his own territory — the Foreign and Commonwealth Office — he had naturally assumed its chairmanship.

That such a high-ranking official was involved reflected the concern felt by the Foreign Secretary who had been informed immediately of the matter of Roy Foster. The official who had told him had apologised for troubling him with a trivial matter, but the Foreign Secretary had waved his apology aside and commented that any attempt to suborn a British diplomat, no matter how junior, was a damned serious business. That was not all, of course. In the three days since Roy Foster's appearance at Scotland Yard, some disturbing facts had been uncovered by the combined, but independent, resources of the Security Service, the Secret Intelligence Service, the Metropolitan Police Special Branch, and the Foreign Office itself.

As the representatives of those various organisations had taken their seats, a middle-aged lady in a blue overall had served tea and placed plates of biscuits on the table, ensuring that most of those on the plate nearest the Chief Clerk were Bourbons. It was a necessary preliminary to any conference held in Whitehall.

"Shall we begin, gentlemen?" The Chief Clerk placed his cup and saucer carefully on the table and beamed at the assembled officials. "I am Brian Chester," he said, "for those of you who don't know me." Chester smiled ingenuously at what to him was the unthinkable. "Perhaps it would be useful if we just went round the table introducing ourselves."

John Gaffney explained his own and Harry Tipper's presence, followed by Hector Toogood and finally James Marchant, a senior official of MI6, the Secret Intelligence Service, and an old friend of Gaffney.

"Good, good." Chester rubbed his hands together briskly. "Well now, who's going to bully-off?"

Gaffney knew from experience that conferences of this sort could be tortuous and long-winded, and decided to get things going as quickly as possible. "It might be helpful if Mr Tipper summarised Foster's story to start with," he said, just as Hector Toogood opened his mouth.

"Splendid, yes," said Chester. "Why don't you do that?" He beamed at Harry Tipper.

As succinctly as possible, Tipper outlined what he had learned from

59

his interview with Foster, and what the police had culled from their various sources since. As he finished, he closed the file in front of him and leaned back in his chair. "And that's the story so far," he said with a grin.

"Yes, well, it seems that what we have here is a young man who has become embroiled with an older woman," said Chester, clearly wishing to retain control of the meeting. "And that, of course, could seriously affect his positive vetting."

"Apart from the possibility of catching AIDS," said Tipper quietly.

Chester wrinkled his nose in distaste. "Quite so," he said. "James?" He glanced at Marchant.

"Not much, Sir Brian, but enough, I think." Marchant opened the manila folder in front of him. "This Gisela Hunter, according to sources, is well thought of by the Pakistani people. She was born in nineteen forty-seven . . . We got this from Special Branch incidentally . . . "

Gaffney smiled across the table. Marchant was a crafty old fox and had only made that acknowledgement because

Gaffney was there. Otherwise he would have claimed the credit for himself.

"She was in London as an au pair in nineteen sixty-seven," continued Marchant, "when she met and married Richard Hunter who was here on holiday from Pakistan. A lightning romance apparently. Hunter's first wife had died a couple of years previously from some disease she had contracted in Karachi. Hunter had established himself there a few years after partition and was in a good way of business."

"Doing what?" asked Chester.

"Exporting textiles. But in nineteen seventy-one — at the time of the Indo-Pakistani war — he was murdered by a native who stabbed him in the street." Marchant laid one podgy hand on top of the other. "The man wasn't caught, but the consensus at the time suggested that he was a Hindu fanatic who saw Hunter, as a successful business man in Karachi, to be a supporter of the Moslem regime of Zulfikar Ali Bhutto. Bhutto, the father of the present Prime Minister, was later executed by Zia."

"Yes, we know," said Chester drily.

"Quite," said Marchant. "If the story is true, it could be a reason for Gisela Hunter's bitter opposition to India . . . "

"Do we know that she harbours a bitter opposition to India, then?" asked Chester.

"Er, well . . . " Marchant consulted his file hurriedly.

Gaffney smiled. Marchant had made an assumption, not uncommon in the intelligence community, only to find that the deputy head of the Foreign Office was now seeking some basis for it. He waited with interest to see what James Marchant would pluck from his rag-bag of so-called reliable information.

"We have a report from our German liaison," continued the SIS man, "which suggests that after her husband's death she returned to her native Germany and was active in the diplomatic circles in Bonn and Bad Godesburg — "

"Active in what way?" Chester smiled benignly.

Marchant looked uncomfortable. He didn't like being probed, particularly by the Chief Clerk. "Without prejudicing sources," he said, "it would seem that she tried to persuade a German Foreign Office official to provide information for the Pakistani Government."

"Oh?" Chester raised his eyebrows. "And when was this? And what was done about it?"

Marchant looked down at his papers once more and struggled on. "The BfV looked into it." Marchant interrupted himself to explain. "That's the Bundesamt fur Verfassungsschutz: German equivalent of our sister service."

There were bored nods around the table. They all knew what it meant and didn't like being talked down to.

"Had he, like Foster, slept with her?" Chester obviously wanted all the sordid details, but would doubtless claim, Gaffney thought cynically, that it was only in the interests of accuracy.

"That's not made clear," said Marchant, "but I think it's safe to assume so. However, when the BfV mounted an investigation, they found that she had disappeared."

"Ah," said Tipper. "The bird had flown." It was meant to be funny, but no one laughed.

"Exactly so," said Marchant, straight-faced. "Incidentally, she had reverted to using her maiden name of Toller then."

"And when was all this?" Chester persisted in knowing everything.

"Nineteen seventy-seven, I believe."

"And now she's over here." Chester smiled at Toogood as though he was, in some way, to blame. "Do we know when she arrived?" His glance travelled round the table, his gaze silently interrogating and accusing the other four members of the meeting.

Gaffney was unimpressed. The Foreign Office was nothing to do with him anyway. "There's no way of knowing," he said. "If she holds a British passport — and presumably she does — she can come and go as she pleases. There's no record kept."

"Even if we know that her activities are, shall we say, suspect?"

"I imagine that we didn't know they were until a few days ago," said Gaffney. "I'll bet her name's not in the Immigration Service suspect index." And you can make what you like of that, he thought, glancing across at Toogood whose service's job it was to supply that sort of information to the Home Office.

"Yes, well we don't want to indulge in inter-departmental recriminations, do we?" Chester sighed. "The question really is what are we going to do next?"

"This man Foster is due to go to the British Embassy in Pakistan, I understand?" Toogood spoke for the first time since the meeting had got under way.

"Yes," said Chester. "As First Secretary Political."

"Still?"

"I beg your pardon?"

"You still intend that he should go?" asked Toogood.

"I see no reason for changing his posting. Do you?" Chester put his head on one side, rather like a dog who has seen a tin of pet food emerge from a cupboard.

"No, it's just that I thought — "

"After all, the temptation is here in London."

"He said it would be six or seven weeks before he went," said Gaffney. "I think the thing to consider is whether we can make use of that remaining time."

"In what way?" Chester glanced sharply at the policeman, sensing that one of 'his people' was being considered as a cat's paw and not liking the idea. He had served abroad as an ambassador and always felt apprehensive about the presence of an SIS man at the mission, necessarily masquerading as a 'straight' diplomat. He did not like the underhand — and to his mind rather dirty — world of intelligence-gathering.

"To turn the tables," said Gaffney simply. "Use him to extract information from her. Set a trap, perhaps?"

"Certainly not!" Chester's hand smote the table-top with a sharpness that made Toogood start.

James Marchant smiled. "I think the Chief Clerk is right," he said patronisingly. Gaffney was about to protest when Marchant delivered a back-handed compliment. "From what John says, he's much too naïve to be any good. In fact it would be dangerous. It's a job for a skilled intelligence operative, and frankly to put one in now would be too suspicious. This Hunter woman would be on to it in a moment." He paused and then smiled again disarmingly. "She sounds to me to be a bit of a *femme fatale*."

"I'm not saying that he couldn't handle it," said Chester abruptly. "It's just that I don't hold with a diplomat acting as a . . . as a . . . " He searched his mind for the appropriate phrase. "Acting as an *agent provocateur*."

"Oh, hardly that," said Marchant mildly. "After all, Foster's the one who's been snared. She couldn't really complain if she got her fingers caught in her own trap."

"I think it would be better if we let things take their course, making sure that Foster's debriefed regularly," said Gaffney, anxious to head off what he saw as an impending wrangle between Sir Brian Chester and the man from MI6. "After all, if we direct him to break off the relationship now, without any explanation, this woman Hunter — if she's the professional we suspect she is — is going to guess that Foster has panicked and gone to the police. The likely outcome of that would, I suggest, be her prompt disappearance."

Chester peered out of the window, a sour expression on his face. He knew that Gaffney had a good point, but was loathe to admit it. "Perhaps so," he said grudgingly.

Toogood drummed his fingers silently on the table. It was the only outward sign he ever displayed of mounting anger. "This, of course, is a matter for the Security Service," he said huffily. "Our charter makes us responsible for countering espionage within the United Kingdom." He stressed the last four words.

"But it isn't, is it?" Marchant leaned back in his chair and flicked at a biscuit crumb, sending it scudding across the polished surface of the table. "It's in Pakistan . . . or it will be. And that makes it the responsibility of my service. Alone!"

"Supposing Gisela Hunter's plan — or whoever her masters are — is to replace a spy, a diplomat, who's already in post, but is due home?" Gaffney dropped the idea quietly into the conversation. It had much the same effect as if he had rolled a hand-grenade across the floor.

"That's preposterous." Chester sat up sharply.

"That may be so. But it wouldn't be unique," said Gaffney with a half-smile.

"Still our business," said Marchant.

"Oh? And who would arrest him? The Pakistan police? That would be novel, given that our man would have diplomatic privilege, and that the Pakistanis are interested parties."

"I think we are rather jumping to conclusions," said Chester, "with this talk of arresting people. All we know, this far, is that the woman Hunter seems — and I stress 'seems' — to have made a half-hearted attempt to persuade one of my people to betray his trust. I am far from satisfied," he continued loftily, "that we have a major espionage scandal here."

Gaffney was beginning to tire of this pointless to-and-fro banter. Nothing had been decided, and if the conference proceeded in its present form, nothing would be. "May I suggest," he began, "that we brief Foster not to do anything untoward. In fact, not to alter his behaviour at all, but that we debrief him, — daily, if necessary — until such time as either he goes, or we've found out more about Gisela Hunter." It was more or less a repetition of what he had said earlier, but it was evident that the point needed to be hammered home. Marchant raised a finger as if to interject, but Gaffney went on. "I would remind everyone that espionage is a crime, and that crime is a matter for the police. Alone!"

"But — " Toogood frowned.

Gaffney held up a hand. "I know what you're going to say, Hector, and Special Branch will work with your service — as always — and yours too, James." He glanced at Marchant.

Toogood wasn't going to let that go. "But, John, this is ours, while it's in the UK." He contrived to look crestfallen, as though someone had taken his lollipop away.

Gaffney began to get cross. "Are we all on the same side, or aren't we?" he demanded. "Frankly, I don't give a bugger whose turn it is to play in the Wendy House. We have a suspect spy here who, *prima facie*, has attempted to suborn a Foreign Office official, and that's an offence under the tattered remains of the Official Secrets Act. Either we're going to do something about it — collectively — or we might as well pack up and go home."

A stunned silence followed Gaffney's outburst, during which time Sir Brian Chester picked aimlessly at a mark on the table. Then James Marchant burst out laughing.

"That's about it, John," he said. "Wendy House. I rather like that." And he laughed again.

But Sir Brian Chester always believed in having the last word at any conference over which he presided. "Isn't the Prime Minister going to Pakistan shortly?" he asked airily. And, without waiting for a reply, added, "I suppose that we should satisfy ourselves that there can be no connection."

4

GAFFNEY wasn't sure whether the agreement had been arrived at with reluctance or relief, but the final decision was that Special Branch would co-ordinate the enquiries. Gaffney was sufficient of a realist to accept that that was only agreed to because Marchant and Toogood couldn't decide whose responsibility it was, and neither was prepared to give way. Nonetheless, Gaffney was surprised that they had allowed him to oversee the operations, even with the tacit agreement that they would wait and see where it all fetched up. Sir Brian Chester's only concern was to stay out of it, providing, of course, that his man Foster did not get into any more trouble than he was in already. Chester's unexpressed view was that if a diplomat was a womaniser, he shouldn't get caught. And Sir Brian Chester knew quite a lot about womanising diplomats . . . first hand.

"Got any ideas, Harry?" Gaffney and Tipper were seated in the Chief Superintendent's office on the eighteenth floor of New Scotland Yard.

"We certainly didn't get any from that fiasco this morning, guv'nor, that's· for sure," said Tipper. "All too concerned with keeping their own little empires intact."

"Yes," said Gaffney reflectively. "And I'll tell you something else, too. James Marchant knows a bloody sight more about this business than he let on."

"You reckon, guv?"

"Convinced of it, Harry. The problem's always the same with Six. They couldn't give a damn about getting a job to court. Their only concern is intelligence, and nothing's allowed to get in the way. And if the information's no damned good, they'll trade it with someone else for something they can use." He shook his head slowly. "If that had been the first that James had heard of Gisela Hunter, he'd have been jumping up and down by now. And I'll tell you something else. There wouldn't have been a conference at the Foreign Office. He'd have vetoed that. That was

73

just a fishing expedition as far as he was concerned. He was sitting there waiting for someone to trot out something he didn't know already."

"And did he learn anything?"

Gaffney laughed. "Shouldn't think so, Harry. Take it from me, if you go to a Foreign Office conference expecting to learn nothing, you'll never be disappointed. Anyway, more to the point, what do we do now?"

"Find out all we can about Madam Hunter. There's nothing else."

"How? It's no good putting surveillance on her. Apart from probably being too fly for that, I doubt if we'd learn anything . . . unless she's got more than one string to her bow."

"I shall make some enquiries," said Tipper with a self satisfying finality.

"I think we ought to see Foster fairly soon," said Gaffney.

"Yes, I suppose so. Put the poor little sod out of his misery."

"Where does he live?" asked Gaffney.

"Richmond."

"That's handy, so do I."

"I know," said Tipper. "But handy it's

not. I presume he lives with his wife, and we don't really want her there when we talk to him about Gisela Hunter, do we?" Tipper grinned insolently at his chief.

Gaffney chuckled and stood up. "Give him a ring, Harry. Get him to call in here on his way home from work. He can always tell his missus that he's going to another diplomatic reception."

"Won't be anything diplomatic about it," growled Tipper.

"Come in, Mr Foster." Gaffney nodded a dismissal to the young detective who had escorted the diplomat up from Back Hall. "Do sit down. You know Chief Inspector Tipper, of course."

Tipper remained relaxed in his armchair and confined himself to nodding briefly in Foster's direction.

"Mr Tipper and I were at a conference at the Foreign Office this morning," Gaffney began. Foster looked apprehensive. "And we discussed this matter with Sir Brian Chester . . . and others — "

"Sir Brian? The Chief Clerk?"

Gaffney nodded. "Yes. It is a serious business, Mr Foster."

"What did he say?"

"Not much." Tipper sounded sour. "Typical diplomat. Talked a lot, said bugger-all."

"We have reason to believe," continued Gaffney, "that Mrs Hunter may be engaged in activities which are somewhat dubious."

"Well I told you that," said Foster with a flash of spirit.

"I meant that there are other things. What we call collateral."

"What, for instance?"

"I'm afraid that I'm not at liberty to reveal that, Mr Foster."

"What did Sir Brian say about me?" Foster looked distinctly worried.

"He said that you would still be going to Pakistan," said Gaffney.

"Did you tell him that I — er, that . . . "

"That you'd been screwing the lovely Gisela? Yes," said Tipper.

Foster swallowed hard. "Did he say anything about that?"

"I got the impression that he didn't see it as part of the job," said Tipper. "However, Mr Foster, you got yourself into this scrape, and we are going to get you out of it. But we can't promise to extricate you in a completely undamaged condition."

"Well, what d'you suggest I do?"

"I'll try and put it to you as clearly as possible, Mr Foster," said Gaffney. "If you break off your relationship with Mrs Hunter now, she may well think that you've reported the matter, in which case she will doubtless turn her attention to some other poor unfortunate, or disappear altogether. However, there are only six weeks or so to go before you leave the country. During that time some further useful information may emerge. The point is this: we don't know whether this woman is a recruiting officer for spies, neither do we know who she works for — yet. She may be interested in hard intelligence, or she may be wanting little more than preferential treatment in the matter of trade quotas — for all we know, she may still have an interest in her late husband's business — or it might even be an immigration racket. The plain fact is, we just don't know."

A look of concern crossed Foster's

face. "You mean you want me to go on seeing her, and . . . sleeping with her?"

"I don't want you to do anything, Mr Foster. I can only outline the options. If you say to me now that you want nothing further to do with her, I shall quite understand."

Foster gazed over Gaffney's shoulder and out of the window for a few moments before speaking. "I don't think I want to see her again," he said at last.

"Well, as I said, it's a matter for you. But what are you going to do if she telephones you at the office?"

"I shall make an excuse."

"Like you're going to a diplomatic reception?" asked Tipper quietly.

Foster turned to glare at the Chief Inspector, "Something like that, yes."

Foster's decision not to see Mrs Hunter again had caused Gaffney to change his mind about not mounting surveillance on the woman, and five days later he got the first report.

Detective Inspector Dave Wakeford was in charge of the Special Branch surveillance unit. About thirty years of

78

age, he was fit — playing squash at least twice a week — and quick-witted, both essential qualifications for a surveillance officer. He was seated now in the armchair in Gaffney's office, a file of photographs and papers balanced on his knees. He was wearing jeans and an old sweater, but was just as much at home in a dinner jacket when occasion demanded, as it sometimes did. His hair was long, longer than would normally be associated with a policeman, but not long enough to make him noticeable. In fact, everything about Dave Wakeford was unremarkable, another necessary attribute for a job which often occupied him for twelve hours a day, sometimes longer.

"Very little to tell you, sir," said Wakeford. "Mrs Hunter does not go out to work. She lives comfortably, and seems to be well off." He opened the file, extracted a sheet of paper and handed it over. "This is the surveillance log. You'll see from that that she rarely goes out. In fact" — he leaned forward and pointed at an entry in the log — "I think she only went out three times in the five days, and that was in the mornings, just to do a bit of shopping." He turned back to his folder. "And we've got some good shots of her." He laid a selection of photographs on Gaffney's desk.

"Attractive woman. I can quite see why our man got involved with her," said Gaffney.

"She has a woman come in for an hour or so each morning. The cleaner, I should imagine."

"Not been out in the evenings, then?"

"No, sir."

"In fact, nothing unusual at all."

"No, sir, not until last night."

"Oh? What happened last night?"

"She had a visitor." Wakeford fingered another photograph out of his file and laid it on the desk.

"That's Foster," said Gaffney.

"Yes, sir." Wakeford looked up surprised that Gaffney should have identified the man. "Lives in Richmond. Haven't found out what he does yet."

"I can tell you," said Gaffney. "He works at the Foreign Office. He's our informant."

"That's all right, then." Wakeford grinned.

"It isn't. He said he wasn't going to see her again. He was adamant." Gaffney pushed his chair back from the desk. "What's his bloody game?"

"I think he arrived there at around six-thirty." Wakeford pointed again at the surveillance log. "And left at about ten."

"Are you going to 'front him with it, guv'nor?" asked Tipper.

Gaffney shook his head. "No, Harry. We don't want Mrs Hunter to know that we're keeping tabs on her, and I reckon that Foster would tell her if he knew. More to the point, what is he telling her, I wonder?"

After a further ten days of fruitless observation, during which time Foster made another visit but little else of consequence occurred, Gaffney went to talk to his commander, Frank Hussey.

"We're getting nowhere fast, sir."

Hussey smiled. "So what d'you want to do next, John?"

"For a start, put an intercept on her telephone and her mail."

"And then?"

"See if we get anything, which frankly I doubt, and take it from there. But more important than that, I should like to go to Germany. Talk to the BKA."

Hussey spent some seconds polishing the lenses of his spectacles. Then he put them on again before peering intently at Gaffney. "Could be treading on some toes there, John."

"How so?"

"What you're talking about is alleged espionage by a British subject for one foreign country in another. That's a bit outside the brief of the Metropolitan Police."

Gaffney laughed. "Yes, I know. But it could have a direct bearing on what we're doing here." He paused. "It's not a junket, sir. I do really think it would be helpful. SIS got hold of this story, and probably got it from their man in Bonn, who undoubtedly got it from the BKA or the BfV."

Hussey nodded. He knew that western intelligence agencies exchanged information fairly freely, and the BKA, the German criminal police, fulfilled a role similar to that of Special Branch, while the BfV was the German Republic's equivalent of MI5.

"Even so, John, I think you'll have to let that go . . . at least for the time being. It's off our patch and there may be more to it than we know. We don't know what Six are up to and they may not have told us everything."

"Now that would be unusual," said Gaffney with a grin.

Contrary to popular opinion, intercept warrants are not obtained lightly. The Press know this, but for the purely commercial reasons of maintaining circulation figures, they perpetuate the myths started by so many minor politicians and allied functionaries, who almost boast that their phones are being tapped. It is only to be supposed that they see such a claim as enhancing their fragile importance in the eyes of their comrades.

Prior to preparing the lengthy and detailed report that was required before the Home Secretary would sign the warrant, Gaffney had telephoned the appropriate office at Queen Anne's Gate, only to be told that such a warrant had already been issued. Had, in fact, been signed a week previously.

Gaffney didn't have to ask who had made the request, wouldn't have been told anyway. He knew. In a mood of black anger, he went straight to the Mayfair offices of the Security Service.

"Just what the hell's going on, Hector?" he demanded. "I thought it had been agreed that I would coordinate this bloody Hunter enquiry."

Toogood looked guiltily at the irate detective. "What's the problem, John?" he asked mildly.

"The problem, Hector, is your lot obtaining intercept warrants for Gisela Hunter's phone and mail. Without having the courtesy to tell me."

Toogood stood up. "John, what can I say? I'm sorry. I really thought that I had let you know. It must have slipped my mind."

Gaffney smiled cynically. "Pressure of work, I suppose. It must be sheer hell over here." He looked pointedly at Toogood's clear desk-top.

"Of course we'll make the product

84

available to you, John."

"Thank you."

"As a matter of interest, it's produced nothing to date. Nor has his."

"His! Have you got Foster on as well?"

"Yes." Toogood sat down again and stared at the centre of his blotter. "It seemed to be the right thing to do."

"Oh, terrific! And have you told Sir Brian Chester that you're tapping the phone of a member of his staff?" Gaffney knew that Toogood wouldn't have done. He wouldn't have done himself — if he'd had the chance — but he didn't want to pass up the opportunity of discomfiting Toogood a little further.

"Well, no. I er . . . "

"Thank God for that," said Gaffney. "However, what about the meetings between Foster and Mrs Hunter? Did you not think it was worth telling me about those?" Gaffney guessed that the assignations had been arranged by phone.

"But you seem to know already."

"Yes, and no thanks to you. Now, look here, Hector, if there's any more of this hole-and-corner carry-on I shall wash my hands of the whole business, and I shall tell my guv'nor why. And he will undoubtedly tell your guv'nor why. This is too serious a business to try and score individual points. We're not in the glory-hunting business. Not you, not me, and not SIS. Got it?"

Toogood got it.

"John, come in. The DAC was asking at 'prayers' this morning how you were getting on." Commander Frank Hussey was standing in the doorway of his office.

"Foster is still seeing her, so she's probably still trying," said Gaffney, following his chief through the door.

Hussey picked his cold pipe out of the ashtray and lit it. "But there's still no firm evidence that the Hunter woman is working for the Pakistani Government, is there?"

"Not really, sir, apart from a gut feeling."

Hussey put down his pipe again and linked his fingers on the desk. "Did you know, John, that the Prime Minister is going to Pakistan in August? Mr Scott mentioned it this morning."

"Yes, I did, sir. Why? D'you think

there's a connection?"

"Not particularly. In fact, in view of what you say about Germany, definitely not. The point is that someone has to go to Islamabad to do advance enquiries for the trip. I suggested you."

"Won't that seem odd?"

"No. I admit that the PM's man usually goes, but it's not an inviolable rule. Why don't you take Harry Tipper with you, and see what you can pick up?" Hussey smiled at the private thought that Special Branch could quite legitimately put something over on the Secret Intelligence Service.

"Do you think it likely that I shall pick anything up, then, sir?"

Hussey laughed, a short contemptuous laugh. "Anybody's guess, John, but just supposing that there's a diplomat on the staff of the British Embassy in Islamabad who is due home, and whom Hunter is seeking to replace . . . with your Mr Foster, for example. That's what interests me."

Commander Edward Scott, Hussey's counterpart in Special Branch, was in charge of the protection of the British Cabinet, visiting heads of state and heads of government. It was an unenviable task in these days of an unceasing threat of terrorism, and the inadequate number of officers he had at his command was, perforce, spread thinly. That the operations commander should voluntarily have surrendered one of his chief superintendents to do an advance survey was a bonus, even if there was an ulterior motive.

"You've done protection duty with the Prime Minister, John," said Scott. "You know what's required."

"Yes, sir."

"But be careful how you play your other enquiries. Don't forget that you'll be there in an almost quasi-diplomatic role, and even today a lot of people in the Indian sub-continent still wear sandals."

"What's that supposed to mean, sir?"

"It's easier to tread on their toes," said Scott drily.

Detective Superintendent Dobbs had been summoned from Number Ten to see Commander Scott about the

Prime Minister's trip to the Indian sub-continent. As he walked across St James's Park he wondered why. It was a routine visit, and Dobbs' report had been a routine report. But for some reason Scott wanted to talk to him about it. Dobbs wondered if he'd ever heard of telephones. Still, it was a nice day for a walk.

"Sorry to drag you over, Terry," said Scott. "It's about the PM's visit to Pakistan and India."

"Yes, sir?"

"You're not going to do the advance trip."

"I'm not?" There was something in the wind. Dobbs knew the signs.

"Mr Gaffney is doing it, along with Harry Tipper."

"But — "

Scott held up his hand. "I know what you're going to say, Terry, but it can't be helped. We've some information that someone on the staff of our embassy in Islamabad, possibly even the High Commission in Delhi, could be spying . . . for the Pakistanis. It's essential that we get Mr Gaffney out there on a pretext.

Just to see what he can dig up. The Prime Minister's impending visit, and the need for an advance survey, gave us just the right excuse. I'm sorry about it, but Mr Gaffney knows the ropes, and he'll be able to give you a full briefing when you arrive."

"Seem a bit odd, sir, won't it? I mean what'll they think at Number Ten? How do I explain away the fact that a chief superintendent from here's doing my job for me?" Dobbs was not at all happy about the arrangement.

"Who is likely to ask, then?"

"The Prime Minister, for one," said Dobbs peevishly.

"Oh, that's all right," said Scott. "The Prime Minister already knows, and knows why. If anyone else wants to know; tell 'em to speak to the PM."

Dobbs frowned. "Does this spy job have any connection with the Prime Minister's visit, sir? I mean, do we have an additional security problem?"

Scott shook his head. "Shouldn't think so. There's certainly no indication so far, but rest assured that Mr Gaffney will look into that aspect of it as well."

Dobbs shrugged. He was far from mollified by the Commander's reasons for imposing Gaffney on Number Ten, but that was the way it went. "Very well, sir." He paused at the door. "As a matter of interest, what pretext would you have used to get Mr Gaffney to Pakistan if the Prime Minister hadn't been going, sir?"

"We'd have thought of something, Terry," said Scott cheerfully.

5

GAFFNEY and Tipper spent the next few days in a flurry of activity. Briefings with one of the secretaries at Downing Street had been followed by a conference with an official at the Foreign Office, carefully arranged so that Foster, who worked in the same department, would be unaware of their impending visit, and a courtesy call on the first secretary at the Pakistani Embassy in London. Then they had been fitted out with lightweight clothing, having learned from the Foreign Office that the temperature in Islamabad when they arrived would be an unbelievable one hundred degrees Fahrenheit.

Gaffney fastened his seat belt and watched the British Airways stewardesses go through the emergency drill, a procedure which did nothing to alleviate his apprehension about flying. Right on schedule at four-thirty, the huge jumbo jet left the ground on its way to Pakistan and the two policemen settled down to a twelve-hour flight interrupted only by a brief stop at Manchester.

"It'll be raining there," said Tipper.

"So it will in Pakistan. But hotter, according to the bloke at FCO," said Gaffney, toying with the paperback he had bought at Gatwick but which he knew he would never settle down to read on the flight.

To Gaffney's amazement — it always amazed him — the aircraft touched down safely at Islamabad International. It was half-past three in the morning, British time, but in Pakistan, which was four hours ahead, they had already started work.

"Bloody hell," said Tipper as they crossed the tarmac, "it's like stepping into an oven." He glanced sideways at Gaffney.

"I suppose this is another of the many places you've been to, guv'nor."

"Yes," said Gaffney, "not that I remember anything of it. I think we were here for about twelve hours, and frankly one five-star hotel is much like another. Mad dash from the airport, quick conference at the hotel, a meal, and back on the aircraft."

Tipper shook his head. "It's a bloody hard life," he said.

"Mr Gaffney?" A tall young man dressed in shirt and slacks approached them as they left the Customs Hall. "I'm Peter Kerr, First Secretary at the embassy." He was brisk and business-like, and shook hands with the two policemen before beckoning a porter. "I've booked you into a hotel in 'Pindi," he said as they walked through to the car park. "We haven't got much in the way of spare accommodation at the embassy and what we do have's not up to much. Flight okay?" he asked as an afterthought.

"Yes. If you like that sort of thing," said Gaffney.

"I'll take you to the hotel. You'll probably want to catch up on some sleep, get yourself organised and so on." He swung his air-conditioned Mercedes into the traffic outside the airport and accelerated fast. "I don't want to rush you or anything, but the local superintendent has asked you to lunch. If I pick you up at, say, twelve-thirty . . . ?"

"That's fine." It wasn't fine at all, but Gaffney could see that he had little option. There certainly wasn't going to be much time for sleep.

"Oh, I nearly forgot. His Excellency's laid on a bit of a supper-party at the residence this evening. Sort of welcome to Pakistan."

"I hope it's not black-tie," said Gaffney, having had dealings with the Diplomatic Service before. "Because neither of us has brought one."

"Heavens no, nothing like that. Very informal. Just a lounge suit. He's not keen on all this dressing up business, thank God."

The Pakistani police superintendent who, among other things, had responsibility for the Special Branch in Islamabad was called Mohammed Khan. He was an inch or two under six feet, overweight, and had a moustache.

"My dear fellows," he said, as he walked across his large office with both hands outstretched. "I am delighted to meet you. And Mr Kerr, how are you?" He turned to Gaffney and with a twinkle in his eye said, "This Mr Kerr is not a bad cricketer . . . for an Englishman."

"And one day Mohammed Khan will be as good as me . . . if he keeps practising." Kerr made the introductions and then excused himself.

"You have been to Pakistan before, Mr Gaffney?" Khan poured glasses of fruit juice and handed them round.

"Once, very briefly. Just saw the inside of a hotel." Gaffney smiled.

"Ah well, we shall have to show you what we can in the short time you are here." He glanced out of the window. "I was thinking, if you have no objection, to having luncheon on the tennis court."

"Wherever you like."

"Good, good. Now I have a programme of your Prime Minister's visit which I got from the people at your embassy. Doubtless you brought one from England. And doubtless they are different." He laughed a deep rumbling laugh.

"Isn't it funny," said Gaffney, "how policemen are always such cynics?"

Mohammed Khan eased himself carefully into a basketwork armchair opposite the two British policemen and started a conversation about cricket. Neither Gaffney nor Tipper was enthusiastic about the game, but Khan was undeterred, speaking knowledgeably about the giants of cricket such as Hobbs, Larwood, Sutcliffe and even W. G. Grace.

"Well," said Khan eventually, "I suggest that we go and have some lunch and you can meet the other fellows on my staff who will be concerned with the visit of your Prime Minister."

Khan's invitation to lunch on the tennis court had been no exaggeration. Overgrown with weeds and devoid of its net — although the posts remained — it now had a long table placed in its centre upon which lunch had been laid. Three or four policemen, some in uniform, stood nearby, all drinking fruit juice.

"Allow me to present . . . " began Khan, and he introduced each of the officers, none of whose names either Gaffney or Tipper was able to remember. They did, however, gather that one of them was in charge of the uniformed presence in Islamabad, another was responsible for the diplomatic premises, and the other two would be assigned to the personal protection of the British Prime Minister. It was, Gaffney noted, much the same as at home.

"What we have here," said Khan, waving a hand over the laden table, "is a selection of typical Pakistani curried dishes. This is not like in England. You have mainly Indian restaurants over there. They can't cook properly, you know — the Indians." Khan ushered his guests towards the table. "I have taken the liberty of sending the servants away," he said, "as we are going to talk of matters of high security."

They sat in wicker chairs, with which the headquarters seemed well supplied, and discussed the arrangements for the forthcoming visit. It was unbearably hot, despite a huge awning which had been stretched over the part of the tennis court where they were sitting. It helped a little, because although the uniformed officers present were in shirt-sleeves, the detectives were not, and Gaffney and

Tipper felt impelled to keep their jackets on.

"I will take you to the President's palace later on," said Kahn, "and to our Prime Minister's office. Your Prime Minister is having discussions with Miss Bhutto, I see. I will leave the embassy to you. And then — " He broke off and peered towards the headquarters building. "Ah, this is looking like a telephone call," he said.

A constable appeared at the edge of the tennis court clutching a mahogany box and trailing a long wire behind him. Placing the box on the table, the constable removed a telephone handset from it, handed it to Mohammed Khan and then saluted. "A telephone call from Karachi, Superintendent," he said. By the look on the faces of the others it was only Gaffney and Tipper who found this little episode amusing.

Mohammed Khan finished his conversation and watched as the constable went back to the office, busily coiling up the wire as he went. "My colleague in Karachi is having terrible problems," he said. "And it is so devilishly hot there, and humid too. Do you know Karachi, Mr Gaffney? Probably not."

"No," said Gaffney, who then pushed out a tentative feeler. "I knew of someone who was in business there. An Englishman called Richard Hunter."

Khan leaned forward and took a sip of his mango juice. "I remember him," he said.

"You knew him?"

"No, Mr Gaffney, but he was murdered, was he not?"

"So I believe."

"Yes, I remember the case. I was not there, of course, not in Karachi, but it was at the time of the war . . . " He paused. "Nineteen seventy-one. He was stabbed in the street by a fanatical Hindu." He paused again. "So the story went. The assassin was never apprehended, you understand." He shook his head gravely. "So he was a friend of yours? Well, well, what a small world it is, Mr Gaffney," he said, and started talking about cricket again.

The Ambassador towered over Gaffney. He must have been six feet six inches at least. "Henry Forbes," he said. "Pleasure to meet you." He stuck out a bony hand which Gaffney was surprised to discover had a vice-like grip. "This is my wife Grace." The Ambassador's wife was tall and slender and her face had a classical bone-structure. Someone must have told her that she looked like Glenda Jackson; she certainly dressed in a style that emphasised the similarity. "Peter Kerr tells me you had to suffer one of Mohammed Khan's lunches today," continued the Ambassador in a booming voice. "On the tennis court was it?"

"Yes."

"Good. Great honour that, having lunch on the tennis court. Don't ask me why. Talks about cricket incessantly . . . only in historical terms, of course, but you'll have found that out."

"Historical?" Gaffney raised an eyebrow.

"Yes," said the Ambassador. "Khan's knowledge of cricket stops dead at partition in nineteen forty-seven — some sort of nationalism, I suppose — that's why he only talks about Larwood and Hobbs and Evans and those people. Play cricket yourself Mr Gaffney?"

"No, I don't."

"Mmm. Oh well, takes all sorts, I suppose. Come and meet the others." He peered over the heads of the members of his staff "Peter, chase up that damned bearer, will you? Let's have some drinks over here."

"I think you're very sensible," said the Ambassador's wife. "Not playing cricket, I mean. Ridiculous game."

Gaffney smiled. "That sounds like heresy, Mrs Forbes."

She smiled at that, in a vacant sort of way.

The Ambassador's conception of an informal and intimate dinner party clearly differed from Gaffney's and there were no less than ten other people in the large and elegant drawing room. The Ambassador touched Gaffney's arm and led him round, trotting out the names of 'his people' as he called them. Anthony Booth, Second Secretary, and his wife Margaret," he began, and then in quick succession, as he had obviously done hundreds of times before, "Julian Bartlett, First Secretary Political, his wife Cynthia . . . " She was a tall, thin woman with a dreamy expression on her face. "Hugh Clements, Head of Chancery, and Barbara . . . "

Gaffney tried desperately to remember all the names; he had found that people expected Scotland Yard detectives to have prodigious memories. Unfortunately, Gaffney knew that unless he made a determined effort, the names would go in one ear and out the other.

Standing next to Julian Bartlett was a tall girl — Gaffney reckoned she was about thirty — elegantly dressed in white linen. "This is Angela Conrad, my secretary," said Forbes.

The girl smiled and held out her hand; Gaffney noticed how cold it was. The coldness had obviously been remarked on before. "Cold hands, warm heart," she said, still smiling, but there was no invitation in the comment.

"And these two young ladies are Jill Pardoe and Jane Morrison," said Forbes. "Two more members of the secretarial staff"

By this time the assembled dinner guests had formed into one large circle, and for twenty minutes or so, Gaffney and Tipper were bombarded with facile questions about what was going on in London. But it seemed a different world from the one that Gaffney and Tipper lived and worked in, and Gaffney supposed that being away from England for long periods of time had left these expatriates with false memories of their homeland. Tipper, in particular, felt like telling them about the chances of getting mugged, or giving them a run-down on race-rioting and terrorism, but decided that they would turn away from such hard facts of life, or even dismiss them as fabrication or sensationalism.

"Well," said Mrs Forbes, "I think it's time we were going in," and she signalled with a brief and imperious nod to a bearer waiting by the door.

Fourteen of them sat down at the long table in the ornate dining room. The fact that Gaffney, Tipper and Kerr were without partners had obviously caused some problems for a hostess who had only a limited number of acceptable women available to even up the balance. That was why Mrs Forbes had produced the striking-looking Angela Conrad and the other two unattached women.

As protocol demanded, Gaffney was seated on Grace Forbes' right, with Jill Pardoe next to him. He glanced down the table and saw, to his chagrin, that the gorgeous Angela was seated next to Harry Tipper. He was tempted to explain the meaning of RHIP to his hostess, but suspected that she would not readily understand that the doctrine 'rank hath its privileges' went beyond the Diplomatic Service and extended, as far as he was concerned, to sitting next to the prettiest girl in the room.

"Is this your first visit to Pakistan, Mr Gaffney?" It was Jill Pardoe who spoke, and Gaffney was surprised to find that she had a deep and attractive voice which offset her plainness and altered her whole character.

"It might as well be. The last time was about five years ago . . . literally an overnight stop on our way from Nicosia to Delhi. Saw the restaurant in the hotel and the road to the airport."

"It's a wonderful country, not everyone's cup of tea, of course. You should try to see some of the sights."

Gaffney smiled and waited to see if she was going to volunteer to act as his guide before saying, "I don't think we shall have much time. I'm afraid we'll be too busy making the arrangements for the PM's visit."

"Must be awfully frustrating." Jill Pardoe made the word 'awfully' sound very long drawn out in such a way that Gaffney presumed she was probably from a sheltered background and had been educated at a public school. Many of the girls he had met in such jobs were like that, and it was often assumed that such a background was obligatory for the job, though one of the most competent secretaries he had come across at Number Ten had been a delightful Cockney girl. Perhaps Jill Pardoe was trying to impress him. He glanced sideways, and noting that the neckline of her dinner dress could not have been higher, promptly dismissed the thought. She was there simply because the Ambassador's wife had told her to be, and high necklines were *de rigueur*.

"D'you do this sort of thing often, Mr Gaffney?" asked the Ambassador's wife.

She made the word 'often' sound like 'orphan'.

"What sort of thing's that, ma'am?" Gaffney wasn't sure whether she meant diplomatic dinner parties or Prime Ministerial 'advances'.

"Going about making sure that everything's all right for the Prime Minister?"

"Not as often as I used to, I'm pleased to say."

"Oh!" Grace Forbes sounded surprised. "D'you not like it, then?"

"Not particularly. I'm afraid that when you're travelling about on this sort of job, it becomes rather tedious . . . and frustrating." He glanced sideways at Jill Pardoe. "You go to all sorts of places that you've always wanted to visit, and once there you get no time to see them." He paused to take a sip of wine. "Still, I suppose it's better than not going at all. But there are always the highlights . . . like this dinner party, of course."

"Yes." Mrs Forbes spoke flatly and smiled in her usual detached sort of way, but Gaffney wasn't sure whether his fulsome compliment had registered.

"It must play havoc with your family life. What does your wife think of it?"

"I'm not married," said Gaffney, in such a way as to discourage further conversation, but he was aware of Jill Pardoe looking sharply towards him.

At the other end of the table, Harry Tipper was deep in conversation with Angela Conrad about London. She had been in Islamabad, she told him, for about three years, and missed her friends terribly and all that went with living in London.

All in all, it was a pretty dreary party, although those senior members of the mission who were present did their best. But living in a closed community, meeting the same people every day, and confining their social activities to the same little circle, produced the sort of tensions that Gaffney imagined might well be present in a group of people adrift in a lifeboat. He thought that they must eventually get on each other's nerves, and as he looked around the huge room he wondered if they knew that the Raj had ceased to exist. There were turbaned bearers moving silently about, anticipating, it seemed, everyone's needs, and a huge fan revolving lazily on the ceiling above, which helped to sustain the illusion. But that was all it did; the air conditioning system worked very efficiently.

At the end of the meal the ladies withdrew and the men moved up to the Ambassador's end of the table for brandy and cigars. As Gaffney said to Tipper later, it was all very civilised and rather like a cameo from the nineteen-twenties.

"Well," said the Ambassador eventually, "I suppose we'd better join the ladies." He uncoiled to his full height and led the way from the dining room, but at the door he paused. "Peter," he said, addressing Kerr, "perhaps you'd tell the *mem* I shall be in shortly. I must just show our two friends here my new Purdeys." He nodded to the two policemen. "Perhaps you can give me some advice," he said. "You policemen chaps know all about guns, don't you?"

"Only enough to know they're bloody dangerous," said Tipper, who was beginning to tire of this loud diplomat.

Unabashed, Forbes led the way into

his study and closed the door. "Do sit down, gentlemen," he said, indicating comfortable leather armchairs. He turned to a side-table and poured three thistles of brandy. Handing one each to Gaffney and Tipper, he sipped his own before sitting down.

"Now, gentlemen," he began, carefully cutting the end of a cigar before lighting it. "How can I help you?" He raised his eyebrows through the gently drifting smoke.

"It's a very routine thing, this visit, Ambassador," said Gaffney, "and the local police — "

"Not that." The Ambassador carefully removed a shred of tobacco from the end of his tongue. "I'm talking about the real reason for your visit." He smiled at them. "I know that it's usually the Prime Minister's own detective who comes on these recognisance trips — alone — not a chief superintendent *and* a chief inspector." He beamed briefly at Tipper. "Also, I know that you told Mohammed Khan that you knew Richard Hunter, which is a coincidence, because I knew him, too. Last time I was here. Well, not here . . . in Karachi, at the consulate. I was there when he was murdered. Damnable business."

Gaffney took a sip of brandy. "How did you know that I had mentioned Hunter to Khan, Ambassador?"

"Very simple. Khan told Peter Kerr. Tells him everything. Peter's cultivated some very good informants." He smiled. "You ought to talk to him." The Ambassador seemed to have taken on a different character, more serious than the jovial and ebullient personality that had been apparent when first they met him. "To be perfectly honest, Mr Gaffney, I thought it unlikely that you knew Richard Hunter. Apart from occasional and brief visits to London — on one of which, incidentally, he remarried — he spent his whole life in the sub-continent. He was born here, you know. You could call him a son of the Raj."

"I'm afraid there must have been some misunderstanding," said Gaffney, matching the Ambassador's hard gaze with his own. "I didn't actually say I knew Mr Hunter. I knew *of* him. It's his widow I know, Gisela Hunter. Met her several times at various diplomatic functions in London."

"Oh, I see. Kerr must have got hold of the wrong end of the stick."

"Or Khan," said Gaffney. "Incidentally, Ambassador, you said something about wanting some advice on your Purdeys. He looked pointedly around the room. He knew that a man of the background and upbringing of Forbes would never keep a shotgun in his study. To him that would be the upper-class equivalent of keeping coal in one's bath.

"Oh, time enough for that tomorrow," said the Ambassador. "I really do think we ought to join the ladies now, don't you?"

6

IT was some minutes before the unfamiliar tinkling of the telephone awoke Gaffney, and it took him a little while to remember that he was in a hotel room in Rawalpindi. He sat up and switched on the bedside light which flickered constantly, probably due to the generators running at less than full power. He grabbed the handset and glanced at his watch: it was half-past three.

"Hello?"

Someone was speaking in Urdu, and Gaffney was about to replace the receiver, assuming it to be a wrong number, when Henry Forbes' strong voice came on the line. "Mr Gaffney, it's Forbes here."

"Ambassador?" Gaffney was still half-asleep, and couldn't imagine why the Ambassador should be telephoning him at three-thirty in the morning.

"There's been a rather serious occurrence here at the embassy."

Gaffney was fully awake in an instant.

"What sort of serious occurrence?"

"I'd rather not discuss it on the phone, Mr Gaffney. Far from secure, you know. Look, I've sent a car. Should be with you very shortly."

"Very well, Ambassador." Gaffney replaced the receiver. He was not pleased. It looked very much as though yet another government official would have to be told that Scotland Yard officers had only one boss, and he was called the Commissioner . . . unless you counted the Lord Chief Justice as well.

It took Gaffney some time to rouse Harry Tipper, but eventually both were dressed. The main door of the hotel was locked, but after waking up the night-duty hall porter, asleep under the counter in the reception hall, they reached the front steps.

The embassy driver, a Pakistani, leaped out of the car, made *namasti*, and threw open the rear door. He then drove like a maniac along deserted roads to Islamabad, covering the twelve miles in about ten minutes.

The Ambassador was standing on the steps of the residence when they arrived.

114

He was wearing pyjamas and a silk dressing gown with his hands thrust in its pockets, and smoking a cigarette in an amber holder.

"Christ!" said Tipper. "It's Noel Coward."

"My dear Mr Gaffney," said Forbes, "thank you for coming so promptly, and you too, Mr Tipper."

Gaffney refrained from pointing out that the Ambassador had left him little option. "What's the problem?" he asked.

"There's been a tragedy, I'm afraid. It's Peter Kerr. He's been shot."

"Is he dead?"

"I'm afraid so, Mr Gaffney."

The Ambassador turned towards the door, but Gaffney remained where he was. Years of training and experience had taught him not to be impetuous, to take matters step-by-step, and only to move when you knew where you were going. An old and very wise inspector — his instructor at the Detective Training School — had said to his young pupils, of whom Gaffney had then been one, 'Don't move out of your old house until you know there's a roof on the new one'. It hadn't been a particularly clever remark, but it was one which Gaffney, throughout his career, had found could be applied to all manner of situations. "What are the circumstances, Ambassador?"

With a slight show of tetchiness, the Ambassador turned again to face the two detectives. "He's in the armoury, Mr Gaffney. It would appear that he shot himself." He paused. "With one of my new Purdeys." The expression of distaste on the Ambassador's face implied that it was a pretty uncivilised thing to do. Not so much to commit suicide, but to do it with a Purdey . . . and a new one at that.

"How did he get in there?" asked Gaffney. "It's kept locked, surely?"

"Yes, it is, but Peter Kerr had a key." Forbes took his cigarette out of its holder and flicked it into the night, the lighted end making an arc in the darkness until it disappeared into the shrubs that bordered the driveway.

"The only key?"

"No. I have the other."

"Why should Mr Kerr — especially — have had the other key?"

Forbes blew gently through his cigarette-holder before dropping it into one of his pockets. "Peter Kerr had certain special responsibilities in the embassy, Mr Gaffney. I don't think it's necessary to elaborate." The Ambassador's face was devoid of expression.

"You mean he was responsible for security?"

"Not exactly."

"I see." Gaffney smiled. "Then I presume you mean that he was the resident SIS man."

The Ambassador stared at Gaffney for some time before letting out a long sigh. "Quite so, Mr Gaffney, quite so."

"How was this discovered, Ambassador?" Still Gaffney refused to budge from the ornate front steps of the residence.

"One of the security guards was doing his rounds. He saw the light on in the armoury and noticed that the door was open."

Gaffney nodded. "What makes you think that Kerr took his own life?"

The Ambassador looked up sharply. "I think, Mr Gaffney, that when you eventually see his body, you will be in no doubt about that."

"Do you know, then, of any reason why he should have done so?"

Forbes appeared to give that some thought before answering. "Only that . . . " he began slowly, and then changed his mind. "No," he said.

"Only that what?"

"There was some suggestion that he was having an affair with Diana Gibson." Forbes spoke reluctantly and a pained expression crossed his face, as though he bore some vicarious responsibility for such misbehaviour by his staff. "But to be frank," he added hurriedly, "I have no evidence of it. It was only — what shall I call it? — embassy scuttle-butt." He seemed impelled to explain. "The compound of an embassy is a very closed community, Mr Gaffney. There is all manner of back-biting, and little things get blown up out of all proportion."

"I shouldn't have thought that having an affair with someone else's wife was a little thing . . . particularly in a closed community." Gaffney emphasised the last few words so that they sounded almost sarcastic.

"Oh, she's not someone's wife. Diana Gibson's not married," said the Ambassador.

"Well, then — "

"But Peter Kerr was."

Gaffney shrugged. "I doubt that that warrants suicide, even so." There was no hurry to track down that particular rumour. "Perhaps we should go and look at the body, then."

"Yes, I think we should."

But still Gaffney did not move. "I must point out however," he said with heavy formality, "that I have no authority to conduct an investigation. My powers here are no different to anyone else's. In fact less. I am not even a diplomat."

"Quite so," said the Ambassador airily. He was on sure ground now. This was an administrative matter, and Forbes knew all about administrative matters. "I have taken the liberty of sending a telegram to the Secretary of State seeking his authority for you to carry out an investigation."

"Which Secretary of State?"

Forbes raised an eyebrow. "For Foreign and Commonwealth Affairs," he. said, in a tone that implied that there was no other.

"It's the Home Secretary who should have been asked," said Gaffney.

Forbes smiled condescendingly. "Yes, yes," he said, "but I have no remit to communicate with the Home Office directly. It's protocol, you know."

"The Home Office will almost certainly withhold approval," said Gaffney. "I have no powers in Pakistan. It's a matter for the Pakistani police." He knew he was wrong, but he didn't want to be saddled with a domestic suicide and all the paper work — complicated paper work — that undoubtedly would go with it.

"Mr Gaffney," said Forbes patiently, "these are diplomatic premises and Kerr is a diplomat. The Pakistani police have no writ here. And," he added drily, "as you yourself deduced, Kerr was a member of the Secret Intelligence Service. Personally, I think Home Office authority is a mere formality."

Still Gaffney fought. "That may be so, Ambassador, but I have no facilities here to conduct the sort of enquiries — "

"What do you mean?"

"A forensic science laboratory. Finger-prints. Photographers. That sort of thing."

Forbes looked unhappy. "What do you want all that for? It's a suicide."

"So you say. But if I am to investigate this sudden death — and as far as I am concerned it's a big 'if' — I shall be the judge of that." Gaffney smiled. "That is to say me and the coroner for the district where the body eventually lands in England. All of which means that I may have to call on the local police for assistance."

"I see." The Ambassador frowned.

"But perhaps we should go and have a look at the body."

Forbes led the way down the drive, past the swimming pool, to the back door of the embassy building. A security man, in civilian dress, nodded to the Ambassador and unlocked the door. The little party carried on along several corridors, eventually turning into a narrower passageway at the end of which was a bunker-like room with a steel door, now open, and guarded by yet another security man.

"This is Brooks," said the Ambassador. "He found the body." He grasped the guard's arm. "This is Chief Superintendent Gaffney from Scotland Yard, Brooks. He's to investigate this matter."

"Blimey, guv'nor, you got here quickly." Brooks' mouth opened in astonishment. "Flying Squad, are you?" he asked, grinning nervously.

The Ambassador looked disapproving at this levity in the presence of violent death, but to Gaffney the man's humour struck a chord. "You an ex-policeman?" he asked.

"Yes, sir. Twenty-five years in the Met."

"What are you doing out here, then?"

"You could say I've come home," said Brooks. "Born out here, I was. Father was in the army."

"Where did you do it?" asked Tipper. He wanted to know where Brooks had served; it was a form of police shorthand that the ex-policeman would understand.

"Walham Green, all my service. Well, they call it Fulham now. Started as a PC . . . and finished as one." Brooks chuckled.

"Yes, well tell Mr Gaffney how you came to find Mr Kerr," said the Ambassador, cutting through the homely chat.

"All in good time," said Gaffney. "If I'm going to investigate this, I'll do it my way . . . when the authority to do so comes from London. In the meantime, I'll look at the body. That won't keep."

Brooks pulled open the heavy metal door and Gaffney took a step inside. The room was about fifteen feet square with narrow, heavily barred windows near to the ceiling. Against the wall on one side were two green cabinets, only one of which was padlocked, while end-on against the wall opposite the door was a table six feet long. On it was a Purdey shotgun wedged in place by a number of wooden ammunition boxes, its barrels parallel with the ground. A length of string ran from the front trigger, round a piece of vertical piping conduit and back past the gun finishing in the hand of the body that sat grotesquely slumped in an office armchair, its chest a mess of blood, flesh and shreds of shirt and jacket. The head was slumped forward on the chest making it impossible to see the face.

"How do you know that's Kerr?" asked Gaffney.

"You can see his face if you kneel down," said Brooks, adding hurriedly, "I didn't touch anything, sir."

Tipper stepped past Gaffney and took the wrist of the body in one hand, feeling briefly for a pulse he knew he wouldn't find. It was an automatic reaction to the discovery of a body, and he would be able to say at any subsequent hearing that he had done so.

"You seem to have done that before, Mr Tipper," said the Ambassador from the doorway.

"You get into the habit," growled Tipper, "when you've spent four years on the murder squad."

"Oh," said the Ambassador softly.

Harry Tipper had spent so long in what the Special Branch referred to as 'mainline CID', and had investigated more suspicious deaths than, as he himself put it, most people had had hot dinners, that he knew the routine instinctively.

"Is there anyone on the embassy staff

who's keenly interested in photography?" asked Tipper.

The Ambassador looked puzzled. "Photography? Er . . . I don't know really. Is it relevant?"

"Extremely," said Tipper. "Until authority comes through from Whitehall, we can't call on outside assistance. And what I need now is someone who can make a reasonable job of taking a few scenes-of-crime shots of this lot." He waved a careless hand towards the body of Kerr.

"Oh, I see." Forbes wrinkled his brow. "I think that young Stebbings does that sort of thing." For a moment or two he looked round helplessly, and then addressed himself to Brooks. "Go and get Mr Stebbings, Brooks, will you? Tell him that we need him and his camera urgently."

"Yes, sir," said Brooks, turning to go.

"Tell him what's involved," said Tipper. "I don't know the first thing about it, but he'll probably need flashlights, or floodlights, or whatever they call the damned things. You know the form, I expect."

Brooks grinned. "Right, guv. Yes, I reckon I've seen a few dead 'uns in my time." He walked away casually, too long in the tooth to be hurried by a dead body.

Nigel Stebbings, when he arrived, was girt about with what Tipper called photographic clutter, and proved to be an effete young man of about twenty-seven. He wore large, owl-like, horn-rimmed spectacles through which he stared nervously, his eyes blinking constantly at the formidable group gathered in the corridor leading to the armoury. If his white face was any guide, he was obviously aware of what had happened, and Tipper could imagine the terse way in which Brooks had delivered the message.

"Mr Kerr is dead," said Tipper, "and his body's in there." He jerked a thumb in the direction of the closed armoury door. "It's a shotgun death, so be warned." Stebbings blinked even more vigorously. "What I'd like you to do is to take some photographs of the body, the room, and anything else I can think of. Reckon you can manage that?"

Stebbings gulped, his oversize Adam's apple bobbing up and down. "Well, I suppose I could . . . " He sounded by no means certain.

"What d'you usually photograph? Birds?" Tipper grinned.

"Yes, as a matter of fact, I do . . . "

"Feathered . . . or naked?" Tipper grinned again.

Stebbings did not find that at all amusing. "Wild life in general," he said. "There's tremendous scope here in — "

Tipper interrupted. "Yeah, I expect there is, but this is a bit different, old son. This will be evidential." He paused, his hand on the armoury door. "Ever seen a dead body before?"

"No . . . actually."

"Well this isn't pretty, I warn you, and if you feel like going out and throwing up before you start, don't worry. It happens to all of us to start with." He grinned and opened the door.

Stebbings moved cautiously into the armoury, his heavy camera case banging on the doorpost as he did so, and with a mild expletive, he pulled it round and held it in the centre of his body.

Reluctantly, he gazed at the body of Peter Kerr, his eyes opening even wider than usual. Then he turned, suddenly, and was violently sick in the corridor, causing the Ambassador to move sharply away for fear of having his expensive leather sandals covered in vomit.

Tipper sniffed, loudly. "Brooksie," he said, "see if you can scrounge a large glass of brandy for Mr Stebbings, will you? Set him up for the job in hand. Oh, and while you're doing that, see if you can get hold of some plastic bags from the kitchen or wherever, will you?"

Eventually, Stebbings recovered sufficient of his composure to begin, and once involved with the technicalities of his quasi-professional task, seemed to suffer no further distress in photographing his gory subject. Under Tipper's direction, he took shots of the room and the body from every conceivable angle, and was able to do all that the police asked of him in about half an hour. Tipper, ever-careful, sent him off to his dark-room to develop and print his exposures before anything was moved, so that more photographs could be taken if the first batch proved to be unsuitable.

The Ambassador had been standing in the doorway during this first part of the investigation, and Tipper now turned to him. "Has the embassy doctor shown up yet?" he asked. "It would be useful if he could officially certify life extinct."

"Oh, he's been and gone," said Forbes.

"Has he?" said Tipper. "Well perhaps you'd be so good as to get him back again." He was beginning to get a little angry.

"Is that absolutely necessary? I mean, won't the morning do?"

"Are you fairly confident that I shall be authorised to conduct this enquiry, Ambassador?" asked Gaffney softly.

"There's no doubt of it in my mind," said Forbes.

"In that case," said Gaffney in the same low tones, "I should like the doctor here now . . . right now."

There was a certain edge to Gaffney's voice that the Ambassador clearly recognised. "Yes, of course, of course," he murmured, and turned away to the wall-telephone in the corridor.

"Archie Gilchrist. How d'you do?"

The embassy doctor was a breezy and confident Scot who shook hands vigorously with the two detectives. The fact that he was fully dressed, complete with bow tie, and that there was a smell of whisky on his breath led Tipper to believe that he had not been back to bed since his first inspection of the corpse . . . if he had been to bed at all.

"You certified life extinct, I understand?" asked Tipper.

"That's right. I hope you're not going to ask some fatuous question about how long he's been dead. That's the way it's done, isn't it?"

"I know when he died," said Tipper. "I saw him alive just after midnight and I saw him dead at four o'clock. From which I deduce that he died between those times."

"Ah!" said Gilchrist. This particular policeman obviously did not appreciate smart remarks.

"What arrangements are you able to make to accommodate the body until the post-mortem, doctor?"

"Post-mortem?" Gilchrist looked

surprised. "In a case of suicide?"

"D'you know that for sure? I mean, are you prepared to tell the coroner that?"

"The coroner? I'm sorry, I don't . . . "

"These are diplomatic premises, doctor, as I'm sure you know. Therefore, the local form of enquiry into sudden death — whatever sort of enquiry that is — has no authority here. The body will be shipped back to England and the coroner will hold an inquest. And I should think that the nearest coroner to here is at Uxbridge . . . given that we land at Heathrow. If by some quirk we arrive at Gatwick, then doubtless it will be the coroner for Crawley, or some such place."

"Oh, I see. Well I suppose that the mortuary at the local hospital would be the place. I could make a phone call, if you like."

"That would be helpful. Thank you. I shall need a statement from you later on this morning." Tipper turned away from the doctor to look at the prints which the embassy's amateur photographer had taken earlier. "Yeah, they'll do fine. In fact they're excellent." Tipper looked

131

up and grinned. "If ever you get fed up with this diplomatic caper, I could always get you a job as a scenes-of-crime photographer," he said.

"I don't think so, thank you," said Stebbings. "Not even if you threw in free brandy." For the first time since they had met, he smiled.

Tipper shuffled the prints into a neat pile. "I shall want a formal statement from you, just saying when and where you took these," he said. "Come and see me just before lunch."

"Where will you be?"

"Christ knows," said Tipper. "You'll just have to find me." He was not too happy at that moment. He and Gaffney were having to do all the things that a full scientific team would have been called out to do in London. Tipper just hoped that he wouldn't forget anything.

The Ambassador was still hovering in the corridor outside the armoury and started to move closer when he saw the two detectives measuring the room and the distances between the body and the shotgun.

Gaffney, holding the other end of the

tape, looked up. "There's no need for you to wait about any longer, Ambassador."

"Ah, no, I suppose not. Er, perhaps you'd join me for breakfast."

Once the Ambassador had wandered off, Tipper closed the door of the armoury. "Have a look at this, guv'nor," he said, and pointed to the string that was around the front trigger of the shotgun.

"What about it, Harry?"

"It worries me. I'm pretty sure that the injuries to Kerr's chest were caused by the discharge of one cartridge not two."

Using two plastic bags as makeshift gloves, Tipper carefully lifted the gun from its resting place between the boxes on the table, and broke it. Slowly and thoughtfully, he extracted one used cartridge case.

"So?" Gaffney leaned against the doorjamb, his arms folded.

"Oh, I don't know, guv. It just seems odd to me. If a bloke sets out to kill himself he might as well use two cartridges as one. There were plenty there." He pointed to the open gun cabinet. "But it's the string that puzzles me: it's round the front trigger, but the

133

cartridge was in the chamber fired by the rear trigger."

"Perhaps he didn't know that," said Gaffney.

"Oh, come on, guv," said Tipper scathingly. "The bloke was in SIS. They know all about guns, surely?"

Gaffney shrugged. "Don't ask me, Harry. Hand-guns, probably, but shotguns . . . ? I don't honestly know." He looked thoughtful. "Don't forget that the Ambassador wanted to talk to us about his new Purdeys — of which this is one — last night. Why us? If Kerr had known about shotguns, Forbes would have asked him before we turned up on the scene, surely?"

"Yeah, maybe so," said Tipper, obviously reluctant to let his half-theory go. "But frankly, I don't think he wanted to talk about shotguns at all. He wanted to know why we were here . . . really here. It didn't take him long to home in on your mention of Richard Hunter to What's-his-name Khan, did it?"

"Yes," said Gaffney thoughtfully, "I've been thinking about that . . . in the light of current events, as they say. Anyway," he continued, "to the matter in hand. Once you exert pressure on the front trigger and keep pulling, the second trigger will activate as well, surely?"

Tipper shook his head. "Search me," he said. "I've never fired a shotgun in my life."

Gaffney levered himself off the door. "If you're going to look for rational explanations for suicide," he said, "why did he go to this trouble at all? Why didn't he do what most shotgun suicides do: put the barrel in his mouth and pull the trigger?"

Tipper sniffed. "Because it makes a nasty mess, and I get the impression that our Mr Kerr was quite a tidy man. However . . . " He lowered his voice. "There is something about this business which is much more important than that."

"Such as?" Gaffney looked up from studying the shotgun's trigger mechanism.

"From what I've heard, there's a fair old kick to a shotgun, guv'nor, and looking at the way that Purdey's wedged in between those boxes, I'd say this whole thing's a non-starter."

Gaffney's eyes narrowed. "Go on, Harry."

"I'm fairly certain, sir, that the force of the discharge of that cartridge would have thrown that shotgun right off the table, not leave it neatly resting where we found it."

Gaffney shook his head and laughed. "Oh Christ, Harry, that's all we need. Glad you came?"

"Life's a bitch, ain't it, guv?" said Tipper.

7

BREAKFAST in the residency was a sombre affair. The Ambassador and Mrs Forbes said hardly a word, which was just as well; Gaffney and Tipper, having had almost no sleep on the flight over and precious little on their first night in Islamabad, were in no mood for witty conversation. In fact, Gaffney was not very pleased at all. Having been sent out to Pakistan ostensibly to confirm the security arrangements for the Prime Minister's forthcoming visit, but secretly to find out what he could about Gisela Hunter's activities, he now found himself facing the possibility of a third investigation. One he could well do without.

"What's your next move, Mr Gaffney?" asked the Ambassador, dabbing his lips with his table napkin.

"To find out if there's a decent pathologist in Islamabad."

"How d'you propose to do that?"

"Have a chat with Mohammed Khan for a start."

"Is that wise?" Forbes looked dubious. "These local chaps are not awfully reliable, you know."

"Really?" said Gaffney. "I should have thought it rather depends on how you handle them. We seemed to get on all right." He was fast approaching the level of intolerance with the Ambassador that Harry Tipper seemed to have reached some time ago; tiring rapidly of his scathing superiority.

"What d'you hope to learn from this post-mortem, Mr Gaffney?"

"I really have no idea. But it's something that needs to be done. You'd be surprised what you discover once you start." Gaffney moved his chair slightly and crossed his legs. "Incidentally, Ambassador, what sort of intelligence material do you keep in the embassy?"

The question was clearly unexpected, and the Ambassador blinked. "Intelligence material?"

"Yes." Gaffney smiled. "Principally, the sort of stuff that might be of use

138

to the Pakistani Government . . . or the Indian one."

Forbes picked up a knife and drew a little pattern on the heavy tablecloth. "Why d'you ask?" He was obviously playing for time in the face of a question that, in his mind, was clearly unconnected with Kerr's death.

"Well, Peter Kerr was with the SIS, was he not?"

The Ambassador nodded.

"And was responsible for gathering intelligence that might be of value to Her Majesty's Government, yes?"

Again the Ambassador nodded. It was fairly clear that in common with a lot of people who should have known, he was unaware of the precise role of Scotland Yard's Special Branch, did not know that John Gaffney was in touch with MI6 in London on an almost daily basis.

"Well . . . yes," said Forbes reluctantly.

"Is it possible that he — ?"

The Ambassador sat up sharply. "Good God!" he said. "You're not suggesting that Peter Kerr was a spy, surely?"

That, of course, was not what Gaffney

was suggesting at all, but it would do for the moment. "I have to consider every possibility, sir," he said.

"That's outrageous," said Forbes.

"Not as outrageous as you might think." Gaffney lit a cigar and gazed mildly at the Ambassador through the smoke. "Not when you consider Burgess, Maclean, Philby . . . "

"But that was years ago. Things have been tightened up since then."

Gaffney smiled. "I wish I had your confidence, Ambassador," he said. "But is there anything here that might interest either the Pakistanis or the Indians?"

Forbes' eyes narrowed. "I don't know what you're thinking, Mr Gaffney," he said. "But it did cross my mind that you and Mr Tipper weren't here wholly to make security arrangements for the Prime Minister's visit."

"Yes," said Gaffney, "I sort of got that impression last night."

Forbes shrugged. "An Ambassador likes to know what's going on in his embassy," he said.

"Well then?"

"Yes. There is information here that

would be useful. Of course there is. But I can really see no reason why it would have caused Peter Kerr to take his own life."

Gaffney, in common with most policemen, didn't trust anyone he met in the course of an investigation, no matter what position they held, but occasionally there came a point when you had to take a chance. "You mentioned Richard Hunter last night," he said.

"Only because you'd mentioned him to Mohammed Khan."

Gaffney nodded. "Yes, I did," he said. "Well, Ambassador, that's the reason I'm here."

"But that was years ago," said Forbes mildly.

"I'm not talking about his murder," said Gaffney. "You may recall my mentioning that I knew his wife Gisela . . . "

"Yes."

"Well I don't, not directly. I know of her. We have reason to believe that she's an agent for the Pakistani Government."

"Good Lord!" said Forbes. "How

extraordinary. Whatever makes you think that?" Hurriedly, he added, "I never knew her, you know."

Gaffney smiled. "No," he said, "I suppose not. But we have information that she has attempted to suborn at least two diplomats . . . one German and one British — "

"British!" Forbes expelled the word like a pistol shot, as though the very idea was unthinkable.

"It happens," said Gaffney. "But fortunately — in both cases — the individuals concerned informed the authorities and no damage was done. If you exclude the fact that the German committed suicide." He paused to allow the Ambassador to draw a conclusion from that if he wished. "What we don't know, of course, is whether she's had any success in the past."

"With someone like Peter Kerr, you mean?"

"It's possible."

"But surely, he'd report it . . . wouldn't he?"

Gaffney was tempted to laugh at such naïvety. "That rather depends on the circumstances of his entrapment . . . if there was one."

"Oh?"

"You see, Ambassador, Mrs Hunter — Gisela — uses the oldest ploy in the world. She gets her victims, all of whom are married, into bed. Then she threatens to tell their wives. In exchange for not doing so, she persuades them to part with a little information. Usually innocuous at first. But that doesn't matter. Once they've started, they're in trouble. They may not have broken the law at that stage, but they've certainly put their careers on the line, and the only way then is to go on . . . and keep on going on."

"Good God!" said Forbes yet again. He seemed to be short of a sufficient range of expletives to cover all of Gaffney's startling revelations. "That's a bit below the belt."

"Couldn't have put it better myself," said Tipper, who had been watching Forbes' reactions with interest.

The Ambassador cast a cold eye towards Tipper before looking at Gaffney again. "And d'you think that Kerr might have fallen victim to this woman?"

"It's always possible."

"But I can't see Peter Kerr ever getting involved with . . . " Forbes stopped. He knew what was coming next.

Gaffney laughed. "It was you who suggested that he might be having an affair with . . . " He paused, the name gone.

"Diana Gibson." The Ambassador shook his head slowly. "Yes, but she works here in the embassy."

Gaffney laughed again. "In my experience," he said, "if a man's a womaniser, he's not too particular about the status of his random partners. If he's made that way, he won't give a tuppenny cuss who she is or what she does for a living . . . within reason." He paused to roll ash from his cigar. "However, that doesn't answer my question. Is there anything in the files of this embassy that might be attractive to another power? Particularly those in the subcontinent."

With a sigh, Forbes leaned back and rested his arms along the sides of his chair. "Yes, there is, Mr Gaffney. The sort of information gathered by

Kerr and his people" — it sounded a little derogatory, the way he said that — "would include such things as tactical deployment of troops, economic forecasts, production figures, particularly of war *matériel* . . . In fact, intelligence that would be useful to India in the event of another Indo-Pakistani war."

"Oh," said Gaffney in a resigned tone. "That's the wrong way round."

"Wrong way?" Forbes looked puzzled.

"Of course. There would be no point in the Pakistanis obtaining information about their own dispositions, would there? They know that already. Not unless our assessment of that information interested them."

"Ah, yes, I see what you mean. But we also get copies of the stuff that the British High Commission in Delhi sends home . . . about the state of affairs in India."

"That's better," said Gaffney, with obvious satisfaction. "So an agent of the Pakistani Government, having a spy placed in this embassy, could find out very nearly as much as one placed in our High Commission in New Delhi."

Slowly Forbes nodded his head. "I'm afraid that's true, Mr Gaffney. But, if you'll forgive me for saying so, you appear to have made a quantum leap in assuming that there is such an agent here . . . if you're basing it merely on Peter Kerr's suicide." He looked searchingly at Gaffney. "Unless, of course, there are things you haven't told me."

"Rest assured, Ambassador," said Gaffney with a smile, "I shall keep you fully informed of any developments." But only if it suits me, he thought.

"I'm most grateful," murmured Forbes. He rose from the table and left the room as his wife had done before the more discreet part of their conversation had begun.

"It strikes me that he's too bloody interested in our little enquiry, guv'nor," said Tipper when the dining-room door had closed behind Forbes' tall figure.

"Well, he is in charge, isn't he?"

"I'd never have guessed it," said Tipper heavily.

Ten minutes later, the Ambassador came back into the dining room. "I think this is what you've been waiting for, Mr Gaffney," he said, laying a flimsy piece of official-looking paper on the table.

It was a telegram, from the Foreign Office in London. Brief and to the point, it said: "After consultation with S of S Home Department and Commissioner of Police of Metropolis, authority granted to Detective Chief Superintendent John Gaffney and Detective Chief Inspector Harold Tipper to investigate death of Kerr. Assigned under Overseas Police Act and expenses to be charged accordingly."

"Well, they didn't waste any time," said Tipper, dropping the message flimsy casually on the table. "And it means that it'll take a bloody long time for us to get our expenses back."

"Mr Gaffney, how good to see you again. And you too, Mr Tipper. What can I possibly do to be of assistance to you?" Mohammed Khan beamed at them.

"I'm afraid that there was a tragic occurrence last night at the embassy."

"Oh?" Khan looked suitably funereal.

"Peter Kerr committed suicide."

"Oh no! It cannot be true!"

"I'm afraid it is."

"But this is dreadful, Mr Gaffney. He was a friend of mine. A good friend."

Gaffney could not help feeling that what they were telling Khan was not news to him. "I need to arrange a post-mortem, and I was wondering if your pathologist — "

Khan brought his hands together. "Mr Gaffney, consider it done. I shall make a telephone call now."

It was all resolved very quickly, despite the Ambassador's pessimistic view. Thanks to Dr Gilchrist's surprising swiftness in making the arrangements, Kerr's body was already lodged at the hospital and within forty minutes of Khan's telephone call, Gaffney and Tipper were watching the pathologist's first incision.

"What now, Harry?" Gaffney and Tipper were seated in Peter Kerr's office, which they had decided to use as their base. There was no subtlety attached to that decision, no psychological ploy of the sort that might appeal to the creators of the inspired and wholly fictional amateur detective so beloved of the crime writer. It just so happened that it was the only office available in an embassy building so inadequate that it was clearly governed by some diplomatic modification of Parkinson's Law.

"Take statements," said Tipper with a sigh. "Until we get the pathologist's report and the photographs, there's not much else." Mohammed Khan had provided a police photographer to take photographs of the body at various stages of the post-mortem examination, Tipper having decided that it would be asking too much of young Stebbings to attend the post-mortem as well."

"Where do we start, Harry?" Gaffney, a career Special Branch officer, readily deferred to Tipper in anything which smacked of a criminal investigation, acknowledging that his chief inspector, most of whose career had been spent in the more sordid areas of crime, was an expert in the field of sudden death.

"At the beginning," said Tipper with a smile. "Ex-PC Brooks."

Ernest Brooks was forty-nine years of age, and as he had told the detectives earlier that day, he had served in the Metropolitan Police for twenty-five years before obtaining his present post at the British Embassy in Islamabad, where he had been for three years.

"One of us does night-duty for a week, guv," said Brooks. "There's six of us altogether — all Brits, of course — on the security side, so one night-duty in six weeks isn't too bad. Knocks spots off pounding the Fulham Road, any day."

"Do you have a schedule?" asked Tipper. "For making routine visits, I mean."

"No!" Brooks grinned. "The Head of Chancery thinks we do, but we wander round as and when."

"What's that mean?"

"Well, for me it means setting my alarm for every two hours. Then I have a stroll round the corridors, just to see everything's okay. It always is. Well, leastways, it was till last night."

"And what time did you have your stroll round last night, Ernie?" Tipper posed the question in an offhand way, giving the impression that he was not really interested in the answer, that it was a routine that had to be gone through for the sake of form, but Gaffney, who had watched him at work before, knew that it was a dangerous assumption for a witness to make. And even more dangerous for a suspect.

Brooks looked thoughtful. "About ten to three, I suppose."

Tipper nodded. "And that's when you found Kerr, was it?"

"Yes, that's right. I made a note of it." Brooks took a notebook from his pocket and opened it on the desk.

"Very wise," said Tipper. "Tell me about it."

"Well, I wandered past the end of the corridor leading to the armoury and noticed that the door was open and the light was on."

"So?"

"So I walked down and looked in. That's when I saw the deceased."

"What did you do then?"

"I ascertained that life was extinct and immediately telephoned the Ambassador from the phone in the corridor." The evidential police jargon came easily.

"Yes?"

"Well, the Ambassador came across from the residence straightaway. He took one look at Mr Kerr and told me to get Dr Gilchrist."

"Why?"

Brooks looked puzzled for a moment. "Well, I suppose he wanted a qualified medical practitioner to say that he was dead." Brooks grinned. "Just like they told us at Peel House," he said. "A dead 'un ain't dead till a doctor says so."

"And of course Dr Gilchrist said so."

Brooks ran a hand round his mouth. "What do you think, guv?"

Tipper smiled. It was an ominous smile, but so far only Gaffney knew that. "I take it that the armoury door was closed on the previous occasion that you passed the end of that corridor?"

Brooks only paused for a moment. "Yes, sir," he said.

"And what time would that have been?"

"Oh, about one-ish, I suppose."

"What time do you start night-duty, Ernie?"

"About eleven."

"About eleven?"

"Yes."

"And that was the time you started last night?"

"Yes, sir." Brooks sat up slightly.

"I see." Tipper gazed into the middle distance, beyond Brooks' left shoulder. "There was a dinner party at the residency last night. Mr Gaffney and I were there. We left just before midnight, but the party didn't break up until one. Would that be right?"

Brooks nodded. "So I believe," he said uncertainly.

"You don't know for sure?"

"Well no, not exactly."

"Why's that?" Tipper appeared to be genuinely interested in this little enigma.

"Well, I was out and about like."

"Yes, I suppose so," Tipper said, almost to himself. "So was it before the party broke up, or after, that you visited the armoury and found the door to be locked?"

"It was just after one. About ten-past, I should think."

"And did you try the door, physically?"

153

"Er, yes, as far as I can remember."

"Only as far as you can remember?"

"Well, it becomes a matter of routine."

"I suppose so," said Tipper. "Thanks for your help."

"Don't you want me to make a statement?" Brooks looked mildly puzzled.

"Not just yet," said Tipper.

"Problems, Harry?" asked Gaffney when the door had closed behind the security guard.

"Yes," said Tipper thoughtfully. "Like he's a lying git."

With surprisingly commendable speed, the pathologist's report and the photographs arrived just before dinner. Gaffney had suggested that Mohammed Khan was clearly out to impress the Scotland Yard officers with the efficiency of the Pakistani police. Tipper said it was because he'd got bugger-all else to do.

"I am beginning to get unhappy about this whole enquiry, sir," said Tipper, studying the full frontal photograph of Kerr taken after the body had been stripped of its clothing but before the pathologist had started to carve it up.

"In what way?"

"I'm not happy about this entry wound." Tipper was using a pencil as a makeshift ruler and was doing some measuring.

"Does it matter that much, Harry?"

Tipper swung round from the window and sat down again. "I think it does, guv'nor, yes."

Gaffney lit a cigar and smiled. He knew already that something was bothering his DCI, had worked with him long enough to be able to tell. "Go on, then."

"It's this spread of shot, guv. I've done one or two shotgun killings before. But they've always been on the hoof. One was a villain legging it and got blasted accidentally by his mate. The other was a villain who tried to leg it with more than his fair share. But this is a suicide." He paused for a moment, before adding, "Or so we are led to believe."

"Oh no!" Gaffney grinned. "Come on then, Harry, what's at the back of your mind?"

Tipper lowered his voice. "It stands to reason that with a shotgun, the further away the gun is from the target, the wider the spread of shot."

Gaffney suddenly became interested. "Go on, Harry."

"I remember one of our pathologists telling me that it's almost an exact science. If you know the gun, and you can measure the spread, you can tell the distance between muzzle and target. I've got a nagging suspicion that the spread of shot on Kerr's chest was too wide for the distance he was from the gun."

Gaffney carefully rolled the ash from his cigar and looked up. "Anything else?"

"Yes, sir. At the risk of repeating myself the string was around the front trigger, but it was the barrel activated by the rear trigger that was charged. I'll wait until we've done a fingerprint examination on the weapon before I try, but I'm damned certain you can't pull through. And I'm just as certain that the kick would have thrown the weapon off the table any way. Well now, that's all a bit iffy . . . " Tipper held his hand out flat and rocked it from side to side in a see-sawing motion. "But to pull the gun towards yourself after you're dead . . . that's bloody brilliant. And that's what happened if my theory about the spread of shot is right." Tipper paused to stifle a yawn. "On the other hand he could have been murdered."

Gaffney exhaled smoke slowly. "Oh dear," he said. "But at least we haven't got too many suspects." He was quite accustomed to Tipper's dry humour, which was just as well.

"No," said Tipper. "Only about ninety-six million of them, if all the security guards here are as good as Brooks."

8

AT the insistence of the Ambassador, Gaffney and Tipper joined him and his wife for dinner that evening. Tipper suspected that the invitation was prompted more by curiosity than hospitality, but then Tipper was like that.

"And how are you getting along, Mr Gaffney?" It was Mrs Forbes who spoke, which surprised both the policemen. So far she had had little to say.

"Making progress, ma'am, but we've decided to call it a day."

"I should think so." She smiled and took a sip of wine. "You don't seem to have had much time off, do you? It's a great shame, that. There's so much to see in Pakistan. Islamabad in particular is interesting. The people here have created a new capital. Of course, it's a new nation — comparatively speaking. It used to be part of British India, you know, until that man Attlee decided to give it away. If he hadn't, we'd still have been here." She spoke as though she were somewhere else, and Gaffney was mildly amused that the Ambassador's wife should have thought he needed a history lesson.

The Ambassador obviously thought that Gaffney was in no need of a lecture on the State of Pakistan. "I don't suppose you've much left to do now, have you?" he boomed from the end of the table.

"Quite a bit, as a matter of fact," said Gaffney.

"Oh, really?" Forbes looked surprised. "Still, you'll be able to let me have my shotgun back, won't you?"

"No, not yet."

"Whyever not?"

"Because Mr Tipper and I have to test-fire it."

Gaffney and Tipper had agreed that the only way to resolve the latter's doubts about the spread of shot on Kerr's body was to fire the Ambassador's Purdey under test conditions and measure the result.

The Ambassador put down his knife

and fork and gazed steadily at Gaffney for some seconds before speaking. "Why on earth should you want to do that?"

Gaffney wished that he could say 'routine' like the make-believe policemen in novels and on television; a meaningless word that seemed to satisfy the most persistent of their fictional adversaries. "In case the coroner should ask for details of the firing characteristics of your particular gun. As you know, each gun will produce slightly different patterns of fire — "

"I thought that was only rifled weapons."

Tipper answered that. "You're talking about the effect of the rifling on the spent round," he said. "As unique as a fingerprint."

"But surely," the Ambassador persisted, "that doesn't apply to a shotgun. You can't say that the pellets that killed poor Kerr actually came from my shotgun, can you?"

"No, you can't."

"Then why are you test-firing it?"

"It's routine," said Tipper.

"Oh," said the Ambassador.

The working day starts much earlier in Pakistan than it does at home, and an embassy car delivered Gaffney and Tipper to police headquarters just after half-past seven. Tipper was carrying the Ambassador's Purdey.

"My dear Mr Gaffney, how good to see you, and you too, Mr Tipper." Mohammed Khan was waiting for them on the doorstep of his headquarters. "But how sad that such an event should have been the cause of your visit." He shook his head. "What a sad affair, very sad indeed. Poor Mr Kerr." He shook his head again. "What can possibly have driven him to do such a thing?"

"It is indeed a mystery," said Gaffney. Khan was overdoing it a bit, and he wondered whether the Pakistani Superintendent was as suspicious as he and Tipper. Khan was, after all, a policeman, and doubtless knew that the British policemen's request for technical assistance indicated a greater depth of enquiry than was usual in a case of suicide. Then again, there was little doubt in Gaffney's mind that Khan knew perfectly well that Kerr had been attached to the Secret Intelligence Service.

"Well, gentlemen. I am sure that Scotland Yard will get to the bottom of it." He smiled archly. "If there is a bottom to be got to . . . " The smile vanished. "Well now, what can I do to assist?"

"The first thing we would like to do," said Tipper, holding up the Ambassador's Purdey, carefully wrapped in a plastic sheet, "is to have this weapon examined for fingerprints."

"Ah, yes," said Khan, "always a necessary preamble to any enquiry." He waggled his head knowledgeably. "I thought that might be the case, and I have my fingerprint staff ready and waiting. Please follow me."

He led the way down a corridor, and Gaffney had visions, from the way the Superintendent had spoken, of a vast department with the most modern equipment imaginable. But it was a small room with just a long bench and two fingerprint officers in white coats.

"These are my fingerprint experts, Mr Gaffney. Allow me to introduce you." He rattled off two names which neither

Gaffney nor Tipper was able to recall ten seconds later.

"It is a great pleasure to meet Scotland Yard detectives," said one of the experts, clearly the senior of the two. "I have had the honour of being trained by the great Metropolitan Police . . . at Hendon." He pointed to a framed certificate on the wall. "The long fingerprint course," he said proudly. "Extremely beneficial in my profession, sir, I can assure you. Please give my regards to this man." He pointed at the indecipherable signature of a chief superintendent at the bottom of the certificate. "And now, sir, to business." He glanced at the weapon in Gaffney's hand.

"I don't hold out much hope," said Tipper, unwrapping the Purdey, "but I should like you to try."

Mohammed Khan stepped closer to the bench on which Tipper had placed the shotgun. "It is a beautiful weapon, Mr Tipper," he said, and just stopped himself from running a hand lovingly along the stock. Then he sighed. "But first, fingerprints."

It didn't take long. "I'm sorry, sir,"

said the senior fingerprint officer, "but there are no identifiable prints on this weapon."

Tipper shrugged. "I didn't expect there to be," he said. "Not on a shotgun, but you never know your luck."

From the Fingerprint Department, Mohammed Khan, who seemed to have nothing else to do, conducted them to the Firearms Section where the introduction procedure was repeated. Eventually the Purdey was put into a clamp and fired, a barrel at a time, then both together, at paper targets at varying distances from the muzzles of the gun. Tipper then took the weapon and fired it himself after which he squatted down and squinted along the barrels. Then he did some measuring and made some notes. Gaffney had no idea what he was up to.

When they had finished, Mohammed Khan pointed at the targets which Tipper was carefully gathering together. "I hope they are of some assistance in your enquiries," he said.

"Oh, it's not to help," said Tipper. "It's to save taking the shotgun back to England for the coroner's inquest. He's bound to want to know something about the gun, and if we can show him these, he won't understand them, but it'll shut him up."

Mohammed Khan laughed. "It is the same the world over," he said, and shook his head, although what was the same he did not make clear.

"Well?" asked Gaffney when they were in the privacy of Kerr's office.

Tipper spread the targets out on a table. Then he flipped open his pocket-book. "The spread of pellets on Kerr's body from the entry wound was four to five inches. I measured it. Look here." He opened the file of post-mortem photographs and pointed. "There, you see, sir. That peripheral spread of shot." He pulled one of the targets towards him. "This is the nearest to the spread on Kerr's body. This shows a spread of shot of four to five inches."

"And?"

"And that, guv'nor, was fired at a distance of thirteen feet from the target. The distance between the shotgun and Kerr's body was four feet three inches."

He pushed the targets away and stood upright, putting his hands into his trouser pockets. "But that doesn't really matter in view of the other things I discovered. Pressure on the front trigger, if continued, does not follow through to activate the rear one. Not unless there's a malfunction. And on the Ambassador's new Purdey there wasn't." He paused. "The cartridge case that was left in the weapon would have been fired by the rear trigger . . . and the string wasn't round that one. In other words, the whole thing was set up. And if that's not enough, sir, I checked the angles. If the shotgun had been fired from the position in which we found it, the trajectory is such that it would have taken his head off . . . not hit him in the chest. And just for good measure, I tried the weapon myself. The recoil would certainly have thrown it off the table, as I suggested it would."

Gaffney lit a cigar, and blew the smoke in a slow spiral up towards the electric fan which suddenly plucked it away in an impatient eddy. "If I hear you right, Harry, you're saying that we have a murder here."

They hadn't seen Diana Gibson before because she wasn't senior enough to have been invited to the dinner party on the night that Gaffney and Tipper had arrived. But she was the girl whom the Ambassador had suggested might have been having an affair with Peter Kerr.

She was a plain girl — not frumpish — but hardly a beauty. She wore make-up no more successfully than the other women at the embassy, all of whom had to contend with the heat, and her clothes, although not striking, were clearly expensive. The two detectives immediately decided that she did not come into the category of a girl it was worth risking one's marriage for, although both were prepared to concede that men often were that foolhardy for the sake of a few minutes' physical ecstasy that in retrospect never seemed quite worth the price.

Gaffney waited until she was seated and then introduced himself and Tipper.

Diana Gibson giggled nervously and put her hand to her mouth. "I'm sorry," she said.

"Something funny?"

"No, it's just that you're already known in the embassy as G and T."

"Oh, I see," said Gaffney, dismissing her feeble joke as unworthy of comment. "Well now, perhaps you'll forgive me, Miss Gibson, if I come directly to the point. It's been suggested that you and Peter Kerr were having an affair."

"Yes, I know." The girl seemed quite unperturbed by Gaffney's bald statement.

"And is it true?"

"No, of course not."

"You seem quite adamant."

"Well if I'm supposed to have had an affair with Peter, I should know whether it's true or not." She spoke defiantly, and Gaffney detected a brief trace of wildness in her eyes.

"Have you any idea why such a rumour should have started?"

"It might help if you told me who told you."

"Well I'm not — " began Gaffney.

"Probably the Ambassador," said Diana. "But since you ask, there are a number of reasons. One or two of the men here have chatted me up, and I've turned them

down. That always hurts a man's ego."
She smiled conceitedly. "But the most
likely reason is that Peter used to come to
my place from time to time to play chess.
We're both keen players, and we're about
the same standard." She crossed her legs
and rearranged her skirt. "I can imagine
that that set the tongues wagging." She
laughed. "No one would believe that
we just sat there playing chess, simply
because no one would want to believe
it, but it was true. As a matter of fact,
I didn't fancy Peter at all." She pulled
her cardigan more closely round her
shoulders. The temperature had dropped
sharply to ninety degrees that morning
and Gaffney had heard one or two people
around the embassy complaining of the
cold when all he wanted was to stand
under a cold shower.

"So it was purely platonic."

"What a lovely old-fashioned expression."
She flicked a strand of mousey-coloured
hair out of her eyes. "I felt sorry for him,
really. He was a very lonely sort of man.
His wife wouldn't come out on this tour.
She hates the heat apparently. It makes
her ill, so Peter said. And it's not easy

for him to make friends. He has to be so careful."

"Why's that?"

"Doing what he was doing. SIS, I mean."

"Oh, you knew that, did you?"

"Of course. We're all told officially. It's to prevent cockups." She grinned at them.

"Did he mention any trouble he was having at all? Any enemies he might have made?" asked Gaffney. He instantly regretted asking that question. It made him sound like a storybook policeman, and it rarely produced any hard evidence, just a bit of gossip that took ages to resolve, and usually came to nought. But he found this girl difficult to talk to. She was very confident, sitting in her chair like a taut spring, and not at all overawed by the presence of two senior Scotland Yard officers.

"In the embassy . . . or outside?" Again the cheeky grin.

Gaffney was slowly revising his opinion of this girl. She might not be much to look at, but she had a sense of humour, and she was direct. "Anywhere," he said.

"Never mentioned any. And never talked about his job . . . ever!"

"No, of course not."

"But embassies are funny places. They're tight-knit communities. Incestuous almost. And the slightest problem, or rumour, or bit of tittle-tattle, is common knowledge in no time at all."

"Such as?"

"Such as this piece of nonsense about he and I having an affair." She stared directly at Gaffney, again with a flash of intensity.

"Did he ever mention his wife, or his marriage?"

"Oh yes. He seemed to be a perfectly normal married man. He loved his wife and he loved his kids. In fact, he often talked about them. And a man who wants to get you into bed doesn't usually talk about his wife." She lifted her chin slightly, inviting him to disagree. "Unless he's telling you that his wife doesn't understand him . . . and Peter never did that."

"You've no idea why he should have killed himself, then?"

"None at all," she said. "Unless he

was missing his wife, but killing himself would hardly resolve that." It was a strange thing to say and she shrugged as though realising the pointlessness of her comment. "Anyway, I think he was due a posting fairly soon."

"Thanks, Miss Gibson. That's all."

She paused at the door. "I suppose neither of you plays chess?"

"Occasionally," said Gaffney, "but I don't have time at the moment."

"And Mr Tipper?"

"He doesn't play chess at all," said Gaffney. "Anyway he's married," he added with a wry grin.

"Pity!" said Diana Gibson, but it was unclear whether she was referring to Tipper's marital status or his inability to play chess.

After Diana Gibson had left, Gaffney stood up and strolled round the office. "It's quite possible that the answer's here, Harry, in this room," he said.

Tipper put his hands behind his head and yawned. "You still trying to tie this up with the Gisela Hunter enquiry, guv'nor?" He didn't sound enthusiastic about Gaffney's idea.

"Think about it, Harry. Foster comes to us and tells us that Gisela Hunter is trying to wheedle information out of him in exchange for fun and games in her bed. And she adds a little gentle blackmail by suggesting that she'll let his wife know if he doesn't play ball."

"You do have a way with words, guv," said Tipper.

"She's got to have had some success in the past. She started back in nineteen seventy-seven, according to James Marchant, possibly even before that. That woman could have a network of spies of differing nationalities all over the place. But just look at who the most useful are likely to be. The British, because of their long association with India and Pakistan. And who better than the resident SIS man right here? If he'd got wind of us coming out here — and it's quite possible that he did through the Number Ten net — that would be a good enough reason for him to sense that the game's afoot."

"You sound just like Sherlock Holmes," said Tipper. "On the other hand, we do know that her old man was in business out here. And we know also that the business is still functioning. She could simply be employing her feminine talent to make sure that the wheels continue to turn. A little favour here, a little backhander there. It's the way these things are done. Anyway, what did Foster really tell us? It was all airy-fairy. Gisela Hunter didn't actually ask him for any hard intelligence. It was just a hint here and there about how helpful he could be, and how grateful her 'friends' would be. It was a load of bloody rubbish when you got it all down on paper. And what happened? Foster, who'd probably had the best tumble of his life, suddenly panics. He gets nicked and breathalysed, and it all comes on top. He sees the whole bloody world disintegrating before his eyes. He probably thought drunken driving was a Bailey job, and it would all come out. 'Foreign Office man in Mata Hari spy scandal — Commons statement'." Tipper laughed. "Let's face it, guv, Foster's got no bottle, has he?"

Gaffney nodded slowly, loathe to see his theory dismissed. "I suppose you're right, Harry. But you can't get away from the fact that we came out here to see what we could find, and within hours of our arrival Peter Kerr is dead."

"But there's no bloody evidence that he was implicated." Tipper remained unconvinced. "Anyway, he was murdered. If anything, he was on to whoever was spying and was killed to keep him quiet. If he was connected at all."

"Or knowing that we were on our way, he decided to come clean, and someone decided to shut him up . . . for good."

Tipper shook his head. "Won't stand up, guv'nor. If Kerr had been at it, he'd have learned to cover his tracks. But he'd be crazy, knowing how SIS works. There's no chance of him getting away with that. I know we take the piss out of old James Marchant, but Six have learned their lesson with people like Philby and Blake and all the rest. What's that lovely expression? Big fleas have little fleas on their backs to bite 'em; little fleas have smaller fleas, and so on, ad infinitum!"

"*Quis custodiet ipsos custodes?*" quoted Gaffney.

"What the hell's that mean?"

"Who will guard the guards themselves?" Gaffney translated with a smile.

Tipper sniffed loudly. "I just bloody said that. Anyway, even if your theory's got anything in it, I doubt if you'd find anything in here," he said waving a hand airily around Kerr's office, "but I suppose it's worth having a look." He stood up and walked across to the safe. "But I don't think you'll banjo this in a hurry."

"I suppose it's locked, is it, Harry?" Gaffney had known safes to be left on the latch before, admittedly against all the rules, but it had happened.

Tipper gently moved the wheel of the combination lock and tried the handle. "No go," he said.

"What's his date of birth, Harry?"

"I know I'm a detective," said Tipper acidly, "but I'm not a miracle-worker What's that got to do with it, anyway?"

"It has been known for people with bad memories to use their date of birth as a combination . . . " Gaffney started opening the drawers of the desk. eventually he held up Kerr's passport.

176

"That should tell us," he said.

There are a number of ways in which the combination of a safe operates. The wheel is turned one way or another to start with, a specified number of times, and is stopped on the first of the numbers which make up the combination. Then the wheel is turned the opposite way, one revolution less than before, finishing on the next number, and so on. After this exacting routine has been completed there will usually be a standard requirement to finish on zero . . . or twenty-five . . . or fifty . . . or seventy-five, and one of the things that Gaffney learned early in his career as a Special Branch Officer was never to try it when you had a few Scotches inside you. But right now he was sober, and he tried every conceivable variation that he knew.

Finally, there was a satisfying click, and with a certain feeling of triumph and self-satisfaction Gaffney swung the heavy door open.

The safe was empty.

Tipper rocked back in his chair, laughing. "Christ!" he said. "It's just like the DAC's drinks cupboard."

They were sitting in Gaffney's room at the hotel in Rawalpindi. Gaffney had taken the view that the murderer would not go away, that the responsibility for Kerr's death rested with someone on the staff of the embassy . . . by the very nature of its closed and secure existence.

Although reluctant to dismiss the possibility of an itinerant intruder, Tipper had agreed that such a likelihood was remote. He was not impressed with the security arrangements at the mission, but acknowledged that an outsider would be unlikely to know of their weakness and, therefore, would not risk breaking in, much less commit a murder . . . unless there was a damned good reason, and so far none had emerged. Apart from anything else, there appeared to be nothing missing, and robbery would have been the most obvious intention of an intruder.

"I think our best bet is to go home," said Gaffney. "Oddly enough, I think we're more likely to find the answer in the UK than here."

Tipper nodded slowly, reluctant to

give up at the scene. It went against his instinct, his experience and all his training. "The answer's got to be here somewhere," he said. "If bloody Brooks had been doing his job, he might have seen something. Someone murdered Kerr in the armoury . . . or elsewhere and put his body there. Kerr was at dinner, with us, and was still there when we left. Where did he go from there? To inspect the armoury . . . at two in the morning or whenever? Shouldn't have thought so, but surely to God someone saw something, heard something. After all, a shotgun's pretty noisy."

"So are diplomats having dinner if the other night was anything to go by. And the dining room is a hell of a long way from the armoury."

"Is there any point in questioning anyone else in the embassy before we go, guv?" asked Tipper.

Gaffney shrugged. "The few we have seen, what I call the material ones, all alibi each other . . . quite genuinely, I think. After all, they were all at the dinner party. The senior ones anyway. And we've spoken to Brooks, and we've spoken to Diana Gibson — "

"And I reckon she was having it off with Kerr, you know. Despite her denial."

"You've got a dirty mind, Harry. Frankly there are quite a few others I'd have preferred to her if I'd been him. The gorgeous Angela Conrad, for example, with whom, I noticed, you were in animated conversation the other night. After all, Kerr was quite a good-looking bloke."

Tipper laughed. "There's only one problem there, sir. The birds you fancy don't always fancy you. One of life's little cruelties, that is. Anyway, got any wild thoughts, guv?"

Gaffney shrugged. "No, not really. Could have been anyone. For all we know the Ambassador himself. So far, he thinks it's suicide."

"Well, that's the line he's pushing," said Tipper, "and we haven't let him know that we know it isn't."

"Sure, but if we tell him we suspect murder, how are we going to prove it . . . if it's down to him? He's our only real contact. Anything useful about the staff must come from him, and he's not been very forthcoming. Look how I had to drag that information out of him about the sort of stuff Kerr was collecting." Gaffney paused to sip at his beer. "And once we let him know that we're not the thick coppers he thinks we are, we're going to get even less."

"That would be obstructing us in the execution of our duty," said Tipper with mock severity.

Gaffney laughed. "What are you going to do, Harry, nick him? He's not your run-of-the-mill villain. Mr Forbes is Her Majesty's Ambassador Extraordinary and Plenipotentiary, and that gives him a hell of a lot of clout. One more of his clever little telegrams to the FCO and we're out on our ears. He's God hereabouts, don't forget."

Tipper held up a hand. "Only joking," he said. "I know all about ambassadors. Mallory, for instance."

Gaffney smiled. "Yes," he said, "I'd forgotten him, and the sexy Penny Lambert. But I think this bloke's a different kettle of fish. Anyway, I don't want to get a reputation for nicking ambassadors."

Tipper stared moodily into his glass before taking another sip of his beer. "What d'you suggest, then?" He placed the glass carefully on the table.

"Tell him that we're satisfied that it's suicide, take all our evidence home and give it to the DPP; let him decide. If he thinks further enquiries should be made, then we'll be in a much stronger position. We can have a go at the Foreign Office for a start. At present, Forbes has talked himself into believing that Kerr took his own life, because a murder, he thinks, would reflect on his authority . . . or he's the murderer."

"It's a bloody dog's dinner, that's what it is," said Tipper angrily.

"Be that as it may," said Gaffney, "that's what we're going to do." He paused. "Once we've done the other job we came out here to do."

Tipper raised an eyebrow.

"Little question of the security arrangements for the PM's visit, Harry."

Tipper grinned. "Oh yes," he said. "I'd

almost forgotten that . . . but I'd like to have one more go at Brooks."

"Why?"

"I reckon he's having us over. Don't ask me why, but there's something. The look on his face when we turned up within the hour was quite something."

Halfway up the embassy drive, Gaffney and Tipper got out of the car. Brooks was patrolling the grounds but stopped as they approached.

"You look as though you're working Number Four beat at Fulham, Ernie," said Tipper, a firm believer in lulling witnesses into a false sense of security.

Brooks grinned. "Those were the days," he said. They walked on a few paces before Brooks spoke again. "How are your enquiries going, guv?"

"We've finished," said Tipper. "All bar a few loose ends." He paused as if struck by a sudden thought. "Which reminds me. Strictly between you and me, Ernie, when you found Kerr's body, that was the first time you'd been round, wasn't it?"

Brooks stopped, turning to face the

Chief Inspector. "I don't know what you mean," he said.

Tipper grinned disarmingly. "It's no skin off my nose, Ernie. I shan't report you to the Ambassador, if that's what you're worried about, but I know that you spent the first couple of hours of your tour of duty getting a few down in the servery with the housekeeper." It was pure guesswork. Tipper had not a shred of evidence to support his assumption, but there had been a dinner party that night and he knew coppers — and ex-coppers — when there was any free booze around.

Brooks raised his hands, surrendering. "You've got me bang to rights," he said. "There didn't seem any point in going round. HE's dinner party was still under way, and it didn't seem worth doing anything until they'd all got their heads down." He stared at Tipper. "I couldn't really say anything else, could I? You know how it is. Absent from beat, and all that."

Tipper laughed. "Weren't playing brag as well, were you?"

It relieved the tension. "Haven't had

a hand of brag for years," said Brooks, a faraway look of nostalgia crossing his face.

They had started walking again, and were almost at the residence. "You must have known Fred Chivers, the DI at Fulham," said Tipper. "Retired about . . . " He appeared to be doing mental arithmetic " . . . five years ago, I suppose. Shortish chap, always wore a pork-pie hat and smoked a stubby little pipe."

After a moment or two's thought, Brooks said, "Yes, of course. Used to stink the station out with that tobacco of his."

"That's him," said Tipper. "Small world, isn't it?"

"Feel happier about Brooks, now you've spoken to him again?" asked Gaffney.

"No." Tipper sat on his bed. "He's hiding something, and I don't know what."

"What makes you think that?"

"D'you remember me asking him if he knew Fred Chivers?"

"The DI at Fulham?"

"Yeah! Except that he wasn't a DI and he never served at Fulham. He retired as a DS and his last few years were at Gerald Road."

"Well, he obviously knew him. The bit about smelling out the nick with his pipe."

"Oh yes. That was right enough, but it was Gerald Road nick. And, guv'nor, Gisela Hunter lives on Gerald Road's ground."

"Oh no," said Gaffney. "Don't try complicating it any further."

Tipper tapped the side of his nose. "You've got to look at all the angles, sir," he said.

9

THE Ambassador was wearing his diplomatic face. "And how are your enquiries going, Mr Gaffney?" he asked.

"Complete, sir, I'm pleased to say."

"Oh, that's splendid." Forbes hesitated. "And your findings?"

"That's not for me to say," said Gaffney, reaching for a bread roll. "But the evidence points to suicide."

"Ah!" The Ambassador let out a long sigh. Whether he was relieved at not having been discovered, or at not having the scandal of a murder rock his intimate little world was unclear, but relieved he definitely appeared to be. "Nothing in this theory of yours about poor Kerr being a spy?" To him it was a rhetorical question and he smiled archly. "What happens now?"

"We go home and present our report to the coroner."

"I see." The Ambassador put down

his wine glass with studied calm. "You mean that there will still be an inquest . . . without a body?"

Gaffney raised his eyebrows. "Without a body?"

"Of course. Unless you're planning on taking Peter Kerr's body home with you."

"That's exactly what I propose to do. Apart from anything else, his widow has requested that he be buried in England."

"But how . . . ? I mean, have you been in touch with her?"

Gaffney nodded amiably. "Oh yes."

"But how?" The Ambassador looked disconcerted. It was obvious that he had been monitoring the signal traffic relating to Kerr's death and appeared puzzled that he could have missed some vital message, or worse, that it had been deliberately kept from him.

"Through Interpol. Mohammed Khan has been very helpful."

Forbes frowned. "Was that wise? Using these local chappies for that sort of confidential stuff?"

"There's nothing confidential about Kerr killing himself," growled Tipper.

"I should think the whole of Islamabad knows about it now. Anyway, we had to make use of Khan's scientific facilities. It's not as if there were any suspicious circumstances." Tipper looked directly at the Ambassador. "Were there?"

"Good heavens, no." Forbes waved away an imaginary cloud of suspicion. "Well, you fellows would know, wouldn't you?" He smiled and patted his lips with his table napkin. Tipper disconcerted him. He was obviously not what Forbes called 'out of the top drawer', but there was a rough incisiveness about the Chief Inspector that upset the diplomat's urbanity. Forbes changed the subject. "Please make use of the embassy's facilities to arrange your flight bookings. My secretary, Angela, usually deals with that sort of thing. She's got a friend at British Airways, as a matter of fact. Should be able to get you an early flight." It was obvious that the Ambassador couldn't wait to see the back of the two policemen.

"I do hope you've enjoyed your stay," said the Ambassador's wife. It was her only contribution to the conversation throughout lunch. She had her usual vacant look about her, and had spoken the courtesy vaguely and automatically. Tipper wondered if she was an alcoholic.

"Thank you." Gaffney inclined his head. "We're not going just yet, of course. We do have to do a security survey for the Prime Minister's visit."

"Ah yes," said the Ambassador. "So you do." And he smiled and nodded.

Mohammed Khan was at the airport when they arrived from their hotel. He stood in the centre of the concourse, feet apart and hands behind his back. Standing to one side and slightly to Khan's rear, as befitted his lowly station, was a constable clutching a sheaf of papers. The four policemen who had been at the tennis court lunch were there too. The two in uniform snapped to attention and saluted as Gaffney and Tipper walked towards them.

"My dear Mr Gaffney, good morning, good morning." Mohammed Khan beamed at them. "And Mr Tipper also."

"Good morning." Gaffney had a sour

190

feeling that the day's events were going
to be protracted, and that did not please
him. Already, at seven-thirty in the
morning, the temperature had climbed
to over a hundred degrees.

Mohammed Khan rubbed his hands
together. "First we do the airport, Mr
Gaffney . . . if you are agreeable?" And
without waiting for a reply, he set off
at a brisk pace through the immigration
and customs controls to airside. An
army officer, immaculate in khaki drill,
complete with Sam Browne, saluted and
shook hands. "May I introduce Major
Naseem Abbasi, Mr Gaffney," said Khan.
"The Major will command the guard of
honour . . . "

"Yes indeed, Mr Gaffney," said the
Major. "My chaps will be here . . . "
He indicated with a wave of his swagger
cane. "Formed up in two ranks, d'you
see?"

Gaffney tried to look intelligently
interested as the soldier went through the
military routine that was to form the first
part of the Prime Minister's arrival. "Yes,
of course," he murmured. He took his
copy of the programme from his pocket

and studied the sketch-map of the airport. "And the dais is over there . . . yes?"

"That is correct," said Khan confidently. He had obviously been over the arrangements a thousand times in his mind and had probably done a physical survey several times before today. Doubtless, he could have recited the programme from memory.

"I see." Gaffney frowned.

"There is a problem, Mr Gaffney?"

"No, no. Just recalling that President Sadat of Egypt was assassinated by his own troops during a review. Such things tend to make one nervous." Gaffney knew that the demands of protocol would never allow a departure from what he called the 'G of H rigmarole', but it did no harm to plant the occasional seed of concern in the minds of those who thought that they had everything buttoned up, or to let them know that he knew his trade. But he smiled to soften the comment.

Mohammed Khan spoke in rapid Urdu to Major Naseem Abbasi who made a quick reply in the same language and then laughed nervously before turning to Gaffney. "I was just telling the Superintendent that my troops are all loyal and hand-picked," he said.

Gaffney raised a placating hand. "I don't doubt it, Major," he said. "Just my little joke." He glanced around. "And the band? Where will that be?"

"Ah yes, of course. Over there." Again the soldier pointed with his cane. "They are to be playing first the British national anthem, then the Pakistani national anthem, and finally an inspection waltz or two." He spoke in deprecating terms. Major Naseem Abbasi did not have much time for military musicians.

Gaffney gazed upwards and around at the flat roofs of the airport buildings. As in almost every airport in the world, they afforded perfect sites for a sniper.

"I know what you are thinking, Mr Gaffney," said Mohammed Khan, anticipating Gaffney's next question. "Roofs are to be cleared. Only policemen will be up there."

"I would never have thought otherwise, my dear Mr Khan," Gaffney said and laughed, restoring some of Khan's self-confidence. Khan, laughed too, but not very heartily. Despite the fact that it might lengthen his working day, Gaffney always believed in asking a few pertinent questions, just to let his hosts know that he took the question of security seriously. There had been too many political assassinations around the world for it to be viewed in any other way.

"There will be no airport vehicles on the apron, either," continued Mohammed Khan, who was beginning to realise that today's survey of the arrangements was not going to be as much of a walk-over as he had thought. "You doubtless remember the unfortunate business in Delhi when a deputy prime minister from Poland, I think it was, was killed by a baggage tractor." He shook his head at both the enormity of the embarrassment and the glaring loophole in security.

"What a funny thing," said Tipper, grinning. "I was just going to mention that."

The tortuous day wore on. Mohammed Khan and his coterie of assistants were, naturally enough, impervious to the heat, but to Gaffney's chagrin it appeared to have no effect on Tipper either, tagging along in the rear of the party, making clever remarks to the CID inspector who had been assigned as bodyguard to the Prime Minister.

The next stage of the reconnaissance was to drive slowly over the route that the Prime Minister's motorcade would take on its journey from the airport to the hotel in Rawalpindi, and from there to the other places that were to be visited. At intervals, Mohammed Khan would stop the car, leap out and wander about in the road, gesticulating at various buildings or junctions that he described as vulnerable points, before explaining in great detail the arrangements he had made to counter the risks they posed. He was shadowed constantly by his constable who would pluck the right sheet of paper from the pile beneath his arm and hand it to Khan whenever the Superintendent flicked his fingers. It was a dangerous business, and Gaffney discovered that stray animals, drivers of motor vehicles, and riders of pedal-cycles — there appeared to be an inordinate number of these — were no respecters of Pakistani policemen, much less British ones. Several times, Gaffney grabbed Khan by the arm to save him from being knocked down, but the Pakistani just laughed. "It is a jolly dangerous place, Rawalpindi, Mr Gaffney," he said.

Khan explained the security precautions that were to be taken at the hotel, at the President's Palace — where the British Prime Minister would be making a courtesy call — and at the Pakistani Prime Minister's residence. Khan then led the party to another hotel where some sort of British-Pakistani trade association was to hold a reception for the Prime Minister. Gaffney had been to these functions before, and knew that the object was usually to corner the PM for an ear-bending session on trade tariffs and the like.

"I have taken the liberty of asking Mr Trumper, OBE, to attend, Mr Gaffney," said Mohammed Khan as they strode into the hotel foyer. "He is the association's president or some such thing."

A corpulent, florid-faced individual with a large moustache stalked across the foyer with his hand outstretched.

To Gaffney, he appeared the epitome of colonial past.

"Mohammed Khan, my dear fellow, how splendid to see you." Trumper seized the Pakistani policeman's hand and pumped it vigorously.

"This is Detective Chief Superintendent Gaffney of Scotland Yard, and Detective Chief Inspector Tipper," said Khan.

"Splendid, splendid. Sidney Trumper," said Trumper, shaking hands with each of them in turn.

"Tipper? I knew some people of that name in Worcestershire years ago. Not one of the Worcestershire Tippers, are you?"

"No. Not one of the generous tippers, either." It was said sarcastically. Tipper never worried about showing his feelings and Trumper exemplified most of what Tipper despised in his fellow man: loud-mouthed and obnoxious.

Trumper had the good grace to laugh, but he made a mental note that it would not be a good thing to get on the wrong side of this London policeman.

Gaffney was shown the hall where the reception was to be held, and Trumper explained in depth what was to happen, most of which was of no interest to Gaffney at all, and seemed to have been included merely to demonstrate what a clever chap Trumper was in organising it all. At one point he drew Gaffney aside, out of Khan's earshot. "Take a word of advice from me, Chief," he said. "Watch these local johnnies, like Khan there. Never know what the devils are up to, y'know. Most of 'em are as bent as arseholes." He stroked his nose with his forefinger. "A word to the wise, old boy, if you know what I mean."

Gaffney detested being called 'Chief', and disliked people of Trumper's calibre even more. "Don't worry, Mr Trumper. I think you'll find that I've been a senior detective long enough to be able to judge the character of my professional colleagues," he said. "Or, for that matter, anyone else who isn't quite what he seems."

"Yes, well . . . " Trumper glanced at his watch. "Dare say you've time for a chota-peg, eh?"

"Thanks all the same, but we've work

to do." Gaffney turned away and then paused. "Does the name Hunter mean anything to you, Mr Trumper?"

Trumper frowned slightly as he appeared to search his mind. "Fellah from Karachi, you mean. Stabbed to death back in . . . "

"Nineteen seventy-one," said Gaffney.

"Oh yes. Heard about it. Everyone round here has, of course. You're not interested in that, surely?"

"Not really, no. I just wondered whether you'd ever met his widow, Gretchen, or Gabrielle, or some such foreign name."

Trumper shook his head slowly. "Can't say I have, old boy. Never met the chap, of course. Karachi's a damned long way away."

"No, I suppose not," said Gaffney. If Trumper knew anything about Gisela Hunter it was clear that he did not intend to be drawn into a trap as simple as the one Gaffney had just set him.

They got back to the hotel at six o'clock and Gaffney threw himself into an armchair.

"There's only one thing I want now," he said.

"I've just poured it, guv'nor," said Tipper.

Angela Conrad had a large office to herself, with a communicating door leading to the Ambassador's suite. She looked up and smiled as the two detectives entered.

"The Ambassador suggested that you could arrange our return bookings to London," said Gaffney.

"Of course. When did you want to go?"

"As soon as possible."

"You're very lucky," she said. "I wish I was coming with you."

Gaffney wished she was, too.

She made a couple of telephone calls and within minutes had given them their flight number, the time of departure from Islamabad International, and when the car would pick them up from their hotel. She was clearly as efficient as she was good-looking.

They thanked her, but as they turned to go, Angela Conrad stood up. "Mr

Gaffney," she said hesitantly.

"Yes?"

She looked embarrassed, and walked across to the door leading to the corridor and closed it. "I've been agonising over this, and I still don't know whether it's important." She fiddled with a ruby ring on the little finger of her left hand.

Gaffney smiled. "Supposing you tell me anyway," he said.

"After the dinner party the other night, the night you arrived . . . " Gaffney nodded. "Well, I don't know if it's relevant in view of what happened, but I thought I ought to tell you anyway. After you and Harry had gone, the party went on for a bit . . . till about one, I suppose, but before that happened, Cynthia Bartlett flaked out."

"Cynthia Bartlett?"

"Yes, she was sitting on Harry's right, two down from me in other words . . . "

"Yes, I know. Tall, willowy girl. Put away a fair amount of wine, if I remember rightly."

"Exactly. Well, between you and me, she's got a bit of a reputation for it. It's not uncommon, to be honest. Life on a foreign station is not all roses, I can tell you, and I'm afraid drink can be a bit of a problem . . . particularly as it's duty-free." She leaned back, resting on the edge of her desk, and crossed her ankles.

"I can imagine."

"And often," said Angela, "it's worse among the wives than the husbands. At least the men have got their job to do, but the women have nothing. They've all got servants and nannies and so on, and they don't have to lift a finger. The social round gets a bit tedious when that's all there is. Anyway, what I was going to say was that at about half-past twelve, Cynthia Bartlett just keeled over. As I said, it's never unexpected in her case, and she collided with a table and fell over. Everybody tries to pretend it doesn't happen, of course, and there's a sort of drill for dealing with it. Margaret Booth and I just helped her up, got her across to her quarters and put her to bed. It's not the first time, I'm afraid, and I don't suppose it'll be the last. Most of the girls here have put her to bed at some time or another." She looked a little guilty. "I know that all sounds like embassy gossip, but on the way back, we saw Peter Kerr walking across the compound towards the quarters."

"Does he live there?" asked Tipper.

"Oh yes, he's got a flat there."

"What time would this have been? When you saw Peter Kerr?"

She thought for a moment before replying. "By the time we'd tucked Cynthia up, about a quarter to one, I suppose." She looked from Tipper to Gaffney and back again. "I'm sorry," she said, "I'm just being silly. I don't know what you must think of me."

"There's no need to reproach yourself," said Gaffney. "We're always very grateful for any information, no matter how irrelevant it may seem." He smiled. "You never know how it fits in with what we already know. You certainly mustn't think that you're wasting our time. Incidentally, where was Mr Bartlett while all this was going on?"

"As far as I know, Julian stayed at the party. In fact, he didn't leave until sometime after we got back there."

"Bit odd, isn't it?" asked Tipper.

She pouted. "I don't think that things are all they might be in that marriage," said Angela. "Bit bumpy at times, if you know what I mean. She drinks too much because they don't get on, and they don't get on because she drinks too much." She held her hands out. "Chicken and egg thing, really."

"Did Peter Kerr go into his own apartment?" asked Tipper.

The girl looked at him quizzically. "I assume so," she said. "Why shouldn't he?" She appeared genuinely puzzled by Tipper's question.

"Only that it's been suggested to me that he might have been having an affair with another member of the staff."

Angela laughed. "Not that old chestnut," she said. "Diana Gibson?"

"Nothing in it?"

"They played chess on Sunday afternoons. Full stop. To be honest, I think that story was put about by certain people who couldn't bring themselves to accept that a man and a woman can just be friends and nothing else. As I was saying earlier, there's very little to do here except gossip."

"And Peter Kerr? Liked the ladies, perhaps?"

"Yes." She smiled. It looked to Tipper as though she was recalling some secret memory. "But he was a perfect gentleman . . . and married." She stood up. "I suppose you think that I'm just as much of a gossip as the others I've been accusing," she said with a smile. "But I thought I'd mention it."

"Thank you," said Gaffney. "I'm very glad you did."

By some quirk of police administration, there was a car waiting at the airport when Gaffney and Tipper arrived.

"You can drop me off at Richmond," said Gaffney, "and then take Mr Tipper home."

The driver, a policeman who normally drove the Home Secretary, shook his head and grinned insolently. "Commander wants to see you, sir."

Gaffney groaned. "Which one?"

"Mr Hussey, sir," — and forestalling Tipper's request, added — "and Mr Tipper."

"Enjoy your holiday?" Commander Frank Hussey was staring out of the window at London Transport's headquarters, but turned as Gaffney and Tipper entered his office. It was a joke, but a joke that was always made by desk-bound senior officers whenever one of their colleagues returned from a trip abroad.

"Some holiday," said Gaffney, dropping uninvited into one of the Commander's armchairs. "Went out to do an advance, and finished up investigating a murder."

Hussey walked across and sat down opposite Gaffney. "You're pretty certain it was a murder, then?" His voice retained its unemotional level.

"There's no doubt, sir, but I'll let Harry explain. He's got all the facts at his fingertips."

When Tipper had finished, Hussey leaned back in his chair and studied the ceiling. "Foster's still seeing the woman," he said after a while, continuing to look upwards.

"D'you think that's relevant, sir?" asked Gaffney.

"I don't know, John, but the murder of the SIS man in Pakistan and her known interest in Pakistani affairs make it a hell of a coincidence if there's no connection." Hussey leaned forward, pulled the ashtray towards his side of the coffee table and gently tapped the dead ash from his pipe. "What d'you propose doing now?"

"I'm going to put what we've got into a report for the DPP, then I'm going to have a chat with James Marchant and put him in the picture."

Hussey nodded slowly. "I doubt that you'll be telling him anything he doesn't know already. With any luck it'll be him putting you in the picture. Anything else?"

"Yes. Harry's going to look into a certain ex-PC who works out there as a security guard."

"I'm afraid your Mr Brooks got caught up in the drive against corruption, Mr Gaffney." The senior executive officer of PT2 Branch — the personnel department of the Metropolitan Police — flicked over a page in the file in front of him. "But it would appear that he got off lightly. He was reduced in rank from detective sergeant to constable and put back in uniform. Six months later, he got his twenty-five years in and went out on pension. Reading between the lines, I should say he was a lucky man."

"What did he get busted for?" Gaffney leaned forward in his chair.

The SEO shook his head. "I don't know. You'll have to draw the Number One docket for that. Here, I'll give you the reference."

A 'Number One' is police parlance for the file which is opened whenever a complaint is made against a police officer. Such a complaint can range from an allegation of rudeness to a member of the public all the way up to serious crime. The file will bear the numeral one followed by a stroke, the last two digits of the year, another stroke and then the number of the complaint itself. These last numbers start from one every year, and there are a lot of them. Cynical policemen will point out that whoever was tasked with devising the police filing system decided that the first category would be for complaints against police but got as far as two-hundred-and-something before acknowledging the existence of crime.

The custodians of these sad stories of policemen's sinfulness work in a branch called the Complaints Investigation Bureau. Paradoxically, the average British television viewer will be more familiar with its American counterpart: the Internal Affairs Department.

Having demonstrated his need to know, Gaffney eventually secured the docket which dealt with the misdeeds of ex-PC Ernest Brooks.

"Ten out of ten, Harry." Gaffney was reading the main report on the file. "Brooks was a detective sergeant at Gerald Road for the three years up to his demotion. Then he was transferred to Fulham as a uniformed PC."

Tipper sniffed. "Comes as no surprise," he said. "But what did he get done for?"

"Massage parlours."

"Eh?" Tipper sat up.

"Except that it didn't stick. Hang on, Harry." Gaffney skimmed through the closely typed pages, and then looked up. "According to the investigating officer, Brooks was copping from a villain who ran a massage parlour on Gerald Road's ground. Then the massage parlour got done and the bloke who ran it screamed blue murder. Apparently DS Brooks was on the take, the deal being that he would let the massage man know when his place was due to get turned over."

Tipper started to laugh. "Oh dear, oh dear! What a crying shame."

"What's so funny about that, Harry?"

"The 'feet' deal with massage parlours," said Tipper, using his customary derogatory term for the Uniform Branch, "and they play it so close to the chest that the CID would never know when a raid was due." For a moment, Tipper looked sad. "It's terrible not to be trusted."

"So Brooks was having this bloke over?"

"Looks like it," said Tipper. "Dangerous game that. What happened?"

"They put it up to the DPP," said Gaffney, turning over a minute sheet at the front of the file, "and he chucked it out. Insufficient evidence. Wasn't going to proceed on the uncorroborated word of a witness with a string of convictions."

Tipper swore, irritated that a bent copper should have got away with it, but accepting phlegmatically that it was not the first time. Regrettably, it would not be the last either. "So what did they do him for?"

There was a silence, broken only by the rustle of paper as Gaffney thumbed through the file. "Ah!" he said eventually. "It seems that when the massage man started singing, they put surveillance on our Mr Brooks, to see if he was at it anywhere else."

"And?"

"He wasn't. They did him for absence from place of duty. Seven counts over five weeks."

Tipper scoffed. "I'll bet the investigating officer was Uniform."

Gaffney nodded. "Yes, he was."

"Should have let the Department do the bastard. They'd have screwed him proper."

"But then," said Gaffney, "we wouldn't have had this little snippet of information." He tapped the file with his forefinger.

"Which is, sir?"

"That the seven occasions of his

211

absence from duty were spent in a lady's flat."

"Surprise, surprise," said Tipper.

"It is, too," said Gaffney. "The lady's name was Gisela Hunter."

10

IT took two or three days of hard work to put together the report on the Kerr affair for the Director of Public Prosecutions, most of which was done by Tipper with the aid of an experienced detective sergeant. It was a tortuous business. The statements had to be collated, and the story that each told had to be embodied in the report with accurate marginal references, so that the DPP not only had a complete account of the investigation, but could check whether the witnesses had anything relevant or important to say if and when the case got to court.

Gaffney, meanwhile, was studying the transcripts of the intercepts on Gisela Hunter's telephone and mail which Hector Toogood was at pains to send to the Yard daily. The only thing of significance arising out of that and the surveillance maintained by Dave Wakeford's team was that despite his original protestations, Foster, the impressionable young man from the Foreign Office, was still seeing her at regular intervals. Furthermore, a telex message had informed Gaffney that Foster had been fined two hundred pounds by the Richmond magistrates, and disqualified from driving for a year.

Tipper was scathing about Foster's obsession with the woman, but agreed with Gaffney that there was no way to prevent him from seeing her. "If he wants to destroy his career," Tipper had said contemptuously, "that's a matter for him."

Nevertheless, the two detectives decided that another interview would do no harm. 'A little jerk on the reins' Tipper had called it with unconscious ambiguity.

Tipper braked to a standstill a few yards short of Fancourt Mansions, switched off the engine and turned out the lights. They didn't have long to wait. The surveillance team had rung in when Foster had arrived, and Gaffney knew from the diplomat's previous visits, almost to the minute, when he would emerge.

"Just look at him," said Tipper as they watched Foster walking down the road towards them. "Like a cat who's just had the cream. Even if we didn't know what he'd been doing, we'd've guessed."

Gaffney wound down the window as Foster drew level with the car. "Mr Foster."

Foster stopped and stared at the detective, concern clearly etched on his face as he recognised Gaffney. "Oh, hello," he said lamely.

"We'd like a word with you. Get in."

Foster glanced quickly back towards Fancourt Mansions and then got into the back seat of the police car. "Look, I . . . " he began.

The two detectives had turned to face the diplomat, their elbows resting casually along the backs of the seats. "What exactly are you playing at, Mr Foster?" Gaffney spoke quietly, almost conversationally, but there was menace in his voice.

Foster looked from one to the other. "I doubt if you'd understand," he said cuttingly, "but I'm in love with Mrs

Hunter — Gisela — and I intend to marry her."

"Then you're a bigger berk than I thought you were," said Tipper brutally. "Incidentally, did she pay your fine?"

Foster didn't answer immediately, uncertain about police sources of information. Eventually, he decided to tell the truth. "Yes, she did, not that I think it's any of your business."

Tipper shrugged. "I couldn't care less," he said, "but as a matter of interest, Mr Foster, what effect do you think your proposed marriage will have on your career?"

"I'm going to resign from the Foreign Office." There was truculence in Foster's voice.

"I see. And what are you going to live on? Gisela Hunter's money?"

"No!" Foster's reply was vehement but unconvincing. "Anyway, it doesn't matter."

"Tell me, Mr Foster, what are you going to do about your existing wife? Daphne, I think you said her name was."

Foster nodded. "Yes. I'll get a divorce."

"Just like that?"

Foster didn't answer. It was fairly obvious that he was infatuated with this dangerous woman Gisela Hunter, and probably only because she was free with her sexual favours. But in Gaffney's experience — Tipper's too — such favours were not given lightly, and in the case of Gisela Hunter, certainly not without something in return.

"And what does Mrs Hunter think about all this?" continued Gaffney.

"I think she loves me, too."

"You think! Don't you know? You have asked her to marry you, I presume?"

"Not yet."

Gaffney laughed and Foster looked uncomfortable. "So she doesn't know about your intention to resign?"

"Not yet, no."

Gaffney held Foster's gaze until he turned away, embarrassed by talking about love and marriage to two hard-nosed policemen. "Let me give you some advice, Mr Foster. Not as a policeman, but as an old married — and divorced — man. Clear the air. Put it to her and see what she says. Otherwise you'll be going on in this dream world of yours for ever. After all, if she turns you down, you're going to have to go to Pakistan, aren't you? There'd be no point in resigning."

It was obviously a possibility that Foster hadn't considered: that after their regular love sessions she might refuse his proposal; but then, for all that he was in his mid-thirties, Roy Foster was an immature man. As for Gaffney, despite having spoken in a way that made his advice seem fatherly, he knew the Gisela Hunters of this world and was certain that if Foster told the woman what he had just told him, it would end the affair for good and all.

Foster walked away from the car seeming much less happy than when he had got into it.

But two days later, the enquiry took a new and unexpected turn.

DI Dave Wakeford, the officer in charge of the surveillance team, appeared in Gaffney's office. "A new face turned up at Fancourt Mansions yesterday afternoon, sir." Wakeford laid four or five photographs on Gaffney's desk. "He spent a couple of hours there and then we housed him to an address in Putney. All I can tell you so far is that the electoral roll shows a Mr and Mrs Hopkins: Albert T. R. and Rose W."

Gaffney spread the photographs across his desk and gazed at them thoughtfully. "Well that's not Albert Hopkins, Dave. It's an ex-policeman called Ernest Brooks, and what he's doing here when he should be in Pakistan interests me greatly."

Gaffney sent for Tipper and for a DI called Keith Holdstock.

"Keith, this man is called Brooks." He showed Holdstock the photographs and explained briefly his interest in him. "He's currently at an address in Putney. Find out all you can. But don't show out. Brooks is an ex-DS, so he knows the form."

Within forty-eight hours, Holdstock was back. "Rose Hopkins is Ernest Brooks' sister," he told Gaffney, "and he's staying with them for a week or so. It's no secret that he's working for the government in Pakistan. At our embassy there. I'm afraid that's all there is."

Gaffney nodded. "It's enough. Well done, Keith. You didn't alert him, I hope."

"No, sir. A few discreet enquiries in the neighbourhood. Didn't even tell anybody we were police. Didn't see Brooks at all."

It was at ten-past eleven the following morning that Gaffney got the telephone call from the PC on duty in Back Hall at New Scotland Yard. "There's a Mr Brooks here, sir. He's asking to see you."

Gaffney met him in the lift lobby on the eighteenth floor, and took him along the corridor to the interview room where Harry Tipper was waiting.

"Well, Mr Brooks, and what can I do for you?" asked Gaffney when they were settled.

Brooks looked at the two detectives. "I thought it was more a case of what I could do for you two gents," he said. He had declined an easy chair and was sitting squarely on an upright one, hands firmly on knees, an almost defiant pose that

220

demonstrated all the old bounce of the junior CID officer he had once been.

"What makes you say that?"

"Well, guv," said Brooks, grinning, "I spotted your obo boys taking me home from Kensington. They're very good. Then you had one of your lads down at Putney yesterday making a few local enquiries, as we used to say . . . "

"Still do," said Tipper in a dry aside.

"So I thought I'd pop in, see if I could save you a bit of time." He glanced around the room. "Few years since I've been in the Yard, I can tell you." He pulled a packet of cigarettes from his pocket. "D'you mind?"

Gaffney shook his head and watched as Brooks flicked his lighter into life. He had not worn well: blazer and flannels, unpressed, and thinning grey hair, and a gut that stretched his shirt buttons, probably as a result of too many hours in too many pubs trying to convince himself that he was only there to garner information from the criminal fraternity. In the process, he had undoubtedly ruined his health, his chances of promotion and his marriage.

He was an out-of-date CID officer. Twenty years too late for the time in which he had served.

"As a matter of fact, you're of no interest . . . officially, that is — "

"Then why put a team on me?"

Gaffney debated briefly whether to tell him the truth, but decided against it. "If you're under observation, then I don't know why. It's nothing to do with me."

For a moment that threw Brooks. "Then why? I mean what should anyone want to keep obo on me for?"

"No idea. Have you?"

Brooks leaned across and stubbed out his half-smoked cigarette before answering. "It's just like old times," he said. He glanced at Tipper before looking back at Gaffney. "I got done before I left the job." Gaffney continued to gaze at him, relaxed and impassive, but said nothing. "Had a bit of trouble over a woman. The one I went to see yesterday. Gisela Hunter. I was a DS and I was over the side with her. Got busted for absence from place of duty. Bit hard that was. A reprimand would have been enough. Four days' pay at most. Bloody wife left me as a result." There was no need for Brooks to tell them whom he had been to see. It was as if he wanted to clear his actions with Gaffney, get official approval, hoping perhaps that he would be told that it was all right.

"It's a hard world," said Tipper, without a trace of sympathy. "Anyway, what are you doing back here, in the UK?"

"Courier job," said Brooks, a little too quickly. "Happens from time to time. Urgent corres." He grinned at the familiar use of the old police phrase. "Gives us a chance for a bit of leave back home at the government's expense."

"I thought Pakistan was home," said Tipper.

"Oh yeah, but you know what I mean."

Gaffney would have liked to have questioned Brooks about Gisela Hunter, but decided that it was too risky. His job at the embassy in Islamabad and her known interest in Pakistani affairs might be linked. This pathetic ex-policeman could just be one of her successes, in post and spying already. Not that Gaffney would have rated Brooks too highly for the espionage business, but then he had already discovered that spies were not always as bright as people supposed. On the other hand, it could just be coincidence. He stood up. "Thanks for dropping in," he said. "Sorry we couldn't help to solve your little mystery."

Brooks stood up too and insisted on shaking hands.

"Oh well," he said. "Perhaps I imagined it." He laughed. "It must be the old copper coming out in me."

But it was evident that Ernie Brooks was a worried man.

The next event of significance was a phone call from DI Wakeford, four days later. "Foster turned up at seven o'clock last night, sir, which is the usual time for his weekly bit of nookey, but he was out again at half past . . . and he didn't look happy."

They decided to catch Foster on his way home. It was better that way. If they had asked him to call in at the Yard, he may not have come, was under no obligation to do so, after all, and even if he did, he would have been prepared. Hyped up, Tipper called it.

Anyway, Tipper was looking for an excuse to have a drink. It was a sultry hot day, not unlike the weather in Pakistan that they had so recently experienced, but made worse by being in the centre of a sprawling, dirty city filled with diesel fumes. So they picked Foster up just as he was walking across Whitehall and steered him into the dive bar of a nearby public house.

"Well?" asked Tipper, looking lovingly at his pint of ice-cold lager. "What news?"

Foster had asked for Campari and soda and took a sip before answering. "It's over."

"Oh." Tipper ran his finger down the side of the glass leaving a line on the condensation.

"Thanks to you." Foster looked accusingly at Gaffney.

"How so?" Gaffney seemed unperturbed by the allegation.

"I did as you suggested. Told her I wanted to marry her and that I was going to resign from the Office."

"And?"

"She went mad. Told me that I was crazy."

"Crazy to want to marry her . . . or crazy to be thinking about resigning?"

Foster thought about that. "Strangely enough, it was leaving the FCO that got her angry."

"Which confirms what you implied in the first place, Mr Foster," said Gaffney quietly. "Mrs Hunter wanted you to work for her. She only allowed you into her bed in furtherance of that purpose."

"But I loved her." Foster blurted out his reply and clenched his fists at his sides. "I don't think that you — "

"Well she didn't love you, old son," said Tipper harshly. "Face it. She's just a bloody whore." Foster clenched his fists again, and for a moment Gaffney thought that he was going to strike the Chief Inspector, but Tipper went on relentlessly. "And what's more, she was having it off with another bloke at the same time. And probably for the same reason." Tipper didn't name Brooks, but thought that his guess was probably accurate, given that Brooks had been disciplined for just that while in the police.

"I don't believe you."

Tipper shrugged. "Matter for you whether you do or not," he said.

"How d'you know?"

"Because we've had her flat under observation ever since you first came to see us. We can tell you every time you went there and how long you stayed. If we were private detectives that little operation would have cost your wife a bomb." Gaffney and Tipper had decided they had nothing to lose by telling Foster that, even if he did pass it on to Gisela Hunter. It might even prompt her into doing something rash, although that was unlikely . . . if she was the professional they took her to be.

"But I — "

Gaffney interrupted. "Was she still trying to get you to work for her?" he asked.

Foster nodded his head and looked down at his feet, leaning against the bar for support. "She mentioned several times how helpful she could be, once I got out there."

227

Gaffney scoffed. "And you believed her?"

"Only because I wanted to." Foster looked miserable.

"If you want any proof Mr Foster, you've only to consider her reaction to your proposed resignation from the Foreign Office. From that point on, you'd have been of no further use to her. That's why she threw you out."

The diplomat shook his head. "What am I going to do now?"

"If I was in your position, I'd go home and tell my wife all about it. Before Gisela Hunter does."

There was a murderous look in Foster's eyes. "I think I've had quite enough of your helpful advice," he said, and banging his glass down on the bar, walked out.

"Excitable, isn't he?" said Tipper and ordered another drink.

James Marchant smiled owlishly. "Yes, I heard, John."

Gaffney and Tipper had paid a courtesy call on the SIS officer to tell him what they knew of the death of Peter Kerr, but their revelations had come as no surprise to him.

"What d'you mean, you heard?"

Marchant leaned back in his chair, his most avuncular expression on his face. "John, the British Secret Intelligence Service is the best intelligence-gathering organisation in the world. You don't really think that one of our operatives could be murdered without our knowing about it, surely?"

"But how? Even I'm not certain."

"Test-firings with the Ambassador's Purdey, John. Questioning the staff of the embassy. Post-mortem examinations. Photographs. Doesn't sound like a straightforward suicide to me . . . and I'm only a layman."

Gaffney grinned at that. "I suppose that Mohammed Khan is your source."

"Who?"

The Assistant Director of Public Prosecutions listened carefully to the summary of Tipper's investigation in Islamabad. The report, with its accompanying statements, lay unread on the desk. The ADPP was a man who much preferred to get the salient facts direct from the investigating officer. When Tipper had finished, he nodded slowly and said, "And what d'you propose doing now, Mr Tipper," adding hurriedly, "and you too, Mr Gaffney?" acknowledging that the Chief-Superintendent was in charge of the enquiry.

"Haven't a clue," said Tipper. "I was hoping you might have one or two ideas. It's fairly evident that someone on the staff of the embassy shot him."

"You definitely rule out suicide?"

"The test-firings show — "

The ADPP silenced Tipper with a raised hand. "I accept that, but is it not possible that he did commit suicide in a similar way, but that the scene was rearranged?"

Tipper scoffed. "What would be the point?" The ADPP might be a brilliant lawyer, but he lacked the basic common sense that drove detectives along a logical line of enquiry.

"Mmm! Perhaps not. What about the Ambassador, then?"

"Unlikely," said Tipper grudgingly. "Not with his own shotgun. There were other weapons there that he could have used. A hand-gun, for instance."

"But a suicide with a hand-gun leaves powder burns at the point of entry, surely? And HE appeared to know about ballistics and rifling . . . "

Oh God! He reads Agatha Christie, thought Tipper. "You can speculate for ever," he said, "but all I've got are facts. The spread of shot indicates that the shotgun was much farther away when fired than where it was when we found it." He decided that it had been a mistake to ask the ADPP for his views without specifying that it was a legal directive he was after, not an enthusiastic amateur detective's ideas. "We'll just have to keep going until we find something. The main thing, of course, is to have your blessing to continue with the enquiries, given that it's not only out of the UK but on diplomatic premises, too."

"But of course." The ADPP riffled the edges of Tipper's report with his thumb. "From what you say, there is evidence of unlawful killing, and that has to be investigated."

11

HECTOR TOOGOOD telephoned at nine o'clock in the morning. "You phoning from home, or is there some grave crisis in the Security Service?" asked Gaffney.

"No, I'm in the office." Toogood completely missed the point of Gaffney's sarcasm. "There's something very interesting on the intercepts, John, that I think that you and Harry ought to see."

"What, exactly?"

"I'd rather not discuss it on the phone."

"But you'll be sending them over later on today as usual, won't you?"

"It looks to be rather urgent, John."

Gaffney sighed. "All right, Hector, we'll be over." He depressed the receiver rest briefly and dialled the number of Tipper's extension.

"Gisela Hunter rang Roy Foster at his office yesterday afternoon," said

Toogood, fingering the sheets of paper that bore the transcript of the intercepts on the woman's telephone. "She apologised for the way she'd behaved and said she hoped that they could continue as before. Then she went on to say that she wanted to marry him but didn't want him to resign from the Foreign Office."

"Crafty bitch," said Tipper.

"But what does it all mean?" Toogood looked puzzled.

"It means," said Gaffney, "that Foster told her that he was in love with her, that he wanted to marry her, and that he would get a divorce and leave the Foreign Office. That, of course, didn't suit her purpose at all. She lost her temper and threw him out of bed. But having thought about it, she's obviously changed tack. She needs a spy in the British Embassy in Pakistan, and he's her only hope. So now she's trying for the best of both worlds."

Toogood looked appalled. "Good God, John, how d'you know all this?"

"We asked him."

"You mean you've actually spoken

to him." It was evident that the very idea of talking to a suspect face-to-face was something that Toogood had neither considered nor would ever contemplate.

"You know damned well we have, Hector," said Gaffney. "You may recall that Foster approached us in the first place. Or were you asleep during that conference at the Foreign Office? Believe it or not, it's a very good way of getting information. The fact that he didn't take our advice is his funeral."

"But you've spoken to him since then? That's what I meant."

"Well of course we have. How else d'you think we can monitor what's going on?"

Toogood shook his head slowly. "It's no good, John," he said. "I'll have to see the DG. There's no way this man Foster can be allowed to go to Pakistan."

Now it was Gaffney's turn to look surprised. "You can't pull the plug now, Hector, for God's sake. You've got to let the hare run. We've got no hard evidence that Gisela Hunter's a spymaster at all. It's all supposition, backed up by a rag-bag of gossip and rumour. For all we know, she might just be trying to oil the wheels of the business she inherited from her husband. And that might have been the case with the German diplomat, too. Not that I believe it for one moment, and it was years ago anyway, so we couldn't use it here. Couldn't have done anyway. Frankly, I don't think we can rely too much on what Foster's told us. He's not the best of witnesses and I can think of half-a-dozen defence counsel who would reduce him to a quivering lump of jelly in the box at the Bailey."

"But John, we know what she's up to." Toogood's face wore a pained expression of desperation. "I know we haven't got proof, not proof that would stand up in court, but there can't be any doubt."

"So what are we going to do? Abort it and let her zoom off in another direction to God knows where? Like the Germans did."

"It's not a decision I can make, John." Toogood was clearly anguished by the whole business. "I shall have to pass it upwards."

"Thought you might," said Gaffney, standing up.

"I entirely agree, John," said James Marchant. "That would be bloody silly." The Secret Service man drummed his fingers on his desk-top. "I think I'll have to pull some strings. These chaps at Five are all very good at sorting out the North Hornsey branch of the Communist Party, but this is international stuff and I'm damned if I'm going to have them balls it up because they haven't got the guts to see it through."

"So what are you going to do?" asked Gaffney.

Marchant placed a finger alongside his nose and grinned. "We have our ways, John, we have our ways."

Whatever those ways were, and Gaffney had a shrewd idea that no less a person than the Foreign Secretary — who also happened to be the political head of MI6 — would have been involved, Marchant rang later in the day to say that Foster's posting to Pakistan would be allowed to stand.

But none of them had bargained for what happened next.

At about three o'clock in the afternoon,

a 999 call was received at the Command and Control Complex at New Scotland Yard from a member of the public complaining bitterly that he had almost been struck by a vase thrown through an upstairs window of a block of flats called Fancourt Mansions near the Albert Hall.

The police operator at the Yard had assigned the area wireless car covering the Gerald Road Division to investigate what he laconically described as a disturbance.

At about the same time, one of DI Wakeford's surveillance team had radioed his control to say that something was going on. A young woman, not previously seen by the team but aged thirtyish, medium height, proportionate build, dressed in jeans, boots, and a green sweater, had called at Fancourt Mansions. She had pressed the bell-push for Number Five and had been admitted. Ten minutes or so later, a vase had been thrown through the window. Shortly after that he reported the arrival of uniformed police.

Wakeford had instructed his officer to stay where he was and not to interfere. Then he rang the CCC and established that police had indeed been called to a disturbance at Number Five.

Gaffney, alerted by Wakeford to what was happening, rubbed his hands. Whatever had occurred at Gisela Hunter's flat would undoubtedly provide him with an opportunity to get his foot in the lady's door without arousing too much suspicion . . . if he needed to. At the moment, he was by no means sure that that would be necessary.

"Harry, get round to Gerald Road nick and have a chat to these two PCs. We'll take it from there."

The police car crew had gone back on patrol after dealing with their assignment and were surprised to get another call almost immediately instructing them to return to the station.

Tipper borrowed the Superintendent's office on the top floor and told the two policemen to sit down. "I'm DCI Tipper, Special Branch," he said. "You've just dealt with a call to Number Five Fancourt Mansions, yes?"

The two Uniform Branch men looked apprehensive. "Has there been a complaint, sir?"

Tipper smiled. "No, not that I know of. We just happen to be interested in the occupant, that's all."

"Oh, I see." The driver, the older of the two PCs, looked a little relieved, but still not wholly at ease. Complaints were made by members of the public these days for no apparent reason, and it was usually a Chief Inspector who was assigned to investigate them, either from the Yard or from Area headquarters.

"What was it about?"

"Usual thing, guv. Fight over a bloke." The driver cocked a thumb at his companion, a flashily good-looking young man of about twenty-five. "Sort of trouble he has all the time."

Tipper didn't smile. "Get on with it, I haven't got all day."

"Er, yes, right, sir." The PC pulled out an incident report book and thumbed it open. "Call received fifteen-oh-three. Arrived fifteen-oh-seven. Member of the public claimed that a vase had been chucked through a window and just missed him. Broken window in Number Five. We were admitted by the owner." He glanced down at his notes. "A Mrs

Gisela Hunter, aged about forty." He looked up at Tipper. "Spoke with a slight foreign accent, sir."

Tipper nodded. "Yeah. She's British but German-born."

"Also present," continued the PC, "was a Mrs Daphne Foster, aged about twenty-seven, address in Richmond."

"Well, well, well," said Tipper. "And?"

"Mrs Foster had a bruise on her left cheek and her hair was dishevelled, like it had been pulled. Mrs Hunter's blouse was torn . . . quite badly." The PC glanced up and grinned, but stopped when he saw Tipper's stony expression. "Both declined medical aid."

"I'm sure that's a very good report you're putting together, lad, but can we get down to the nitty-gritty of the thing?"

"It seems that Mrs Hunter has been having it off with Mrs Foster's old man, and Mrs Foster didn't like it too much. Apparently she went there and fronted her with it. One thing led to another, a punch-up ensued and Mrs Foster finished up by flinging a bloody great vase at Mrs Hunter. Fortunately it missed and went through the window, otherwise we could have had a murder on our hands."

"This Mrs Foster, what was she like? Good-looking woman?"

The older PC shook his head. "No, sir, not really. Could have been if she tried, I suppose, but she was a bit dowdy, plain, no make-up. Downtrodden housewife bit. Know what I mean? I can see why this Foster bloke fancied Mrs Hunter. A good ten years older, but she'd got it. Black underwear, too."

Tipper smiled. "How d'you know that?"

The PC grinned. "Like I said, guv, the other bird had practically torn her blouse off."

"Randy bastard," said Tipper. "Did Mrs Foster say what her husband did for a living?"

The PC looked down at his book again. "Don't think so. Oh, just a minute. Yes, here we are. Civil servant. Just goes to show, doesn't it?"

"Goes to show what?"

"What exciting secret lives these little pen-pushers have."

Tipper laughed. "You don't know the

half of it." Then, becoming serious again, he said, "I don't want anyone to know of my interest in this. Understood?"

"Stand on me, guv," said the PC.

"Yes," said Tipper thoughtfully. "Any proceedings pending?"

"No, sir. Neither party wished to prefer charges. Mrs Hunter said it was all a misunderstanding and they'd made up their differences. Mrs Foster agreed. I just referred them to their civil remedy. Got the impression that whatever it was, they didn't want the police involved."

"What about the informant, the bloke who was nearly hit by this flying vase?"

"Haven't seen him, guv. He'd done a runner by the time we arrived. I think it was a male anon anyway."

"And what did you tell the CCC?"

The PC grinned. "All quiet on arrival, sir," he said.

"It's Roy Foster," said the voice on the telephone.

"Yes, Mr Foster?"

"I was wondering if I could come and see you."

"Certainly," said Gaffney.

Twenty minutes later, Foster, having walked across the park from the Foreign Office, was seated in Gaffney's office on the eighteenth floor of New Scotland Yard. "I've left my wife," he said without preamble.

Gaffney nodded. "I gather there was an unfortunate scene at Fancourt Mansions yesterday?"

"Oh!" Foster looked surprised. "You know about that."

"Of course. The police were called."

"I'm going to marry Gisela."

"Just like that?"

"I'm going to Pakistan, and she's going to follow me out. She has a house in Karachi."

"Long way from Islamabad, isn't it?"

"Oh, we wouldn't live there."

"I suppose not. But the Foreign Office isn't so enlightened as to give you official quarters, surely? At least not until you are married."

"She's going to get a place in Rawalpindi, until the divorce comes through, then we'll get married."

"You don't see any problems with the divorce, then?" asked Gaffney. He had a niggling feeling that he was getting too involved in Foster's matrimonial affairs, drifting away from the espionage aspect that had first interested Special Branch in the diplomat's activities.

"I'm going to allow Daphne to sue me as the guilty party."

Gaffney laughed. "I don't see that you've much choice," he said. "You could hardly claim to be innocent in all this. But it's going to cost you a lot of money."

"Gisela's told me not to worry about money."

Gaffney was amazed by the man's naïvety. "I'll bet she has." He lit a cigar. "But why have you come to see me?"

Foster looked puzzled at the question. "I thought you ought to know," he said.

"Mr Foster." Gaffney blew smoke towards the ceiling. "When you first approached the police, you said you thought that Gisela Hunter was trying to suborn you. I advised you to leave well alone, and you agreed. If I remember correctly, you said you didn't want to see her again. But see her again you did."

"I know." Foster's face bore an appealing expression, seeking Gaffney's sympathy. "But I didn't realise then that I was in love with her."

"Are you, though? Or is it just infatuation? Your wife is consumed with housework and the children. No time for the romantic side of marriage. Am I right?"

Foster nodded dumbly.

Gaffney had taken a guess, deduced that that was the case from the description of Daphne Foster that Tipper had been given by the policemen who dealt with the incident at Fancourt Mansions. "D'you still think that she's trying to persuade you to work for her?"

"No!" Foster sounded adamant. "I've given that a great deal of thought," he said. "The night I was arrested, when I spoke to the sergeant at Barnes, I'd had too much to drink." He half-smiled.

"That's certainly what you were arrested for," said Tipper.

"To be honest, I wasn't thinking straight. When I thought about it later, I realised that I was panicking over nothing."

"Oh really?" Tipper moved his chair slightly. "I would remind you, Mr Foster, that you were stone-cold sober the next day, when you came to see me. You certainly thought then that Mrs Hunter wanted something from you . . . apart from your body, of course."

Foster reddened slightly. He was unaccustomed to straight talking people like Tipper. "Yes, I know," he said, "but I've had time to think it over. There is nothing that the British have that would be of any real interest to Pakistan. They are a friendly nation, after all. They're even talking about seeking re-entry to the Commonwealth." Foster sounded more confident now that he was on familiar ground. "One tends to be over-sensitive in my sort of work, you know."

"In mine too," said Gaffney drily. "But usually not without cause." He stood up. There was nothing more to be gained from Foster. "I can only wish you luck," he said.

Foster smiled for the first time since his arrival, obviously sensing that he had been released from his self-imposed obligation to the police.

After Foster had left, Tipper let out a long sigh. "We've got problems, guv'nor," he said. "Once she's left the jurisdiction, there ain't going to be a great deal we can do. Even though she's British, there's no way we can extradite her from Karachi for spying for Pakistan."

"Quite so," said Gaffney grimly. "But there's always the question of an unsolved murder in Islamabad to occupy our minds." He yawned. "D'you know, Harry, if I'd been the chief superintendent at Kensington, instead of in Special Branch, my biggest worry right now would have been parking problems outside Harrods?"

"Never mind, guv," said Tipper. "Make a cock-up of this one and you could still finish up there."

Gaffney had directed that a warning be sent to all ports and airports to report the departure of Gisela Hunter, just to keep the books straight, he had said. He had decided to do so immediately after Foster had told him of her plans. It was a matter of regret, though, that he would be unable to arrest her on her way out, but had been forced to agree with the Director of Public Prosecutions' man that despite the wealth of suspicion, there was no evidence to substantiate a charge.

What Gisela Hunter had told Roy Foster was confirmed the following day. Hector Toogood, nervous that he might neglect to pass on some vital snippet of information, called Gaffney and told him that the intercept operators had just phoned through a piece of urgent information. Gisela Hunter had telephoned the offices of Pakistan International Airways in Piccadilly and had made a reservation on flight PK 782 which was scheduled to leave Heathrow Airport for Karachi at half-past five the following day.

"Well, that looks like the end of that," said Gaffney when he had told Tipper the news. "That bloody woman's going to walk out of it, and there's not a damned thing we can do."

Tipper shrugged. "Some you win, some you lose, guv," he said.

Detective Inspector Dave Wakeford and his surveillance team were not overjoyed to get the news of the telephone call that Gisela Hunter had made. They had hoped that their hours of apparently fruitless observation would bring a satisfactory result, preferably in the shape of an arrest, but it looked very much as though it was not to be. Gaffney had directed that Wakeford and his team should follow Gisela Hunter to Heathrow on the Wednesday, just to make sure that she went. Then he settled down to contemplate how best to resolve his other outstanding enquiry: the death of Peter Kerr. But he was still convinced that they were connected in some way.

Wakeford had arranged for a Vauxhall Carlton with a police advanced driver at the wheel to be standing by near the Albert Hall, and he and several members of his team were maintaining a casual presence in the vicinity of Gisela Hunter's flat. The remainder of his watchers were in various parts of Terminal Three at Heathrow Airport, waiting to see her board the five-thirty Karachi flight.

At half-past one, Gisela Hunter left her flat and crossed the road to where her BMW was parked, the same BMW in which the unfortunate Roy Foster had been arrested. The fact that she had emerged much earlier than the surveillance team had anticipated and that she carried nothing but a handbag, caused them to wonder whether she was going to the airport after all. There was no doubt that if she was the practised spy they believed her to be, she would assume, always, that her telephone was being tapped, and might just have made the booking to Karachi to confuse the police.

She looked up and down the road but failed to see anyone who might have been watching her. Wakeford, proud of the professionalism of his team, would have been extremely annoyed if they had been spotted. They watched her cross the road and Wakeford had to admit to himself that his interest was not wholly professional: she was a good-looking woman. Again, she looked up and down the road before opening the door of her car and throwing her small black handbag carelessly on to the passenger seat. Then she got in and started the engine.

The journey to Heathrow Airport was hair-raising. Once clear of the Hogarth Roundabout, she put her foot down, and it was as much as Wakeford's experienced driver could do to keep up with her with any degree of discretion. At one point, Wakeford glanced down at the speedometer and saw that it was flickering at around the one hundred miles an hour mark.

"Can't we do her for excess speed, sir?" asked the driver plaintively, unable to forget that he had once been a traffic patrol officer.

"According to the guv'nor that's about all we will be able to do her for," said Wakeford irritably.

At Junction Four of the M4 motorway, she swung left and dropped down to the airport, but then threw her followers by driving into the Terminal Two long-term car park off Northern Perimeter Road.

"What the hell's she going in there for?" asked Wakeford, half to himself "She's supposed to be taking off from Terminal Three."

The driver laughed. "Don't ask me, guv," he said, "I'm only the driver."

Gisela Hunter came out of the car park, carrying the small leather case that PC Inman had searched when he arrested Foster, and which she presumably kept in the boot of her car as a permanent escape kit. Then she caught one of the courtesy buses to Terminal Two, leaving Wakeford's team in a state of disarray. After a moment's hesitation, he radioed the officers who had been lying in wait at Terminal Three and ordered them to get across to Terminal Two as soon as possible. They were not pleased. It's a long way on foot and they were left to run through the tunnels, waving their warrant cards at the bemused security men on duty at the various checkpoints.

Gisela Hunter made her way into Terminal Two and walked across to the Lufthansa desk where she produced a ticket and checked in.

One of Wakeford's officers had been right behind her and he now walked across to where the DI was standing reading a timetable. "Booked on the fourteen fifty-five to Cologne, sir," he said. "Which you'll be happy to know has a thirty-minute delay on it."

252

"What the hell's she up to?" asked Wakeford. "She must have made that booking from a public call box. She's obviously sussed out that we've got taps on her own phone." His mind racing, he walked across to where WDC Marilyn Lester was sitting on a bench seat, and dropped down beside her. "How's your German?" he asked.

"Non-existent, sir. Did a bit at school, but that won't get me anywhere."

"Never mind. That's where you're going. Get across to the Lufthansa desk and book yourself on the same flight to Cologne as Gisela Hunter. I just hope they've got a spare seat."

"And what do I do when I get there, sir?" Marilyn Lester sounded alarmed. "She could be going anywhere."

"I know," said Wakeford, "but with any luck she'll be picked up by the BKA at Cologne Airport . . . if I can get Mr Gaffney on the phone . . . and he can get hold of the Germans . . . and they can get a team organised."

"Terrific," said the girl "What do I use for money?"

"Got a Barclaycard, or something?"

"Yes, sir."

"That's all right then," said Wakeford. "You've cracked it." And he laughed.

"I thought that Karachi business was too good to be true," said Gaffney, when Wakeford eventually got through to him. "What have you done so far?"

"I've put WDC Lester on the same plane, sir. I thought that you would want to jack up the BKA, but it occurred to me that they might not know what she looked like. Lester can point the woman out to them."

Gaffney sucked through his teeth. "Yeah, all right, Dave." But he sounded doubtful.

"Is that all right, guv?" Wakeford was apprehensive.

"Yes, it's all right," said Gaffney. "I was just wondering what the guv'nor will say when he sees the bill. A bit over the top, a trip to Cologne, even for your lot."

WDC Lester stood up when the flight was called and, keeping Gisela Hunter a few yards ahead of her, walked through to immigration control.

"Passport, please." The Immigration Officer looked up as Marilyn Lester laid her ticket on the desk, but the Special Branch officer on duty at the outward control, already briefed by Wakeford, had seen Marilyn Lester approach and stepped up to the desk. "This is the officer I spoke to you about, Fred," he said quietly.

The IO smiled. "All right by me," he said. "I just hope the Germans will let you in."

Marilyn Lester picked up her ticket. "Oh, they will," she said. "Right now they can't do without me."

The thirty-minute delay added to the two hours and five minutes' flight time meant that the aircraft containing Gisela Hunter and Marilyn Lester did not touch down at Cologne until gone half-past five. Somewhat apprehensively, the woman detective followed her quarry through to the immigration control, wondering what sort of reception she would receive if Gaffney had not been able to make contact with the German police.

She watched Gisela Hunter produce her *Ausweis*, the identity card with which Germans could travel in and out of their own country, and be waved through the control.

Then it was her turn.

She laid her warrant card on the desk in front of the German official. "I think you're expecting me," she said. It sounded rather lame.

The official looked up at her and smiled. "Yes, we are," he said, "but they did not say that you were so good-looking." He turned to a man in plain clothes standing nearby and spoke quietly to him in rapid German.

The man nodded and walked across to Marilyn. "Allow me to introduce myself," he said in perfect English, and took her arm as if she were a girlfriend he was meeting off the flight. "I am Kurt Gotter, with the BKA. We are most grateful to you for your assistance. If you will just point out the woman to us, we will take over."

"That's her, all in black," said Marilyn as they entered the Customs Hall. "Didn't you pick her up going through immigration?" She knew that that is what Special Branch would have done.

"Unfortunately, she is not using the name Hunter, Miss Lester. So we did not immediately identify her. That is why we appreciate your help." He walked over to a man who was obviously another BKA officer and spoke briefly to him before returning to Marilyn Lester's side. "Good," he said. "My colleagues will take care of everything." He smiled. "My job is to take care of you. First we arrange a hotel, so you can have a bath, and then we go out to dinner."

Although it had come as a surprise that Gisela Hunter had gone to Cologne, the carefully contrived and executed plan that she had employed to deceive the police served to confirm Gaffney's suspicions that she was a professional spy, rather than a business woman making friends for some commercial advantage. In a comparatively short space of time, she had come to the notice of the police twice, albeit in the shape of uniformed constables on each occasion, but it was something that all spies feared. The only answer was to take off. And she had done so . . . from Heathrow Airport.

Gaffney picked up the phone and spoke to Willi Fischer at the *Bundeskriminalamt* in Bonn.

12

"I'VE been making some questions since her return," said Fischer in his slightly fractured English, "and I think we will bring her in."

"Straightaway?" asked Gaffney.

"No, no, John. First we wait to see where she goes and what she is doing. Keep a little eye on her, and then whoof! Into the police station for some talking. You like this?"

"Yes, marvellous," said Gaffney without enthusiasm. It might solve Willi Fischer's twelve-year-old enquiry, but he doubted very much that it would assist his own investigation.

It was as if Fischer had read Gaffney's thoughts because he then said, "If you want to come over, John, maybe you would want to ask some questions yourself, *ja*?"

Gaffney hesitated. He was still hoping to get Gisela Hunter in a position where he could question her, and arrest her if her replies were sufficiently incriminating. In Germany, where her British nationality would count for little, given that she was German-born, there would be no chance of that. And there was the usual problem of being unable to extradite her for what international agreements called 'offences of a political nature'. On the other hand, Gisela Hunter did not know Gaffney, and if he sat quietly in the corner while Fischer did the talking, he might learn something. There was really nothing to lose. Right now, he had next to damn-all that would be any good in a court of law.

"I'll see if I can make it, Willi. Give me a call when you've got her in custody."

It was exactly twenty-four hours later when Fischer telephoned to say that the BKA had detained Gisela Hunter for questioning. She had protested strongly, Fischer said, but admitted nothing.

James Marchant greeted Gaffney with his usual bonhomie. It was a ploy that always made Gaffney feel as though he should be constantly looking over his shoulder.

"But of course, my dear fellow," said Marchant when Gaffney told him of his proposal to go to Germany. "Damned good idea. You'll let us know if you pick up anything which might be useful, won't you?"

Wilhelm Fischer was delighted to hear that Gaffney, whom he had met several times before, was coming to Germany and had immediately arranged a hotel. "Not too expensive, but good and clean," he had said on the telephone. As a policeman himself, he knew all about the limitations placed on expenses by parsimonious authorities.

And he was waiting at Cologne Airport. A tall, well-built, craggy-faced man with thinning hair, he seemed always to be sun-tanned. "John!" He seized Gaffney in a bear-hug and laughed. "You're late."

"Not my fault, Willi. Talk to the driver."

"You should travel by Lufthansa, John. It is the best." Fischer appeared to notice Tipper for the first time. "And who is this?"

"Chief Inspector Harry Tipper. Harry,

261

meet Willi Fischer. He's a director in the BKA. Roughly equivalent to a chief superintendent."

"*Ja, ja,* that's right!" Fischer beamed and shook Tipper's hand vigorously. "And how is my good friend Mr Marchant of the Secret Service, eh?"

"Oh, you know him, do you?" asked Gaffney.

"Of course. All secret and no service."

"Yes," said Gaffney, "you do know him."

Fischer laughed uproariously and then, with a few brief words of introduction, led them past customs and immigration officials and out into the car park.

Fischer's car was a 3-litre BMW, and Tipper whistled softly when he saw it. "You do all right for yourselves here," he said. "Is it yours?"

"No!" Fischer laughed scornfully. "It is the office runabout." He spoke good English, but with a heavy accent.

Willi Fischer drove fast — a little too fast for Gaffney's liking — but confidently, and delivered the two Scotland Yard officers to their hotel in Bad Godesburg. "So!" he said, glancing at his watch. "It is now quarter-past seven. You want to have a wash or a shower? We go out to dinner at eight o'clock. Okay?"

It had been a riotous and relaxing evening, and Gaffney and Tipper had the headaches that Willi Fischer had promised them. The German, however, seemed unaffected by the copious quantities of beer they had each consumed, and the two British policemen assumed, rightly, that he was more accustomed to the local brew than they were.

Fischer had spent the evening regaling them with funny stories about the German police and its problems, all of which had a familiar ring to them, and listening in turn to their tales. He had eaten mountains of food and had caressed the waitress, with whom he appeared to be on familiar terms, at every available opportunity.

But now it was a serious Willi Fischer who sat in his office at the BKA headquarters in Bonn, slowly stirring his coffee and listening intently as Gaffney unfolded the details of their interest in Mrs Gisela Hunter.

When Gaffney had finished, Fischer drew a file across his desk and opened it. "Frau Gisela Hunter, born Toller, on March third, nineteen forty-seven, Bad Salzuflen. Attended school at Herford Gymnasium to the seventh grade. Went to England as au pair in nineteen sixty-seven, and lived with the family Jenkins in Holland Park . . . " He looked up. "You know this place?"

Gaffney nodded. "It's in London. D'you have the exact address, Willi?"

"*Ja*. Maple Road, Seventeen." Fischer turned over the page. "Was married in the same year, nineteen sixty-seven, in London to Richard Hunter, a *Witwer* . . . ?" He looked up again, a quizzical expression on his face.

"A widower, could that be?" asked Gaffney.

"Widower? What is this?"

"His first wife died."

"So! Yes, of course. I understand. This Hunter was a merchant from Pakistan. But he was English, *ja*?"

"So I understand, Willi, yes."

"And he took his new wife, the Frau Hunter, back to Karachi with him."

"Yes. Well, we knew most of that, Willi."

Fischer grinned. "Okay, so now you know twice."

"But she came back. Back here to Bonn."

"In nineteen seventy-two, March," continued Fischer. "She was in a flat in Damen-strasse, Number Six." He calculated quickly in German. "She was then twenty-five years of age."

"When did she first come to your notice?"

"Not until nineteen seventy-seven, when she was thirty."

"And?"

"An official in the Foreign Ministry of the *Bundesrepublik* — here in Bonn — called Dieter Muller, reported that he had met this woman at some party at the Foreign Ministry. She had been very . . . amenable?" He looked up. "Is that a good word — amenable?"

Gaffney grinned. "From what we hear of her, a very good word, yes."

"Oh, by the way, she was calling herself Gisela Toller again, Fräulein Toller. She did not tell Mr Muller that she had been married, or that she was now British, although she had kept her German nationality, also. Anyway, they became friends. Good friends!" Fischer looked up and leered suggestively. "But then she started to ask him certain questions about what he did, and whether he could find out some things about Pakistan."

"What sort of things?"

"About what the Federal Republic knew about their relationships with India mainly."

"And that's when this Muller decided to report it?"

"Not straightaway. He waited for two or three weeks."

"Why? D'you know?"

. Fischer smiled. "Of course. He was married."

"Yes, he would have been. What happened then?"

"We decided to keep a watch on Fräulein Toller — Mrs Hunter — but she had gone."

"Where?"

"We didn't know. Until you telephoned the other day to say she was in London."

"I see. Willi, was there anything to show why she was doing this? Why does a German woman, who had been married to a British businessman, try to get information from the German Foreign Ministry about Pakistan and India?"

Fischer held up his hands in an attitude of surrender. "I don't know, John. Of course the BfV — you know the BfV?" Gaffney nodded. "They got all excited, but the woman was gone. The BfV said they would talk to their friends, whatever that means, but we heard nothing more. We couldn't use Interpol because it was political. Anyway, it was all a lot of nothing. That time we had the Baader-Meinhof Group, the Red Army Faction. Silly girls going to bed with government clerks and talking about Pakistan . . . " He shrugged. "It was nothing."

"What happened to the man from the ministry?"

"Oh him. He killed himself." Fischer said it in an offhand way as though it was the natural outcome of an event of this sort. "Personally, I think he warned Fräulein Toller that he had told the police. Anyway, he threw himself under a train," he added, shutting the file and slapping it decisively with his hand. He stood up. "So! Now she is in custody and we talk to her, *ja*?"

Gaffney shook his head slowly. "You talk to her, Willi. At the moment, I'd rather she didn't know of our existence. I hate to think of the complications that might arise if she confessed to a crime she'd committed in England while in your custody in Germany. I can imagine defence counsel having a marvellous time with that."

Fischer laughed. A great rumbling laugh. "Lawyers," he said dismissively. "Always getting in the way of justice."

It was a tedious business. Gaffney had overlooked the fact that the woman's native tongue was German and that Fischer would naturally question her in that language. The interrogation suite was very sophisticated, far superior to anything the Metropolitan Police had, and the two British detectives were placed in an observation room from which they could see the suspect and her interrogator through a two-way mirror.

Fischer had thoughtfully provided an interpreter whose unenviable task it was to translate question and answer as it came to him through the headphones he was wearing.

Gisela Hunter was dressed in the all-black outfit she had worn for the flight over: tight trousers and a long-sleeved sweater high to the neck. Apart from tiny gold keepers in her ears, she wore no jewellery, but had clearly spent some time on her make-up and, judging by her elegantly long, painted fingernails, even longer on her manicure.

There were no hard chairs and no table, just two comfortable armchairs with small side-tables on one of which — the one nearest Fischer — was a tray bearing cups and a coffee pot. He poured out the coffee and placed one of the cups on the table next to Gisela Hunter before sprawling back into his chair, one leg crooked over the arm.

"It is just general talk about how long it is since she was last in Germany — twelve years — and why she came back," said the interpreter, staring intently through the two-way mirror as if he were lip-reading.

"She is making no positive answers. She asks why she is here. She says she has done nothing wrong, and the police have no right to detain her. She will make a complaint. She is telling Herr Fischer that she is a British subject. Now, Herr Fischer is reminding her that she was also British when she was here before but then called herself Fräulein Toller. If you are so proud to be British why were you not calling yourself Frau Hunter the last time? And why did she use the name Toller when she arrived in Cologne a day or so ago?" The interpreter pressed the earpieces of his headphones as if that would clarify what he was hearing. "Her answer to that is that it is easier to travel on her German *Ausweis* . . ." He paused. "You know that word?" Gaffney nodded. "Now she is saying that when she came back to Germany before, her husband had not long been murdered, and she thought it better that she used her former name. Later she changed her mind. She asks if that is a crime." There was a pause, then a look of relief came over the interpreter's face and he grinned. Taking off his headphones, he put them on the table in front of him. "Now she tells Herr Fischer that she is British, and if he wants to talk any more, she will only speak in English." He flicked down a switch and instantly Gisela Hunter's voice came through the loudspeaker.

"I don't know why I am here. I repeat that I have done nothing wrong," she said.

Fischer had not stirred, but maintained his sprawling posture, a half-smile on his face. "You came back here in nineteen seventy-two, Mrs Hunter," he said, "but in nineteen seventy-seven you disappeared. Where did you go?"

Gisela Hunter sat up sharply at that. Whether it was the defeat of her ploy by a German detective who spoke near-perfect English — certainly as good as her own — or the fact that the authorities in Bonn had clearly been keeping a record of her movements, was not apparent.

"To America. Why?" she asked.

That reply stunned Gaffney. It was the first intimation anywhere in the enquiry that Gisela Hunter had spent any time in the United States. And that opened up a whole new can of worms. He willed Fischer to ask for more details. But at first it seemed that the German policeman had ignored what she had said, perhaps had missed it altogether. But Willi Fischer was too shrewd a detective for that.

"Was it because Dieter Muller told you that the police were interested in your activities?"

"The police? I thought it was the Gestapo." It was a throwaway remark and she turned to drain her coffee cup.

Fischer did not react to the insult, although Gaffney guessed he might have done if someone other than a German had said it, and for a moment he wondered whether Gisela Hunter had any Jewish blood in her veins.

"You would like another cup of coffee, Mrs Hunter?"

She shook her head briefly. "No."

Fischer shrugged. "You know what happened to Dieter Muller, I suppose?"

"I don't know anyone of that name."

"He killed himself under a train," said Fischer casually. "The Munich express as a matter of fact." He smiled as he added that as though it made a difference, was less painful perhaps.

There was no reaction. Gisela Hunter remained unmoved. "Really? Why are you telling me this?"

"Because you tried to get him to work for the Pakistani Government, Mrs Hunter. And he came to us and told us. You and he were lovers, and you threatened to tell his wife. Then he told you, and you ran away — to America — and he killed himself. Now you are back again. I wonder why, Mrs Hunter." Gaffney was relieved. Fischer had picked it up. And now he followed it through. "Where did you go in America, Mrs Hunter?"

Gisela Hunter gave her questioner a cool look of appraisal, and for a moment Gaffney thought that she was going to refuse to answer him. But then she said, "New York," in a tone of voice that implied that it was the only place worth visiting in America. The readiness with which she had parted with that information surprised Gaffney. New York was the city where the United Nations had its headquarters, and there were more diplomats in New York than there were Yellow Cabs. But there again, perhaps she hadn't got anything to hide. She could just be a goodtime girl after all. But all Gaffney's professional instincts made him doubt that.

"And why have you come back to Germany now, Mrs Hunter?" Fischer continued his questioning quietly and patiently, but Gaffney, a skilled interrogator himself, recognised a certain resignation in his voice that implied that the German detective knew he was getting nowhere . . . and would get nowhere.

"It is my home. I was born here."

"But a moment ago you were telling me that you were British."

"Pah!"

Fischer put his head on one side and smiled, awaiting an explanation for her sudden outburst of annoyance.

"I am being harassed by the British police," she said. In the observation room, the German interpreter looked at Gaffney and grinned. Gaffney grinned back, and Tipper looked at the ceiling. "She'd know all about it if she was," he growled.

"Harassed? In what way were you

being harassed, Mrs Hunter?" asked Fischer.

"First they arrest a friend of mine on some nonsensical charge of stealing my car," she said. "And then, because I am having a friendly argument in my flat with another friend, the next thing is that the police arrive. They are watching me . . . all the time."

"Why would they be doing that?" asked Fischer.

"Because I am German, and the British do not like the Germans."

If it was an attempt to provoke sympathy, it failed. Gisela Hunter did not realise just how much comradeship existed between the police forces of the world, or that the allegation she had just made had been made against them all at some time or another.

"Oh dear," Fischer said, and smiled.

The questioning went on for another hour, Fischer patiently probing in an attempt to secure some sort of admission, but Gisela Hunter would have none of it, countering his questions with protestations of innocence until eventually, with carefully disguised exasperation,

Fischer said, "Very well. You can go."

They had lunch at a smart little *Gasthof* just outside the city. Fischer shook hands with the owner, the owner's wife, and half the clientele, and kissed the waitress. There was much back-slapping and heavy Teutonic bonhomie before the German policeman sat down.

"It was a waste of time, John," said Fischer. "I think that all we have done is to tell her of our interest. She will not do anything suspicious now."

Gaffney shrugged. "Maybe so. But she might give something away. I presume you're having her watched anyway?"

Fischer nodded. "*Ja*, but for how long?" he asked through a mouthful of *Kartoffelsalat*. "This man Muller has been dead so long his body has rotted." He grinned, and with policeman's black humour added, "Those bits that they found anyway."

They all laughed and Fischer called for more beer.

"Not for long, though," continued Fischer, wiping his lips with his table napkin. "It is all too old. No harm was done — not to Germany anyway — and the chief won't let me waste men on it."

"Sounds familiar," said Gaffney.

"Anyway, why are you wicked British policemen being so cruel to Frau Hunter, John? Following her everywhere and making her life so miserable that she has to come back to Germany, eh? And I always thought that you were such gentlemen at Scotland Yard."

The waitress brought the beer and Fischer pinched her bottom. She laughed scornfully at him and wiggled her hips as she walked away.

The failure of the German police to elicit any information from Gisela Hunter had probably hindered Gaffney's investigation, and the alarm which they had caused the woman was confirmed when, two days later, she left her hotel in Bad Godesburg and flew to Karachi.

"Get hold of Wisley," said Gaffney to Tipper.

DI Francis Wisley appeared in the office minutes later.

"Fancourt Mansions, Number Five,"

said Gaffney. "Get a warrant and search it, discreetly. And make some enquiries. See if she's gone for good, or whether there's a chance of her coming back."

The search of Gisela Hunter's flat was disappointing. The indications were that she had just walked out and left it, with every intention of returning. But it was her own flat, and no one knew whether she was coming back. The phone was still connected and the power still switched on. The transcripts of the intercept on her post and her phone — and on Foster's — did not record that she had told the diplomat she was going. Not that that was foolproof There were other ways of communicating, and several times before her departure the surveillance team had seen her using a public telephone box. And Wakeford had probably been right in assuming that that was how she had booked her flight to Cologne. Any professional spy would be familiar with cut-outs, and the sterile state of her flat pointed to her being very professional indeed. Or innocent.

Gaffney discussed the case with Frank

Hussey, the operations commander, who was all for abandoning it.

"Let's face it, John," said Hussey. "Foster now denies that she was attempting to recruit him, but from what you say of him, he's just a bloody idiot. Hunter's gone, and the only tittle of evidence is a bit of twelve-year-old scuttle-butt in Germany with a diplomat who's now long dead anyway. I'd forget it, if I were you."

Gaffney looked doubtful. "I'm intrigued by this statement of hers that she went to New York from Germany, sir. It's the first intimation that she didn't come straight to this country."

"Didn't your other enquiries turn that up?"

"No, sir. We can place her here in the UK from about three years ago, but before that not a thing. We've tried everything, including, incidentally, the States, but the FBI have got nothing. I could have another go, I suppose."

Hussey shrugged. "Well, if you think it's worth it, John, you've got my blessing. But my advice is don't waste too much time on it."

"There is the little matter of a murder in Islamabad, sir," said Gaffney.

"Ah, yes, so there is. What d'you want to do about that?"

"Make a few enquiries at the Foreign Office, sir," said Gaffney enigmatically. "But there's only one place to investigate a murder. Where it happened. With your permission, sir."

"Every time you come through that door, John Gaffney, I sense trouble." Joe Daly, the resident FBI man at the American Embassy in London, shook hands vigorously and grinned.

"Never mind your smart remarks, Joe, how about some of that inimitable American coffee of yours."

"Jesus! American coffee, he calls it. I tell you, John, that goddam secretary of mine will only ever buy instant." He waved an invitation to Gaffney to sit down. "But then she is English."

"Racist!" said Gaffney.

Daly relaxed behind his desk and grinned. "What's on your mind, John?"

"Gisela Hunter," said Gaffney.

Daly leaned forward and drew a pad

towards him. But he paused, pen in mid-air. "We've spoken about her before, surely?"

Gaffney nodded. "Yes. But you turned up no trace."

Daly dropped his pen on the desk. "You got something new, then?" He ran a hand through his thick grey hair.

"Yes and no. I was in Germany last week, sitting in on an interrogation. The BKA pulled her in about a West German diplomat she'd tried to get information from about Pakistan, back in nineteen seventy-seven."

Daly scoffed. "You putting me on, John?"

Gaffney smiled. "No, seriously, Joe. During Willi Fischer's interview — you know Willi, don't you?" Daly nodded. "During the interview she admitted going to New York when she left Germany . . . end of seventy-seven, I suppose."

Daly looked doubtful. "I can try again, John, but I don't think I'll be any more successful than the first time."

Gaffney nodded. "Probably not. But if it's any help, I can give you a photograph, and the benefit of a hunch. How's that?"

"Worth a try. What's the MO?"

"I think that she spent some time in New York and — I'm taking a wild guess here — may have tried to turn any one of the diplomats working at the UN headquarters who might have had some knowledge of Indo-Pakistan affairs."

"Beautiful!" said Daly. "That's just about any of them. Gees, John, there are about a hundred and sixty nations with representatives at the UN, and every one of them reports approaches damn near every day of the week. Can't you do better than that?"

Gaffney held up his hands. "I know it's asking a hell of a lot, Joe, but it's my only chance. I've got an espionage job hanging on this . . . and a possible murder."

Daly raised his eyebrows. "You wanna hang a homicide on this broad?"

"Not directly, Joe, but I think she's got an agent placed in our embassy in Pakistan. The resident SIS man there was murdered, and I'm pretty certain that there's a connection."

"Okay, John," said Daly, starting to write again, "but sure as hell, you guys really strain the special relationship." But he smiled as he said it. "You said you had a photograph?"

Gaffney handed across several prints. "They're shots our surveillance team took of her. They're a good likeness on the whole."

Daly glanced at them and put them to one side. "Okay, John," he said, "I'll fax them across, see how we do. I'll give you a call."

The phone was ringing when Gaffney walked into his office. It was eight days since he had spoken to Joe Daly and he was beginning to think that the Americans had drawn a blank yet again.

"John?" The unmistakable voice of Joe Daly blasted into Gaffney's ear. "Where the hell've you been all day?"

"I've just arrived," said Gaffney. "We don't start work until ten, you know."

There was a guffaw from the other end of the line. "I don't wonder our General George Washington caught you guys with your pants down." It was an old joke between them, and Gaffney joined in the laughter. "I've been here since eight o'clock," said Daly.

"Drinking instant coffee, no doubt?"

"Okay, okay, wise guy. This Hunter woman, John . . . "

"Yes?"

"She's wanted in New York."

"What for?"

"Homicide."

When Gaffney went to the American Embassy, Joe Daly was able to add very little to what he had said on the phone. In fact it looked, if anything, less promising. "The SAIC in New York" — it meant Special Agent in Charge, and Daly pronounced it "Say-ick" — "thinks it might be her."

"Terrific!" said Gaffney.

"He got a feedback from the NYPD. A guy in Homicide there picked a flyer out of the open file from way back . . . nineteen seventy-nine or thereabouts — "

"Would you mind translating that into English, Joe?" Gaffney grinned.

For a moment Daly stared at the British detective. "Yeah, right. It means that NYPD have an unsolved homicide on their hands. One of many," he added, and laughed. "When they get to the point where they think it's going nowhere, they put the docket into the open file. It means it's available for anyone to have a go, and any detective who gets some information — perhaps a snitch comes up years later with something — can add to it. Might even finish up getting a collar out of it."

Gaffney nodded. "I think I've got the drift, as you Americans say. Go on."

"The guy who got murdered was a diplomat, an American from the State Department, working out of the UN in New York. He was shafting this broad . . . claimed to be Austrian and went by the name of Mia Neidhart. He was married, of course." Daly shrugged. "They found his body in her apartment, shot to death with a three-two automatic, they reckon. But Mia Neidhart had disappeared, and they never found her."

"Is that it?"

"Up to last week, John, yes. Homicide showed the shots of your Hunter woman to the super at the apartment block and he said, yeah, it could be her. But we're talking ten years here." Daly spread his hands in a gesture of hopelessness. "With the smart-ass lawyers we got in the States, she'd walk . . . if they ever found her."

Gaffney nodded. "It's not much, is it?"

"Much?" Daly laughed gratingly. "It's nothing, John."

"Is there any chance of anything more, d'you think?"

Daly shrugged. "Look at it this way," he said. "I get it from the SAIC in New York. He gets it from the guy in Homicide in the NYPD, who wasn't even the guy who caught it in the first place . . . he's long gone, buried with full department honours five years back, after he went down in a shoot-out at a liquor store." He laid his hands flat on his desk. "There could be more, I reckon, but right now the NYPD've got more to worry about than a ten-year-old domestic homicide. Sorry I can't be more helpful." He paused. "If you could persuade your commissioner to let you go across there, you might get something more, but I reckon your people'd sniff heavy if you asked for a ride on Concorde for that." He laughed again.

"I think you're probably right, Joe, but thanks anyway."

13

THE senior official in the Establishments Department of the Foreign and Commonwealth Office, to whom Tipper had been referred by its Security Branch, looked askance at the detective. "Murder? Good God! In an embassy?" The expression on his face could not have betrayed greater shock if Tipper had just told him that the Foreign Secretary was a raving homosexual. "How can I help?"

"I would like a list of everyone on the staff of the British Embassy in Pakistan," said Tipper, "together with thumb-nail sketches of their backgrounds."

The official blinked. "I can't possibly release this sort of information without the Secretary of State's authority. It's a matter of security."

"Is that so?" Tipper withdrew a piece of paper from his pocket and laid it on the desk. "If you get out the FCO telegram bearing that reference," he said, "you will find that it is the Secretary of State's authority for Detective Chief Superintendent Gaffney and me to investigate the death of Peter Kerr, a First Secretary at the British Embassy in Pakistan." It was a habit of Tipper's. Whenever he saw a piece of paper that told him to do something — particularly a piece of paper he was not allowed to keep — he jotted down the reference, the date, and the name of the person who signed it. He called it insurance.

"Oh!" said the official, blinking again and peering at the note.

"Shall we begin, then?" asked Tipper jovially.

"It'll take time." The official continued to stare at the note, stalling. "But I'll see what I can do. Can I ring you?"

"Of course." Tipper wrote his phone number on the top of the note.

It was three days before Tipper was ushered back into the same office.

"Ah, Mr Tipper, sit down." The Foreign Office official was more relaxed than on the detective's first visit, and it was obvious that he had looked up the telegram of authority and found that it salved his conscience. He waved a hand at a pile of files on a side-table. "I have all the personnel files there . . . except the Ambassador's, of course."

"Why 'of course'?"

The official looked shocked. "But surely, you don't think that His Excellency — ?"

"I don't see why not," said Tipper mischievously. "It was his shotgun after all, and if I knew who'd pulled the trigger, I wouldn't be wasting your time."

"But you see, ambassadorial files are held — "

Tipper waved him down with a smile. "Don't worry," he said. "We'll have a go at these first. If we need to look at Forbes' file, I'm sure it can be got hold of."

The official winced at Tipper referring to an Ambassador by his surname. "What exactly do you want to know?"

Tipper had given the enquiry a great deal of thought, and in common with most experienced detectives was hoping to short-circuit what could develop into a protracted enquiry. "Have any of them served in Germany?"

"Germany?" The official raised his eyebrows. "But I thought — "

"If I have to explain every reason for asking a question," said Tipper patiently, "we're going to be here all night."

"Ah, yes, quite so. Germany. Well, we'll see."

After half an hour, three files rested on the official's desk, each the personal record of a diplomat now in Pakistan who had served at the British Embassy in Bonn.

"I still don't see your interest."

"No, I don't suppose you do, but then you don't know what I know," said Tipper in a way that implied that the official wasn't going to be told either. "Is there anything odd about these fellows?"

The official thumbed through the files again. "Not that I can see," he said pensively. "This chap though . . . Bartlett, Julian Bartlett, didn't do his full tour. Came home after only a year. Odd that. Most unusual."

Tipper's languid attitude did not betray his sudden interest. "Does it say why?" he asked in an offhand sort of way.

"No." The official continued reading. "When was it, then?"

"In nineteen seventy-seven."

"Was it now?" Tipper looked smug. He was pretty sure that nineteen seventy-seven was the year that Gisela Hunter, formerly Toller, was seducing the late Herr Dieter Muller of the German Foreign Ministry in Bonn, but he would have to check his notes when he got back to the Yard. "What does he do, this bloke Bartlett?"

"Do? What does he do?" The official found it increasingly difficult to understand Tipper, but then so did a lot of people.

"Yeah. What's his job?"

"He's a first secretary," said the official hesitantly, uncertain that that was the answer the detective was seeking.

"Right. That a photograph of him there?" Tipper leaned towards the file in front of the official.

"Yes." Protectively the official drew the file towards himself and unclipped a passport-size photograph from inside the file cover. Tipper recognised him immediately as one of the diplomats with whom he and Gaffney had dined the night of their arrival in Pakistan. His didn't appear to be the face of a murderer, but then none of the murderers that Tipper had ever arrested in his service had the face of a murderer. Whatever that was. He recalled the death masks of the twenty or so of last century's killers that resided on a shelf in the Yard's Black Museum, and the injunction to the very first detectives, back in the eighteen-sixties, that that was what criminals looked like, so go out and find some.

"Is he married, this Bartlett?" Tipper returned the photograph. He knew the answer to that as well. Remembered the tall, thin woman who had sat next to him that same night. He remembered, too, the story that Angela Conrad had later told them about putting her to bed . . . drunk as usual. But he had no intention of letting this official know any of that. People like this fellow, who wore old school ties and operated the old boy net, had a tendency to gossip.

"Yes, he is. Wife's on station with him. Two children, both sons, aged twelve and fourteen. At school in England."

The official read the mundane details off the file.

"Good," said Tipper. "I think we'll have a chat with him."

"But he's in Pakistan."

"Yes, and he's about to be visited by great iron bird from out of sky."

"The first thing to do, Harry," said Gaffney, "is to find out why he was backloaded from Germany before his tour was over."

"How do we do that, guv'nor?" asked Tipper. "Given that the FCO are reticent about telling us anything."

"A simple phone call," said Gaffney, reaching for the hand-set.

It was obvious that James Marchant had sources at the Foreign and Commonwealth Office that were denied to policemen, and the fact that Gaffney was investigating the death of one of Marchant's operatives doubtless added a little impetus. Whatever the reason, the answer to Gaffney's query came twenty minutes later. It did not exactly fill him with glee.

"The ambassador in Bonn in nineteen

seventy-seven was Sir Brian Chester, Harry," said Gaffney, putting the phone down. "Who is now, you will recall, Chief Clerk at the Foreign Office."

"Hoo-bloody-ray," said Tipper.

Sir Brian Chester had agreed to see the two detectives immediately, which caused Tipper to suggest that he had got sod-all to do.

Gaffney laughed. "You're a miserable bugger, Harry," he said as they mounted the broad staircase in the FCO main building. "If he'd put us off you'd have accused him of being obstructive."

Tipper muttered to himself.

They were ushered into the Chief Clerk's ornate office overlooking St James's Park, and Chester, beaming, shook hands and enquired whether they would prefer Indian or China tea.

"Now, Mr Gaffney, I presume you wish to talk about the Foster affair."

"No, Sir Brian. At least, I don't think there's a connection. I want to ask you about another diplomat, Julian Bartlett."

Chester frowned. "Bartlett? Bartlett?"

"First Secretary at the Islamabad Embassy."

"Ah yes." Chester stirred his tea thoughtfully. "What, may I ask, is your interest in him?"

"We are investigating the death of another first secretary there, Peter Kerr."

"So you are." Chester spoke mildly, but his eyes narrowed. "What's the connection?"

"I don't know that there is one, Sir Brian. At the moment we are seeking anomalies."

Tipper smiled to himself He had to admit that Gaffney was quite good at this diplomatic double-talk.

"I see. Well, he's not exactly under my tutelage . . . "

"No, Sir Brian . . . but he was when you were ambassador to the Federal Republic of West Germany."

For a moment or two Chester gazed steadily at Gaffney. "You've been doing your homework, Chief Superintendent," he said.

"Why did he come home before he'd completed his tour?" The question was bald, to the point, but Gaffney had no intention of pussy-footing about any longer on this esoteric diplomatic wavelength. Apart from anything else, he hadn't got the time.

"You think that relevant?"

"Until you answer the question, I shan't know, Sir Brian." Gaffney smiled but it failed to disguise his impatience.

"Gambling," said Chester reluctantly. Gaffney waited for him to continue but the Chief Clerk added nothing more.

"Would you care to expand on that?"

Chester looked pensive and placed his empty teacup carefully on the table. "More tea?" he asked.

"No, thank you."

"I'm afraid Julian Bartlett was a bit of a naughty boy." Chester carefully poured himself another cup of Lapsang Souchong, before glancing up in time to catch the acid expression on Tipper's face. "He rather got himself into debt, silly young fellow. Of course," he continued expansively, "we encourage our people to be friendly towards the natives . . . when we're in friendly territory, that is." He smiled tolerantly. "Provided they're the right sort of people."

Gaffney could guess what Chester's idea of the right sort of people was. "But he mixed with the wrong sort, I take it?"

"In a manner of speaking. There are some very rich Germans in Bad Godesburg. Much richer than the average diplomat."

"Very rich, then," said Tipper.

Chester glanced briefly at the Chief Inspector, unsure whether he was being sarcastic or not. "Yes," he said, "very rich. And he got rather involved with gambling."

"And drinking and loose women as well, I suppose?" asked Tipper.

"Good heavens, no." Chester replied a little too quickly, and Tipper guessed that he either didn't know or didn't want to know. "I thought it best to send him home. Gave him a ticking off, silly young devil."

Gaffney looked sideways at Tipper. "You said that there was nothing about this on his personal file, Harry, didn't you?"

"That's what the bloke in the Establishments Department said."

"No, well there wouldn't be." Chester smiled, a smile of tolerance that seemed to make an allowance for these mere policemen not understanding the ways of the Diplomatic Service. "It was all rather informal. It could have blighted the fellow's career. Seems a shame for just one peccadillo. I'm sure you have a similar system in the police."

Tipper opened his mouth to say something, but Gaffney cut across him. "You're probably right, Sir Brian." He knew what Tipper was about to say, that he knew of detectives who had suddenly found themselves wearing a tall hat on the basis of some unsubstantiated hint of corrupt practice, but he needed Chester's help and nothing would be achieved by antagonising him. He would have liked to point out the errors of the past when early action would have prevented a national scandal, but he put that to one side, reserving it for the day when he had someone in custody and could say 'I told you so'.

"What happened about Bartlett's gambling debts? Did the Foreign Office settle those for him?" Gaffney knew that government generosity did not extend that far, but gave himself the luxury of an impish remark at the Chief Clerk's expense.

Chester smiled, appreciating the joke. "I don't know, to be perfectly honest," he said, gently smoothing the cloth of his trouser leg that was stretched over his knee. "They *were* settled, that much I know. Perhaps he took out a bank loan." Chester's smile became a chuckle at his own little attempt at humour.

"And when he came home, what happened to him then? Another posting?"

"Not immediately. He spent a few years here, in London. A sort of penance."

"How awful," said Tipper. "Then you shunted him off to Pakistan."

"Exactly." Chester snapped out the answer. He didn't like Tipper, or his thinly veiled sarcasm.

"And how long has he been there?" asked Gaffney.

"Nearly three years it must be."

"So he's due back fairly soon?"

"I don't know about that, but he's certainly due for a change."

"Any ideas where he might go?"

"None I'm afraid. The Establishments' people do all that. I only get the details for formal approval. Don't often interfere."

"I take it you'd veto a return to Germany?"

Chester lifted his empty teacup from the table and placed it on the silver tray. "I don't see why," he said. "I think he's learned his lesson."

"Let's suppose for one moment that Bartlett's our man," said Gaffney. It was nine o'clock in the evening and he and Tipper sat in the Chief Superintendent's office, an open bottle of Scotch on the desk between them. Most of Special Branch had either gone home or were out on the various assignments that made up their assorted responsibilities.

"Why suppose that, sir?" Tipper drained his glass and put it hopefully on the desk.

"He was in Germany at the same time as Gisela Hunter. She disappeared when he came home but we now know that she went to New York. Bartlett's due back now from Pakistan, and the Hunter woman's busily trying to recruit

Foster." Gaffney poured more whisky into Tipper's glass. "Except that that all seems to have come to nothing." Gaffney yawned and drained his glass. "Only one thing for it, Harry." He smiled. "We're going back to Pakistan."

"Terrific," said Tipper. "When?"

"As soon as we get back from New York, Harry . . . if I can persuade the DAC to let us go."

ACSO's secretary looked up and smiled. "Hello, Mr Gaffney," she said. "Mr Frobisher won't keep you long. Do take a seat. Would you like a cup of coffee?"

"Thank you." Gaffney settled in the armchair. It was always the same, seeing the Assistant Commissioner Specialist Operations, head of the department which included Special Branch. The first time that Gaffney had waited in this office was when he had been appointed a detective constable, nearly twenty years ago. In best suits, he and three others, palms sweating, not daring to sit down much less accept an invitation to take coffee — not that it would have been offered to a lowly DC — had waited to be ushered into the presence and formally welcomed to 'the Department', as it had been called before faceless uniformed imports had tried their desperate best to destroy any form of élitism in the Metropolitan Police. They had even tried it with Special Branch, redesignating it SO 12. But no one had taken any notice: to its members, and most other people, it was still 'The Branch'. Now, as a detective chief superintendent, Gaffney's place in the hierarchy of the Criminal Investigation Department put him much closer to the Assistant Commissioner. But the waiting was just the same. Since that first day, he had seen successive Assistant Commissioners on numerous occasions, but not once had Gaffney been received at the time of his appointment.

As if reading his thoughts, the secretary glanced across. "He's just changing," she said, and smiled. "It's the Investiture today . . . he's getting his medal. Shouldn't be long."

"Ah, Mr Gaffney." The tall silver-haired figure of Peter Frobisher stood in the doorway of his office, immaculate in morning dress. "Sorry to have kept you." He glanced at the cup and saucer that Gaffney was holding as he struggled to his feet. "Do bring your coffee in with you."

Well, that was something. You could always tell. If you were up there to be reprimanded, Frobisher would press his buzzer to summon you. And you didn't take your coffee with you.

"Do sit down, Mr Gaffney." Frobisher indicated an armchair.

"Congratulations on your CBE, sir," said Gaffney, as he seated himself. The Assistant Commissioner had featured in the Birthday Honours List a few weeks previously, but it was the first time since then that Gaffney had seen him to talk to.

"Thank you. Very kind," murmured Frobisher, settling himself into the armchair opposite Gaffney. "Goes with the job, of course. A tribute to the department, really." He gestured dismissively with his hand. "I've been considering your request to go to America," he continued.

"Yes, sir." So that's what it was about.

"D'you think you'll get anywhere?"

"To be frank, I don't, sir. But I think

it's one of those loose ends that ought to be cleared up. I take it you've seen the docket?" Frobisher nodded. "There is an outside chance that Gisela Hunter is the woman responsible for this murder in New York. But that's based on the porter of the flats where she lived, identifying her from our surveillance photographs." Gaffney shrugged. "Which, to be honest, he would probably have done from any photo we sent him." The Assistant Commissioner smiled and nodded: he liked to show that he knew what detective work was all about. "The only other connection is the fact that she was allegedly Austrian . . . which could also mean German, of course."

"It's a very tenuous connection, isn't it, Mr Gaffney? An identification from a photograph of someone the witness saw ten years ago."

"Yes, sir, it is." Gaffney nodded. He wondered if the Assistant Commissioner had been listening to him.

"The Foreign Secretary has taken a great interest in this case," said the AC. "Not so much about the murder, of course . . . although that's very important . . . " He smiled condescendingly. "But about the espionage angle. Clearly if there is a spy in the British Embassy in Islamabad, then he — or she — needs to be rooted out." He looked thoughtful for a moment. "I suppose this Hunter woman can be ruled out of the murder of Kerr, can she?"

Gaffney sighed inwardly. If Frobisher had read the docket at all, he certainly hadn't read it thoroughly. "Yes, sir," he said. "The surveillance team puts her in London at the time of Kerr's death. It's in the report, sir."

Frobisher nodded. "Ah, yes, quite so," he said, but it was obvious that he had not grasped the salient facts of the investigation. "MI5 not giving you any trouble, are they?"

Gaffney smiled. "No, sir. In fact, they're not giving me anything."

"Really? Oh well, I suppose you're quite used to that." The Assistant Commissioner smiled thinly. "Well I'm sorry, Mr Gaffney, but in the circumstances, I can't really justify the expenditure of your going to America. Frankly, I doubt that you'd learn any more than you have already." He spread his hands apologetically. "I suggest that you talk to Joe Daly again . . . see if he can get you any more information. If he does — and it would make a trip across a viable proposition — well then do feel free to come back to me again." He walked over and sat down behind his desk, and scribbled a few lines on the minute-sheet of the docket which now lay in front of him. "I've just made a brief note of the reasons for my decision," he said, closing the file and smiling. "I see you've got Chief Inspector Capper working with you on this. Good man, good man."

"Tipper, sir."

"I beg your pardon?"

"Tipper, sir. The Chief Inspector's name is Tipper."

"Ah, yes." The Assistant Commissioner slipped a half-hunter out of his pocket and peered at it. "Well, Mr Gaffney, I mustn't keep Her Majesty waiting, must I?"

14

I T was another week before Joe Daly came up with a few more snippets of information. They weren't a great deal of help to Gaffney, but he derived a wry satisfaction from drawing attention to the fact that the Americans not only had a bit of bother on their hands but had apparently done nothing about it at the appropriate time.

"I got Sol Whiteman, the SAIC in New York, to go see the NYPD again, John." Daly was looking more serious this morning as he ushered Gaffney into an armchair in his office at the embassy. "He saw a lieutenant called . . . " He broke off and thumbed through the open file on his desk. "Koniotes, that's the guy. He's the lieutenant in charge of detectives at the precinct where this homicide's recorded." Daly looked up. "He wasn't there at the time, of course. Koniotes, I mean."

"No, I suppose not," said Gaffney.

He imagined the regular movement of detectives was as much a part of New York's policy as it was London's.

"Whiteman told him about your homicide in Pakistan, but nothing about the espionage angle." Daly grinned. "That doesn't have anything to do with the police," he said.

"Speak for yourself," said Gaffney quietly.

"Harry Rossman, the guy who was killed, was working for the State Department, attached to the US mission to the UN." Daly skimmed a few more paragraphs in his file. "The super from an apartment building in Manhattan called it in. Nine o'clock in the morning. December twenty-fourth, nineteen seventy-nine." Daly looked up. "Christmas Eve, would you believe? Said he hadn't seen Mia Neidhart for a few days, and got worried. Says he visited to wish her a happy Christmas." Daly scoffed. "Looking for a hand-out for a Christmas box, more like. He got worried . . . " He laughed. "I'll bet he did. So he let himself in with the pass-key. There was no sign of Muzz Neidhart, but of Mr Rossman there was plenty: his blood was all over the carpet in the sitting room and Mr Rossman was very dead. At the autopsy they took four slugs out of him." Daly glanced up. "It's a wicked world, isn't it?" he said with a grin.

"The porter at the apartment block saw the photographs of Gisela Hunter, I understand," said Gaffney.

"Oh sure, but ten years on, and women have this way of looking different every time y'see them . . . never mind after ten years. He said it could be her. And that's it."

"And the NYPD have no idea what happened to her?"

"Nope! She just went. They tried Immigration, they tried the IRS, they tried City Hall, and they checked for a driver's licence. Zilch! She was supposed to be Austrian, but for all we know she could as easily have been a US citizen. Who's to tell?" Daly fingered a piece of paper out of his file and handed it over to Gaffney. "They sent a description, John."

Gaffney read through it. It was a typical police description, and could have been Gisela Hunter . . . or a thousand other women. "This Rossman — from the State Department — what d'you know about him?"

"Twenty-nine years old. Married to Helen Rossman, born Hurst. Two children. A normal all-American guy."

"What exactly did he do, this Rossman? I mean, what was his job in the State Department?"

"I was afraid you were going to ask that question, John, because it's the question that Sol Whiteman asked." Daly looked embarrassed. "And, quite frankly, it's the question the Bureau should have asked ten years ago, when it all happened. According to Rossman's supervisor, he specialised in — and I quote — 'the affairs of the Indian sub-continent.'" He closed the file.

"Interesting," said Gaffney. "It certainly points to our Gisela Hunter."

"Sure." Daly dropped the file back into his brief-case. "It also points to the possibility that Rossman was feeding her information. What beats me — assuming it was your Hunter woman — was why she should kill him . . . if she did."

"I should think she probably pushed him a bit too hard, and he threatened to come and see you."

Daly shrugged. "So what? Why not just split? She did anyway. It doesn't make sense, John."

"Maybe she didn't intend to kill him — "

Daly scoffed. "Putting four slugs into him doesn't sound accidental to me."

Gaffney shrugged. "Are you going to do anything about it, Joe?"

Daly stretched his arms upwards, his fingers touching the picture of the President that hung on the wall behind him. "Sol Whiteman's speaking to Washington about it, but it's a long time ago. I don't know if they'll want to bother after all this time. If Rossman was spying, the perp only did what we'd have done . . . took him out of circulation. Except that she did it permanently." He laughed at that, proving yet again that policemen everywhere have the same sense of humour. Daly walked across the room and refilled his coffee cup. "More coffee?"

Gaffney shook his head. "No thanks."

"Doesn't help you though, John," continued Daly, sitting down at his desk once more. "There's still nothing that links that homicide with yours."

"Supposing we get an admission from her . . ."

"You going to pull her in, then?"

Gaffney nodded. "Sooner or later, yes . . . if she comes back to the UK, that is. But if she admits to the murder of Harry Rossman, would the NYPD go for extradition?"

Daly grinned. "Now that's downright charitable of you, sir." He affected a deep Southern drawl. "Why are you interested in clearing up a New York homicide?"

"Because at the end of it all that might just be all there is," said Gaffney, "and I hate seeing people get away with things."

"Yeah. Me too, John. But it's a complicated business. I don't have to tell you about extradition, I guess. First it has to go to the DA, then on to the Attorney-General's office, then across to State. If you get across all those hurdles we might — just might — get her back there." He shrugged and spread his hands. "There again, Jesse Jackson might just get to be President one day."

Gaffney laughed. "I suppose that's the American equivalent of 'Beware of low-flying pigs'."

Daly wrinkled his brow. "How's that?" he said.

Henry Forbes was not best pleased to see them. Despite his knowledge of government in general and the Diplomatic Service in particular, he had nurtured the vain hope that the question of Peter Kerr's untimely death was now all in the past. But then he was still labouring under the delusion that the SIS man had taken his own life.

"Well, this is a surprise, Mr Gaffney, I must say. Welcome back, and you too, Mr Tipper." But there was no warmth in the courtesy. "What brings you to Islamabad again?"

Gaffney and Tipper had discussed strategy on the way over, and had decided that the only way to proceed was to take the Ambassador into their confidence.

"Peter Kerr was murdered, Ambassador," said Gaffney baldly.

Forbes, who had been standing with his back to the two policemen, pouring sherry, put the decanter down heavily and turned. If he was the killer, then his self-control was masterly. "Are you serious?" He walked across and closed his study door firmly. Then he sat down in an armchair, the sherry forgotten. "What on earth makes you think that?"

"You will recall that we conducted a number of tests with your shotgun?" said Gaffney. Forbes nodded. "They proved that there was no way Kerr could have killed himself. The distance was wrong. The angles were wrong. The whole thing was wrong."

The Ambassador's eyes narrowed. "But you knew that before you left."

"Yes," said Gaffney with a bland smile.

"Why on earth didn't you say so?" Then, mentally, he answered his own question. "Good God! Surely you don't think that I . . . ?" The sentence trailed as the enormity of the detective's reasoning struck him.

"It was your shotgun," said Tipper, who never saw any reason for being nice to suspects.

"My God!" Forbes shook his head. Then, his natural courtesy returning, he stood up. "I'm sorry, gentlemen," he said, crossing to the cocktail cabinet, "but that was quite a shock." He paused. "I don't know about you," he said, "but on second thoughts I'd rather have a Scotch."

"Thought you'd never ask," said Tipper bluntly.

The Ambassador handed out chunky tumblers of whisky and sat down again, his poise restored. "What do you propose to do now, then? I mean, which way do you see your enquiries proceeding?" Without giving Gaffney time to reply, he added, "This is a dreadful business . . . reflects badly on the mission."

Gaffney was mildly amused by that. Forbes was clearly one of those people who worried about impressions and what others thought of him, and was probably already visualising in his mind the reputation that would accompany him for the rest of his career, and beyond, as the ambassador, one of whose staff had been murdered. And hearing the laughter against a background of ice

316

tinkling in glasses at cocktail parties all over the world when someone inevitably said, "And with HE's own shotgun."

"Do you think the fact that Kerr was one of the 'friends' could have had something to do with his death?" asked the Ambassador.

"Friends?" Tipper knew what Forbes meant, but he disliked the euphemism that diplomats used for members of the Secret Intelligence Service.

"Yes, you know . . . Six." The Ambassador almost whispered the final word.

"It's possible," said Gaffney. "I really don't know." The Gisela Hunter affair, and the woman's connection with Pakistan, was too much of a coincidence in his view, but there was nothing to support his speculation, save what policemen called 'copper's nose'.

"Well," said Forbes, "if there's anything I can do to assist, just say the word." He walked over to the cocktail cabinet and took hold of the whisky decanter. "The other half?" he enquired, holding it up.

Gaffney thought that the Ambassador had mellowed a little; Tipper wondered what his urbanity was hiding.

Gaffney and Tipper had been in Islamabad for five days. They had conducted routine interviews with all British members of the staff of the mission and got nowhere. They didn't bother to see Diana Gibson again, the chess-playing girl whom the Ambassador had thought had been having an affair with Kerr. Nor did they have another talk with Brooks, the ex-policeman, despite the fact that he had lied to them about his police career. The remainder were bland, hiding behind their diplomatic impassiveness and, although helpful, largely of no great help. By the time they had finished, the two detectives had amassed a pile of useless written statements and very little else.

The next day, Roy Foster arrived. They ran into him in a corridor at the embassy, being shown round and introduced by the Head of Chancery, Hugh Clements, whom Gaffney and Tipper had met at the dinner party. He stopped, suddenly, his mouth opening, and the blood draining from his face.

"Hello, Mr Foster," said Tipper cheerily.

"What on earth are you doing here?" The question was rhetorical. Foster was convinced that he knew.

"I take it you've met," said the Head of Chancery.

"Yes, we have . . . in London," said Gaffney. "Some time ago."

"Mr Gaffney is investigating the death of Peter Kerr," said Clements. "The poor fellow committed suicide." Gaffney and Tipper had not revealed the full circumstances of Kerr's death to anyone but the Ambassador, although some members of the staff must have wondered why two senior Scotland Yard detectives were dealing with it. They probably put it down to Kerr's connection with the SIS which, in accordance with Foreign Office and SIS policy, they had been officially advised of.

Foster, however, was even more sceptical than the rest, and made a point of speaking to Gaffney after dinner. "What exactly are you doing here?" he asked, his voice a curious mixture of fear and truculence.

"Exactly as Mr Clements said." Gaffney was beginning to tire of Foster, not only because he had wasted a lot of police time, but because Gaffney was convinced that the diplomat was allowing himself to be used by the scheming and ruthless Gisela Hunter. "I'm afraid that we have more to concern ourselves with than your distasteful affair with Mrs Hunter. Where is she, by the way?"

"Here in Karachi, as far as I know. I haven't heard from her for a day or two."

It sounded like bluff. Gaffney was pretty sure that Foster had no idea, was convinced that he had now been abandoned by Gisela Hunter, and almost felt sorry for him.

On Sunday, the Prime Minister arrived at the embassy surrounded by Pakistani police motor-cyclists, and accompanied by two truck-loads of armed soldiers, Superintendent Khan, several Pakistani bodyguards and the four Scotland Yard protection officers, led by Detective Superintendent Terry Dobbs. In addition were the Principal Private Secretary, the Parliamentary Private Secretary, the Political Secretary, the Press Secretary, a doctor, a duty clerk and a couple of those largely unseen and hardworking secretaries who were known throughout Number Ten as the Garden Room girls. The Foreign Office man attached to Number Ten, Charles Morris, was there too. In addition to that little circus was the Foreign Secretary, his two protection officers and a whole team that was almost a mirror image of the Prime Minister's staff.

Terry Dobbs and Bill Carson, the Prime Minister's two senior protection officers, made a point of finding John Gaffney the moment they arrived.

"Well, sir," said Dobbs, looking round, "you look as though you've got yourself well organised in this outpost of Empire." He glanced across at Tipper. "Hello, Harry."

"Nice to see you, guv'nor," said Tipper. "Welcome to the foothills."

"Drink?" Tipper placed a bottle of Scotch on the desk.

Dobbs shook his head. "No thanks, guv, we're still working. I'll have something soft if you've got it."

"You can have Roy Foster, if you like,"

said Tipper quietly.

"I've got a lot to tell you," said Gaffney. "And I'll introduce you to Mohammed Khan. He's the local SB superintendent." Gaffney paused. "You're into cricket, aren't you, Terry?"

Dobbs nodded. "Yes," he said. "And if you're talking about the Pakistani copper who talks incessantly about the game, I've met him already . . . at the airport. He's here somewhere. Came with us. Started talking about cricket the moment we shook hands. He's a walking Wisden, that bloke."

"I've no doubt that he's pleased to meet someone who knows what he's talking about, then."

"How's this job of yours going?" asked Dobbs. "The one that did me out of my brief moment of leisure before the circus got here," he added ruefully.

"Don't ask," said Gaffney. "Harry and I have got a murder on our hands now."

"A murder!"

"Yes, but for Christ's sake don't tell anyone," added Gaffney hurriedly. "They all think it's suicide here, apart from the

Ambassador. He knows. But it was the Six man . . . " He waved his hand round the room. "This is his office . . . or was."

"What the hell's that all about?" Dobbs glanced across at Carson. They were both wondering whether Gaffney's news would affect the safety of the Prime Minister.

Gaffney ran briefly through the story of Kerr's death, and the results of the investigation to date. "So you see, Terry," he said finally, "we haven't made a great deal of progress." He drained his glass. "Which is a bloody sight further than we've got on the Gisela Hunter job."

Dobbs laughed. "Rather you than me, sir," he said. "How much longer are you planning on staying?"

"That rather depends," said Gaffney with a laugh, "on how we get on. At the present rate of progress, we could be here for ever."

"Alleluia!" said Tipper.

Gaffney was obliged to leave the Kerr investigation for a while in order to brief Terry Dobbs fully on the security arrangements he had made, and take him to the various places that the Prime Minister would be visiting. It was, after all, the official reason he and Tipper had been sent to Pakistan in the first place. As for the visit itself Gaffney had been involved in that sort of junket in the past, knew that the embassy would be in a state of flux, and that scant attention would be paid to his problems for the next two or three days, even though he was conducting a murder enquiry.

He did, however, catch the Ambassador after breakfast the following morning, and posed a vital question. "Who is Roy Foster replacing, Ambassador?"

Forbes looked perplexed by the enquiry, but then he wasn't privy, as far as Gaffney was aware, to the relationship that existed between Foster and Mrs Hunter.

"It's Julian Bartlett. Why d'you ask?"

That was interesting but not wholly surprising. "I've not seen him since I got back." Gaffney recalled the tall, supercilious character who had sat along the table from him — the other side of Jill Pardoe — at the Ambassador's welcoming dinner the first night of their visit to

Pakistan. The night of Kerr's murder. He had thinning, mousey-coloured hair and a breathless sort of laugh that Tipper put down to nervousness.

"No, he went home a few days before you got back, Mr Gaffney. Had some leave owing. It often happens."

Gaffney nodded, almost disinterestedly. "It's just that I'll need to interview him. To round off the enquiry. I'm sure you understand."

"I see." Forbes smiled. "Well, I'm afraid you'll have to catch him in England. He's back there now . . . I suppose."

"You suppose?"

"He might be going on somewhere. I don't really know. Probably find him *en poste* in Mumbo-Jumboland." The Ambassador shrugged. He had recovered from the initial shock of being told that Kerr had been murdered, and was not wholly displeased that Gaffney and Tipper had, so far, failed to find the killer. A suicide in his mission was bad enough; a murder was ten times worse. "If you'll excuse me," he said, "I have to see the Prime Minister."

Gaffney was unimpressed. "Of course," he said.

"That's it, Harry. I've had enough. We're going home."

"Thank God for that, guv'nor," said Tipper.

"If we're going to solve this bloody thing at all, I reckon we're going to do it in the UK. We'll start at the Foreign Office and work outwards. The answer's got to be there somewhere, and I reckon it's got something to do with Gisela Hunter."

Tipper sighed. "That's what you said in the first place."

15

"ONE more unidentified caller, sir." DI Wakeford laid some photographs on Gaffney's desk. "Well, not quite unidentified. His name's Bartlett."

Gaffney glanced at the results of the surveillance team's camera work. "I know. Until recently a first secretary at the British Embassy in Pakistan. How did you identify him?"

"Housed him to the Royal Dominion Club, sir. He's staying there . . . or was last night."

"Interesting. What happened?"

"He turned up at Gisela Hunter's place at about seven o'clock yesterday evening, sir. Rang the bell, got no answer, and went to his club. We didn't bother to keep obo. Just had a few words with the hall porter, got his pars and left him."

"Well, Harry?" Gaffney swung his chair to face Tipper. "Now what d'you think?"

"Seems half the world's beating a path to Frau Hunter's door," said Tipper cheerfully. "Perhaps we ought to do her for tomming."

"According to the Foreign Office file, Bartlett's UK address is somewhere in Petersfield. Why's he staying at the Royal Dominion?"

Tipper shrugged. "Could be half-a-dozen reasons," he said. "Like he's moved, his wife's left him — or vice versa — or he's working late at the office ... or he just fancied a bit on the side with Mrs H."

"Well, if that was the case, he was disappointed." Gaffney turned to Wakeford again. "Can you have a word with your friend the hall porter and see if Bartlett's booked in for any length of time? Discreetly, mind you."

Wakeford looked hurt. "Naturally, sir."

Gaffney grinned. "And then we'll have a word with him."

At lunch-time the following day, Wakeford rang in to say that Bartlett was staying at the Royal Dominion Club on a semi-permanent basis. At seven o'clock, he rang again to say that the diplomat was now in the club.

"Right, Harry, we'll go and talk to the man."

The Royal Dominion Club, in one of the back streets of St James's, was past its heyday. At its foundation it had been exclusively for the use of those associated with the dominions and colonies, but now, with the demise of Empire, it admitted anyone who had enough money to pay its spiralling subscription. The entrance hall was tatty, and the leather sofas there and in the grandly styled Poona Room were well past their prime. Tipper, resentful as ever, sulkily pointed out that Poona was in India which hadn't become a dominion until nineteen forty-seven . . . and even then had only lasted a couple of years or so before becoming a republic.

Bartlett had been paged, and appeared from the direction of the dining room, a mystified look on his face. He walked to the desk and spoke briefly to the hall porter who pointed at Gaffney and Tipper, sitting uncomfortably on a sofa which appeared to have no springs left.

As he walked towards them, the two detectives stood up.

"Mr Bartlett," said Gaffney. They had met in Pakistan of course, but the puzzled look remained on the diplomat's face.

"I know you from somewhere, don't I?"

"We met in Islamabad. I'm Detective Chief Superintendent Gaffney, and you'll doubtless remember Detective Chief Inspector Tipper."

"Ah, of course. You came out to look into that awful business of Peter Kerr's death, didn't you?" Bartlett avoided Gaffney's eyes, watching instead a waiter emptying the ashtrays in the entrance hall.

"Not really. We came out to make arrangements for the Prime Minister's visit. It just so happened that Peter Kerr committed suicide while we were there." Gaffney had no intention of giving Bartlett — their best suspect so far — the advantage of knowing that the police knew it was murder.

"I see." Bartlett seemed relieved. "Well, what can I do for you now?"

"We went back to Islamabad . . . after

330

you'd returned home. Consequently, we missed you. All we want from you," said Gaffney casually, "is a statement about what you knew of the incidents of that night."

"But I — "

Gaffney smiled. "I know. You had dinner with the Ambassador and the senior staff. I was there too, with Harry." He nodded in Tipper's direction. "It's all a bit of a nuisance, really, but you know what officialdom's like. All got to be down on paper."

For the first time, Bartlett smiled. "Oh yes," he said. "Red tape's something I do know about." He glanced round. "I don't know where the best place would be . . ."

"It'll have to be the police station, I'm afraid," said Gaffney. "My clever chief inspector here forgot to bring any official forms with him. It's not far, and we've a car outside."

Bartlett frowned briefly. He would not have put up with incompetent subordinates like this Tipper fellow . . . but then he didn't know that the reason for Tipper's deviousness was to enable he and Gaffney to get Bartlett on their home ground without arousing his suspicion too much. He glanced at his watch. "Will it take long?"

"It shouldn't. Do you have an appointment, then?"

"No, but I was going to pay a surprise visit on an old friend, just on the off-chance so to speak."

Gaffney nodded. He could guess who the old friend was. It was fairly obvious that Gisela Hunter had taken flight without telling Bartlett either. "No problem," he said, "we'll even drop you where you want to go when we're through."

"That won't be necessary," said Bartlett, a little too quickly. "I can get a cab."

Tipper, standing to one side, looked at Bartlett with a feeling of pleasurable anticipation. Their suspect was starting to wriggle already, like a fish on the hook. Not that Tipper had ever fished in his life . . . not for fish, anyway.

West End Central Police Station was overcrowded, but then it always was.

Harassed custody sergeants with sheaves of paper dashed back and forth, shouting and swearing. A dishevelled drunk sat in the charge room, a vacant expression on his face and vomit down his clothing, while at the front office counter a dozen people, mostly foreigners, were waiting to report that they had been robbed or ripped-off or were wanting to know how to get to somewhere else . . . which was very wise of them. Bartlett, judging by the expression on his face, found the whole scene quite distasteful, and probably wished he was somewhere else, too.

They found a quiet office and sat down.

"There isn't really anything I can tell you, you know," said Bartlett. He had obviously been giving the matter some thought during the journey to the police station.

"No, perhaps not, but it's surprising what comes out when you start talking about it. Some little thing you may have forgotten, or think is unimportant, can often be extremely valuable to us — when put with other things we have learned."

Gaffney smiled patiently.

Bartlett watched Tipper as he took a pile of statement forms out of a cabinet and shuffled them into a neat pile before laying them on the end of the desk. "You seem to be going to a lot of trouble over this." The diplomat rubbed the palms of his hands on his knees. "More than I should have thought it warranted."

"Maybe so," said Gaffney, "but a sudden death is not to be treated lightly." He paused. "Particularly one on diplomatic premises . . . and particularly when the Secretary of State has taken an interest."

Bartlett understood that and nodded. "I suppose so."

"If you'll just tell me what you did that evening, and what, if anything, you saw, we'll get a form of words down on paper and I'll ask you to sign it."

"I really don't know anything." Bartlett leaned forward earnestly.

"Mr Tipper and I left the dinner party at the embassy at about midnight," said Gaffney. "What with the difference in time and the flight over, we were just about all in. But I understand that it went on a bit after that?"

"Yes." Bartlett nodded. "Until about one, I suppose. It had gone a bit better than most."

"Oh?"

"One gets fed up with seeing the same old faces all the time and listening to the same boring conversation, but you and Mr Tipper being there, and talking about London and so on, made it much more interesting. Anyhow, at about one, HE suggested that we ought to be turning in, and that was that."

"What did you do?"

"Went to bed." The answer came out in a way that suggested there was no alternative. "Cynthia was pretty tired by then, and . . . " He paused, uncertain whether to complete the sentence.

"And what?"

"She'd had just a little too much champagne, I think." Bartlett smiled ruefully.

"Where did you go to bed?" asked Gaffney. "I mean where d'you live?"

"In the compound, at the back of the residence. It's a flat."

"I see. And when, Mr Bartlett, were

you first made aware of Peter Kerr's death?"

"Next morning when I went into work." Bartlett answered instantly, giving his reply no thought at all.

"And what time would that have been?"

"About seven-thirty. We start quite a bit earlier in 'Pindi — " Bartlett spoke in drawling tones as though the British Raj still existed and he was a part of it.

"'Pindi?" It was Tipper who posed the question. "Not Islamabad?" He knew the answer, but Bartlett's affectation irritated him.

"We tend to call it 'Pindi, but, yes, it is Islamabad. Same thing really."

"Go on," said Tipper. Rawalpindi and Islamabad were not the same at all to him, and he still recalled, with disquiet, the hair-raising ride that he and Gaffney had endured on the night of Kerr's death when the Ambassador had summoned them back to the embassy.

"I was absolutely stunned. We all were. Peter never seemed to have a care in the world. It was a dreadful shock."

"Yes, it must have been." Gaffney

336

picked up a paper-clip and started twisting it. "You back here for good now?"

"For a bit, yes. I'm not keen on the FCO, and travelling in on the train after somewhere like 'Pindi is an absolute nightmare."

"It must be awful," said Gaffney with a sarcasm that was lost on Bartlett.

"I'm hoping to get back there."

"Where? Pakistan?"

"Oh no, I shan't go there again, at least not unless I'm promoted. No, I rather fancy Delhi, if I can pull a few strings."

"How long have you known Gisela Hunter?" Tipper's question came like a whiplash.

Bartlett's reserve was masterly. For a moment or two he stared into space, almost as if he hadn't heard the question. Then he turned, very slowly, to gaze at Tipper. "Who?" he asked.

"Hunter, Gisela Hunter." Gaffney took the questioning back. "I can't remember now, but someone mentioned the Hunters that night at dinner. I know that the Ambassador said he'd known

Richard Hunter when he was at the consulate in Karachi. I thought you said that you knew them, too." He waved a dismissive hand, as though it was a matter of no importance. "Must have got you mixed up with someone else."

Bartlett looked genuinely puzzled, as if desperately searching his memory. "Name means nothing to me," he said eventually.

"No matter, Mr Bartlett," said Gaffney, and glanced at his watch. "Anyhow, we've taken up enough of your time already. Mr Tipper's been writing while you were talking." He turned. "Just read it over, Harry, will you?" He glanced back at Bartlett. "If you agree with what's written, I'll get you to sign it, and we'll call it a day."

They had dropped into a pub for a quiet pint before going home.

"Interesting," said Gaffney, taking the head off his Guinness. "D'you remember what Angela Conrad said about Cynthia Bartlett being smashed out of her mind that night, and the follow-up we did. There was a statement from Anthony

338

Booth . . . or was it his wife . . . ?" He paused. "Forgotten her first name."

"Margaret," said Tipper. "Yeah, she said that Cynthia Bartlett had to be helped to bed. Does it matter?"

"It does if she was so drunk that she can't remember whether her husband went to bed with her or not."

"She's not a compellable witness," said Tipper with a shrug. "Not against him."

"No . . . " Gaffney drew the word out pensively. "But I think we're getting somewhere at last, Harry."

"Just so long as 'somewhere' is not back to bloody Pakistan," said Tipper with feeling, and he ordered another round.

"Anyone'd think you didn't like the place, Harry."

Tipper shook his head. "Give me the East End any day of the week, guv'nor."

"Surprise, surprise," said Joe Daly, as he pushed open the door of Gaffney's office.

"Surprise that you've actually found

339

your way out of that embassy of yours? Or an even greater surprise — you have something of use to me?" Gaffney grinned as he beckoned the FBI man in.

"This Rossman homicide in the States, John." Daly lowered his big frame into one of Gaffney's armchairs. "It seems the NYPD didn't spot Rossman's connection with Indian affairs at the time." He shrugged. "Not that it would have meant anything to them anyway. An Austrian broad getting screwed by a guy in the State Department who's on the Indian desk. Probably nothing new in that. So what? Either way, the Bureau weren't told . . . "

"I wondered why you were looking so pleased with yourself Joe," said Gaffney. "I suppose that gets the Bureau off the hook."

Daly frowned. "Not altogether. When Sol Whiteman mentioned it across at State, and told them your story, they damn-near took off." He laughed and adjusted his spectacles. "They're funny about spies," he said.

"Our Foreign Office are a bit touchy

about them too," said Gaffney mildly.

"The whole damn thing went up like a rocket, straight to the Secretary of State . . . in person. Next thing, the Attorney General — he's our boss — is screaming like mad for a piece of the action. Result: the United States of America will assuredly apply for extradition if you turn up anything that could possibly prove that Gisela Hunter was Mia Neidhart, and may be implicated in the homicide of Harry Rossman. Yes, sir."

"We're not likely to get any proof over here, Joe," said Gaffney. "I suppose we might get an admission from her. But somehow I doubt it. More likely to deny it, knowing damn well that there's nothing any of us can do. And if you get her back there and put her in a line-up, will she get picked out by witnesses whose memories are ten years old? And what if they do? So she was there. Yes, it was her flat, but did anyone see her kill Rossman? And where's the gun?"

Daly shrugged. "Search me, John," he said.

"Okay, Joe, I'll do what I can. A mention of Harry Rossman might just shake her enough to make her admit to what I want her for, but frankly I don't think your job stands a cat-in-hell's chance of getting off the ground. Apart from anything else, you've got to have that proof before you start proceedings for extradition. If you haven't got it, the High Court here will throw it out . . . assuming the Bow Street magistrate grants a provisional warrant in the first place. Personally, I think he'll want more than you've got right now."

"I do so love you Scotland Yard men," said Daly, grinning. "You're brimful of confidence. Anyways, don't shout at me, I'm only the messenger."

"Would I be right in thinking that there's a bit of panic emerging on the other side of the Atlantic?" asked Gaffney drily.

"Damn right there is, John."

"So what'll happen . . . if you do get her arraigned in front of a court with a battery of clever lawyers?"

"She'll walk . . . "

Gaffney laughed. "Yes, I think she probably will," he said.

"Yeah!" Daly eased himself out of the

chair. "Mind you, by the time she's over there, we might have turned up something that'll enable us to hang an espionage rap on her."

Gaffney shook his head slowly. "And that won't go anywhere, either."

"Oh?"

"She can only be tried for the crime she was extradited for, Joe," said Gaffney. "And those clever lawyers I was talking about will be falling over themselves to tell the judge so. Anyway, what am I telling you that for? I thought all you FBI blokes were qualified attorneys."

"Sounds to me though you should think about becoming a lawyer yourself John," said Daly.

Gaffney smiled. "I'm much too honest, Joe," he said.

"Smart-ass," said Daly. "Come on, I'll buy you lunch."

They found the statement. In fact, there were two statements. One had been made by Anthony Booth, who said that his wife had helped Cynthia Bartlett when she had 'fainted'. Booth, and there was obviously no love lost between him and the Bartletts, had said that Cynthia had a reputation for drinking too much. On the night of the dinner, she had got to the point — at about half-past midnight — when she had collided with an occasional table and fallen over. Mrs Booth's statement said much the same, confirming that she and Angela Conrad had helped Cynthia with the short walk across to her flat and put her to bed. Julian Bartlett, according to Booth, had not left the party until after Booth's wife and Angela had returned from their self-imposed mercy mission, a fact that was again confirmed by Margaret Booth.

Gaffney laid the statements on the desk. "What did Bartlett say about all that, Harry?"

"Very non-committal, sir." Tipper scanned Bartlett's statement until he found the relevant paragraph. "He said, 'HE suggested it was time we turned in.' Then he went on to say, 'We went to bed in our flat in the compound.'" Tipper sniffed. "If you don't take his use of the word 'we' too literally, he doesn't actually say that he went to bed at the same time as his wife . . . but he doesn't say he didn't either."

"Stick it in the book, Harry. We'll need to clear that up when we see Bartlett again."

"And when's that going to be?" Tipper dropped his pen on the desk and closed the action book. He and Gaffney had gone meticulously through the statements they had taken in Islamabad looking for inconsistencies, but there was little of importance in any of them. Not surprisingly, this was the first difference they had found. Even then it would probably amount to nothing, and they wouldn't have had that if Angela Conrad hadn't mentioned putting Cynthia Bartlett to bed. It wasn't until Gaffney, on their second trip to Islamabad, had prompted the Booths that they had recalled what to them was a trivial — and frequent — occurrence.

"I think we'll let him run a little, Harry," said Gaffney. "See if he makes contact with Mrs Hunter . . . or better still if she gets in touch with him. If he's working for her — and don't forget he said he wanted to go to Delhi — then sure as hell, she'll want to know where he is and what he's up to."

"But she's in Karachi," said Tipper. "Surely to God we're not going there . . . are we?"

Gaffney laughed. "You're always putting obstacles in the way, Harry," he said.

The tow-truck stopped at the entrance to Terminal Two long-term car park and the driver's mate wandered across to the girl in the cashier's cabin. "Come to pick up a BMW," he said, laying a piece of paper on the window ledge. "That's the number there."

The girl shrugged. "You'll have to speak to the supervisor," she said. "Hang on, I'll get him on the phone." She dialled a number, and picked up the piece of paper with the details on it.

Five minutes later, a car pulled into the forecourt of the car park and a man got out. He walked across to the cashier's cabin. "You the bloke who's come to collect a BMW?" he asked.

"Yeah. You the supervisor?"

"No. Police." The man produced his warrant card.

"Here, it's not bent, is it, guv?"

The policeman shook his head. "No. Who asked you to pick it up?"

"I've got a letter of authority here," said the garage hand. He produced another piece of paper from the pocket of his overalls, smoothed it out and handed it over.

"Okay," said the policeman. "As far as I'm concerned, you can take it away . . . but I'll hang on to this."

The policeman walked across to the cashier. "It's all right by me," he said.

"Right." The cashier glanced at the garage hand. "That'll be sixty pounds and seventy-five pee," she said with a smile.

"Bloody hell," said the garage hand, "the boss never said nothing about that."

Gaffney had set traps following Gisela Hunter's departure for Germany, and had arranged with the chief superintendent in charge of the Special Branch unit at Heathrow Airport for him to be informed if her car was removed. Gaffney had anticipated that the woman herself might return, and it came as something of a surprise to learn that she had openly written to a garage near the airport asking them to collect her car, sell it and send her the money.

"What's the address on the letter, guv'nor?" asked Tipper.

Gaffney tossed it on the desk. "Poste restante in Karachi," he said. "Which comes as no surprise to any of us."

16

DETECTIVE Inspector Dave Wakeford was feeling particularly pleased with himself as he stood on the concourse of Victoria Station, hands in pockets, looking like any other bemused traveller. First thing that morning, just before he had left the anonymous building that was the headquarters of the surveillance team, he had been telephoned by Commander Scott. Scott was responsible, among many other things, for the overall administration of Special Branch. Three or four days previously, Wakeford had appeared before a promotion selection board to be considered for the next rank. After the customary jokes about what an appalling show he had put up on the board, Scott had told him that he had been selected to be a detective chief inspector and would be promoted in order of seniority. Given that there were three other inspectors ahead of him, Wakeford reckoned that he would have about six months to wait. Not that there was any guarantee. It could be sooner, or it might be later, advancement depending upon such whimsical occurrences as retirements and sudden deaths.

Apart from the financial advantages, his success meant that at long last he would escape from this God-awful job in charge of the surveillance team. As soon as his promotion came through he would return to the Yard, probably to a desk job, and work a civilised day instead of being out at all hours and in all weathers. He would be able to make arrangements to take his wife out, no less certain than most other policemen that he would stand a reasonable chance of being able to keep his promise.

On the other hand, he hoped that he would be left with the Gisela Hunter job long enough to get a result. He didn't know that Gaffney had more or less written it off and was now only interested in solving the murder of Peter Kerr.

WDC Marilyn Lester, attired in jeans and a T-shirt, stopped beside him, gazing up at the departures board. "Booked to

Brighton, sir," she said, hardly moving her lips.

"Right," said Wakeford. "Have you got a ticket?"

"Yes, so's Pete."

"When's the next train?"

"Fifteen-forty, sir."

"Good. Stay with it. We'll try and beat you down there. If we don't, keep in touch."

Wakeford strode quickly towards the exit of the station. Two other detectives, both men, converged on him as he reached the car, an anonymous-looking grey Ford Granada.

"What's on, guv?" one of them asked as they got in.

"We're off to the seaside," said Wakeford, doing up his seat belt. "Brighton."

"Bloody terrific," said the driver, who had stayed with the car all the time that Wakeford's team had been fanned out on the station concourse. "And I was daft enough to tell the missus that I'd take her out tonight."

Wakeford laughed. "Should go for promotion, my son." He glanced at his watch. "Blues and twos," he said. "I want to get there before the train."

"Bloody terrific," said the driver again, a man of unimaginative vocabulary. He got out of the car and ambled towards the rear. Then he stopped and came back for the keys. After a bit of ferreting around in the boot, he reappeared and put a magnetic blue lamp on the roof of the car, feeding a cable in through the window. Settling himself he plugged in the Kojak lamp, as it was universally known, and did up his seat belt.

"We can go today, can we?" asked Wakeford.

The driver just grinned and started the engine. The banter between him and Wakeford was a habit; the DI knew that he'd got one of the best advanced drivers in the business.

They pulled out of the forecourt at the rear of the police office and drove straight across into Vauxhall Bridge Road, ignoring the one-way circuit, their siren and blue light carving a priority passage through the afternoon traffic.

"Which way are you going?"

"Over Vauxhall Bridge, then due

south, guv," said the driver, yawning. As they passed the end of Francis Street, the needle was flickering at around sixty-five.

They just made it, pulling into the forecourt of Brighton Central Station as their quarry got into a taxi. Anticipating that that might happen, they had stopped briefly in Trafalgar Street to remove the Kojak lamp, and arrived looking as nondescript as any other vehicle . . . unless you counted the four large men in the car, a dead giveaway to the average criminal. But that didn't matter. The target was not an average criminal.

"Hop out, Ray," said Wakeford over his shoulder to one of the DCs in the back. "Collect Marilyn and Pete and make for the nick. I'll call you there."

The DC scrambled out. "Where is the nick?" he asked.

"Dunno," said Wakeford cheerfully. "Ask a policeman."

Fortunately for the sake of discipline, the DC's reply drifted away on the light afternoon breeze.

The Royal Gallop was one of Brighton's more elegant hotels, and since Wakeford was the only one of the team wearing a suit, it was he who followed their target in.

Once the registration formalities had been completed, and the hotel's latest guest had followed the porter into the lift, Wakeford approached the receptionist, produced his warrant card and demanded to see the register as he was empowered to do, aptly in this case, under the terms of the Official Secrets Act. The register, in common with most of the larger hotels these days, proved to be a computer print-out. As Wakeford had anticipated, the target had booked in for one night. It was quarter-past five and he debated whether he should telephone Gaffney immediately, or wait a while. He decided to wait.

At ten to six, Gisela Hunter entered the hotel. Looking neither to the left nor the right she walked confidently past the reception desk. The last time Wakeford had seen her was at Heathrow Airport boarding a flight for Cologne. But now she was back in the country, and, as far as Wakeford was aware, Gaffney didn't know. Casually, the DI stood up and strolled across to where she was waiting at the lift.

"Which floor?" asked the lift attendant.

"Six, please," said the woman.

"Same, please." Wakeford stared absently at the indicator panel until they arrived and then stood aside to allow Gisela Hunter to get out of the lift, a courtesy which she acknowledged with a taut smile and a brief nod. Following her at a discreet distance he was not at all surprised to see her tap softly on the door of Room 614 before he carried on along the corridor and down the service stairs.

"Bartlett arrived at seventeen fifteen and was joined in his room at seventeen fifty-five by Gisela Hunter, sir. What d'you want me to do now?" Wakeford gazed out at the hotel foyer through the glass panels of the telephone booth, and smiled to himself.

"Gisela Hunter, did you say?" Gaffney could not keep the surprise out of his voice.

"Yes, sir." There was always some satisfaction to be derived from telling a Chief Superintendent something he didn't know.

"Bloody hell," said Gaffney. He was wondering how she had got back into the country without being spotted by Special Branch officers on duty at one of the ports. He knew the answer, of course. It seemed that every time she moved, she assumed a new identity. And as Joe Daly of the FBI had said, every time you see a woman she looks different.

Gaffney shrugged. "Stay with it," he said and replaced the receiver.

To the surprise of the watching policemen, cynics to a man, Gisela Hunter did not stay the night but left the hotel at a quarter to eight and took a taxi which the linkman called for her.

WDC Marilyn Lester, along with DCs Pete Cane and Ray Pattenden, had been summoned from the police station in John Street and were covering the hotel, inside and out.

WDC Lester had changed into a dress and was sitting talking to Wakeford in the bar, in such a position as to command a view of the foyer.

"Off you go," said Wakeford, hoping that the man outside would have spotted Gisela Hunter and alerted the driver of the surveillance team's Ford Granada.

It worked out. As Gisela Hunter's taxi pulled away, the police car stopped at the entrance, and the linkman, making an unwarranted assumption, opened the rear door for Marilyn Lester. The taxi pulled into Marine Drive towards Newhaven followed by the Granada about two cars behind.

"Would your ladyship like the travelling rug?" asked the police driver, glancing in the rear-view mirror.

"Balls!" said Marilyn Lester.

The radio report from WDC Lester that Gisela Hunter was making towards Newhaven caused a flutter of alarm when it was relayed to Wakeford who was still sitting in the bar. He had visions of the Hunter woman boarding a ferry for Dieppe, but DC Pattenden had done his homework.

"There are no more ferries tonight,

guv," he said. "I reckon she's making for somewhere local."

"I bloody well hope so," said Wakeford.

The next message put his mind at rest. Gisela Hunter's taxi had turned off some way before it reached Rottingdean and deposited her outside a small, detached villa. She let herself in just as the police car passed the door.

"Well?" said Wakeford, when Marilyn Lester walked into the bar. "What now?"

"I think a gin and tonic would go down rather well, sir," she said, pushing her half-finished orange juice to one side.

"It's a gamble, sir," said Gaffney to Commander Frank Hussey, "but I think we've got to pull her in. She's had proven contact with Foster and with Brooks, both of whom are on the staff of the British Embassy, and with Bartlett who's only just left there."

"And who denied he knew her? Bartlett, I mean."

"Yes, sir."

Hussey looked thoughtful, and then smiled. "I agree with you, John, but I've got this nagging feeling that if we wait a little longer, we might get her bang to rights. After all, there's no damned evidence is there?"

"Not a bloody shred, sir. Not that'll stand up in court anyway. Harry Tipper thinks she's a call-girl."

Hussey laughed. "He always thinks that," he said. "But I suppose it is just possible that Bartlett and Foster have no other motive for meeting her than sex. And Brooks too. From what you say, she's an attractive woman."

"Yes, she is," said Gaffney. "But there's got to be more in it than that, surely? There is another way, of course," he added, and went on to outline his plan.

Hussey listened in silence. "You'd have to take the local SB into your confidence, John. You happy about that?" he said when Gaffney had finished.

"Yes," said Gaffney. "Sussex SB are all right." It sounded like faint praise, but policemen are very conservative when it comes to compliments. There were some police forces around the country with whom Gaffney had had distressing experiences, and whose competence — or lack of it — would have brought forth some quite damning epithets, but the Sussex police did not come into that category. The most that a policeman would ever say was that it — or they — were 'all right'. That was praise indeed.

"Okay, John, do it," said Hussey.

Gaffney had met Detective Chief Superintendent Don Sullivan before, during a political party conference in Brighton. As head of the county CID, Sullivan also had responsibility for its Special Branch.

"Only too glad to help, John." Sullivan pushed an ashtray across his desk. "I must say you get some exotic jobs. Diplomatic murders in Pakistan, and an OSA job, all rolled into one."

"It wasn't a very diplomatic murder, Don, and I've got no evidence of a breach of the Official Secrets Act. As far as I'm concerned, it's a bloody nuisance, and the sooner I can get it squared up, the better."

Sullivan nodded. "I've asked my HSB

to come up," he said.

A moment or two later, the Head of Special Branch, DCI Jack Mant, came into the room.

"This is Detective Chief Superintendent Gaffney from Met SB," said Sullivan. "He wants some help," he added with a smile.

Relaxing in an armchair with his hands spread across his ample stomach and his chin sunk on his chest, Mant looked as though he was listening to a lecture on rose-growing, rather than to a plan that was designed to trap the agent of a foreign power. But when Gaffney had finished, Mant sat up.

"No problem, sir. I know the house, and as luck would have it, a golfing mate of mine lives damned-near opposite . . . I think!" He laughed. "If that's the case, I'll put a man in his front room. Couldn't be easier."

And so it proved to be. But it took a week. The first thing that the combined team of Metropolitan and Sussex police officers did was to make a few enquiries. It was a phrase and a practice common to the investigative process. As a young detective, Gaffney had been told to find out as much as he could before moving from his desk. It was a theory prompted as much by laziness as efficiency on the part of the old hand who had been tasked with teaching him the trade, but it was a sound theory.

The first piece of evidence that DCI Jack Mant's man turned up was that Gisela Hunter was known to the estate agent from whom she had rented her house as Mrs Mia Calvert. And she had told the agent that she was separated from her husband, a snippet that caused Tipper drily to observe that she hadn't much option, given that he was interred in Karachi. But by far the most intriguing piece of information was that she had held the lease there for nearly three years.

To the police, a woman who rents a second house fifty miles away, in a different name, is clearly up to no good. Furthermore, the name Mia was the name that the alleged murderess of Harry Rossman had used in New York. Admittedly, Mia was not an uncommon

German name, but it could be an indication that she was a professional who had slipped up . . . and even professionals did, from time to time.

Gaffney rubbed his hands together. "I think we might have got her, Harry," he said. "If we're going to find anything at all, it'll be in this little hideaway in Rottingdean."

"Yes," said Tipper cautiously. "It could just be coming together."

Convinced now that Gisela Hunter, if not the key to the murder of Peter Kerr, was certainly involved in espionage, Gaffney deployed Wakeford's surveillance team in Brighton. Mant's golfing partner had been co-operative and given over his front bedroom to the police that they might maintain observation. Diagonally opposite the target house, the team had a good view of the front door but, not surprisingly, found that Gisela Hunter's pattern of behaviour had changed little from that which she had followed in London. In four days, she went out twice, and then only to the local shops. On each occasion she was out of the house for less than an hour, certainly not long enough for the police to search it.

It was very frustrating. More than once, Gaffney was tempted to abort the observation and go steaming in with a warrant. But he knew perfectly well that if nothing incriminating was found, as had been the case at Fancourt Mansions, he'd finish up with egg on his face. After that, there'd be absolutely no chance of getting any evidence to convict the woman he was convinced was a spy. It was better to wait, and search the house in Gisela Hunter's absence.

On the Thursday, one week exactly from her meeting with Julian Bartlett at the Royal Gallop Hotel, the luck of the police changed. At nine o'clock in the morning, a taxi drew up at the front door. The intercept on her telephone, which had told the police nothing else in seven days, had at least forewarned them of that, and a nondescript van belonging to Sussex Police which had been stationed in a turning off Marine Drive, was able to fall in discreetly behind the taxi and follow it to Brighton Central railway station. There she boarded a train for London accompanied, unbeknown to her, by several surveillance officers.

Secure in the knowledge that Gisela Hunter was well out of the way, the police moved in. Half of Wakeford's team were with her, and the moment she boarded a train to return to Brighton, a telephone call would ensure that the Sussex end of the operation would have at least an hour to tidy up and quit the premises . . . unless they had discovered enough evidence to justify her arrest, in which case there would be a reception committee awaiting her arrival.

The front door was easy. Tipper's credit card slipped the lock and they were in.

Neither Gaffney nor Tipper had seen the inside of Gisela Hunter's flat at Fancourt Mansions, but they quickly surmised that the decor and furnishings were not what she would have chosen, a view probably influenced by Jack Mant's discovery that she had taken the house furnished.

With a practice borne of years of experience, the handful of detectives fanned out through the house on their search. There was nothing. At least, nothing incriminating. Until they came to the second bedroom.

That was where they found the computer.

Tipper surveyed it with distaste. "Anyone know how to work one of these things?" he asked.

"Yes, sir." DC Peter Cane moved closer to the small personal computer, mounted on a black metal trolley. "I've got one of these at home."

"Well, wind it up and work it," said Tipper, "and don't tell me how you do it, because I don't want to know."

Cane sat down in front of the keyboard and rubbed his hands together like a concert pianist about to give a rendering of a hitherto unperformed work. Having set up the computer, he selected a disk at random from a box of six that one of the other detectives had found in a drawer at the bottom of the wardrobe. Life being what it is, it was not until Cane put the last disk into the drive that the screen showed anything, and that, disappointingly, appeared to be an attempt at romantic fiction.

"Can't you fast-forward it or something?" said Tipper, "just to make sure it's not that sort of crap all the way through?"

"It's not a video recorder, sir," said Cane.

"You know what I mean, smart-arse," said Tipper. "Get on with it."

After about eighteen pages of what Tipper described as 'bloody drivel', the story stopped abruptly. There followed a few blank pages, then came what they were looking for.

"Interesting," said Tipper, and turned to another officer. "Ask Mr Gaffney to come up, will you?"

Gaffney, who had been following his usual practice of sitting in an armchair while the search was going on around him, joined Tipper. "What have you got, Harry?"

"What we've been looking for I think, guv." There was page after page of it. Firstly came a political assessment of India from the British point of view, and Britain's perception of how India viewed Britain. There were a fair number of obvious statements: India was a member of the Commonwealth; Pakistan was not, followed by a lengthy summary of the history and strategical stance of India and Pakistan, one to another. Comments and opinions about Britain's action in the event of another Indo-Pakistani war were gone into at great length. But more disturbing was a list of Indian military formations and troop deployments, and the likely effect that war would have on Kashmir, Afghanistan and Bangladesh. There was some suggestion too, that Pakistan may have been attempting to foment trouble in the Sikh province of Punjab, where the Golden Temple of Amritsar was a frequent focal point of insurrection, but it looked speculative and may even have been the writer's own view.

But at the very end, Gisela Hunter had made an unbelievable error. She had recorded the name of her source. It did not surprise the detectives that the name was Julian Bartlett, but it did surprise them that she had incriminated him. It proved to Gaffney's satisfaction, and probably would to a jury, that she had actively suborned Bartlett, a Crown servant, to pass information to an enemy. And an enemy had been defined, over and over again, as *any* foreign power . . . friendly or otherwise.

"Well, Harry? What d'you think?"

"Got her," said Tipper. "Bang to rights . . . and him!"

17

GISELA HUNTER alighted from the train and moved swiftly through the crowded concourse of Victoria Station. Pausing briefly to survey, and then to dismiss, the long queue for taxis, she crossed Vauxhall Bridge Road and hailed a cab at the bottom end of Victoria Street.

One of DI Wakeford's team had watched her depart from Brighton and promptly telephoned Special Branch at Scotland Yard. As a result, there had been time to deploy a surveillance vehicle at the London end. Even so, the woman's apparent intention of walking, but then hailing a cab, had almost caught the team wrong-footed. More by luck than anything, they had just managed to get organised before losing sight of her taxi as it headed towards Belgrave Square.

It was an unremarkable and frustrating day as far as the police were concerned. Gisela Hunter appeared to be quite open about her movements. If she suspected that she was being followed, she didn't seem to care. Her short taxi ride ended in Lowndes Square where she stood, waiting for the cab-driver to sort out her change from the large cloth bag he hauled from somewhere in the inner recesses of his cab, and gazed around. But there was no concern in her glance, nor did she appear to be searching for anyone who might have followed her. Then she walked quickly into the Pakistani Embassy.

"Sod it!" said Wakeford phlegmatically. "There's no way we're going to find out who she's seeing in there. But I'll put money on it being the military attaché."

Gisela Hunter emerged from the embassy at about ten to one, accompanied by a man who was fairly obviously a member of the staff. They walked to a restaurant and had lunch. Then the Pakistani went back to the embassy and Gisela Hunter got into a cab and went back to Victoria Station.

"Did you get close enough to hear any of their conversation?" asked Wakeford.

Marilyn Lester smiled. "Heard every word, sir. We were at the next table."

"And?"

"And I don't speak Urdu, or whatever it was, and I didn't understand any of it." She indicated her male companion. "Nor did he."

Wakeford shook his head wearily. "When I joined this Branch," he said, "there were at least half a dozen Urdu speakers . . . some of whom were still alive."

Gisela Hunter got a taxi from Brighton Central Station and drove out to her house near to Rottingdean.

She closed the front door behind her and peeled off her gloves. Dropping them and her handbag on to the scratched hall-stand, she examined her face in its peeling mirror and patted her hair into place. Then she walked into the sitting room.

"Mrs Gisela Hunter?" asked Gaffney as he and Tipper rose from the armchairs in which they had been sitting for the last thirty minutes. Wakeford had arranged for Gaffney to be told her movements well in advance so that he could be prepared.

There was no hysterical reaction such as might be expected from a woman finding two strange men in her sitting room. She appraised them slowly and searchingly. "And who might you be?" she asked. "More to the point, what are you doing in my house?"

"We are police officers," said Gaffney, "and we are executing a search warrant granted by the Bow Street Magistrate under the Official Secrets Act."

Gisela Hunter's gaze remained level and unwavering. "Why?"

It was hardly the reaction that Gaffney had expected and he half-smiled at her cool reserve. "Because we have reason to believe that you have at least committed acts preparatory to the commission of an offence under that act," he said.

"I see." She walked across to the window and dropped the upper half six inches before frowning at the cigar Gaffney was smoking. "And what makes you think that?" She sat down and crossed her legs, revealing a tantalising glimpse of black nylon-clad thigh before decorously arranging her skirt over her knees.

"We have discovered a number of disks upstairs — computer disks — one of which contains information which almost certainly came from the British Embassy in Islamabad. And since you obligingly added his name, we are in no doubt that it came from a British diplomat called Julian Bartlett who, until recently, was on the staff there."

"I've never heard of him." She spoke haughtily, but Gaffney noticed that her German accent was a little more marked than previously.

"And whose room at the Royal Gallop Hotel you were seen to enter a week ago," continued Gaffney, as though she hadn't spoken.

Gisela Hunter laughed. Gaffney suspected it was more to relieve her tension than that he had said something amusing. "You look like a man of the world, Mr . . . ?" She paused, one eyebrow raised quizzically.

"Gaffney. Detective Chief Superintendent Gaffney."

"Well, Mr Gaffney, I imagine that it is not outside your experience that ladies occasionally visit gentlemen in hotel bedrooms." She paused and smiled. "I leave it to your fertile imagination to work out why."

Gaffney nodded, slowly. "For the same reason that Roy Foster visited you from time to time at Fancourt Mansions?" There was no trace in her demeanour that the name meant anything. "But as you and he are to be married, I suppose it is necessary to be circumspect in your liaison with Mr Bartlett."

Gaffney was playing with her and she knew it. She put her head on one side and smiled. "Whatever gave you that idea?"

"Mr Foster told me."

She shook her head. "Poor innocent boy," she said. "A little bit of fun and he thinks he has fallen in love. I could not convince him. Why do you think I moved down here and used another name?"

"Setting aside that you took this house nearly three years ago," said Gaffney, "probably because he'd told you he'd been to the police."

For the first time since their conversation had begun, Gisela Hunter looked apprehensive. "He's been to the police?" Her voice rose very slightly. It was fairly evident that Foster had not told her of his visit to Scotland Yard after all, and presumably she ascribed Gaffney's presence in her house to some other source.

Gaffney nodded. "Oh yes," he said. "That's why we took an interest in you." It did no harm in his view to put a wedge of uncertainty between this woman and Foster.

She recovered her poise quickly from its momentary lapse. "Poor boy," she said again. "We met at the Pakistani Embassy one evening and . . . " She paused, searching for the right words. Then with a shrug she added, "We finished up in bed. I'm sure you understand such things." She looked past Gaffney's shoulder. "Funny really, he's not my type."

"You're quite a regular visitor to the Pakistani Embassy, aren't you?"

Gisela Hunter did not seem at all put out by that observation. "I've been there today, as a matter of fact," she said with a smile.

"I know."

She looked up, a sharp glance that was almost one of admiration from one professional to another. But she said nothing.

"Why did you go there?" asked Gaffney.

"My late husband had substantial business interests in Karachi," she said. "Business interests which I have inherited. There are things that need to be discussed from time to time." She waved a hand airily.

"So presumably you saw the trade attaché, or some such person."

She smiled, but made no reply.

Gaffney was beginning to tire of this cat-and-mouse conversation, and it was obvious from Gisela Hunter's unruffled and relaxed poise that she thought either the police were fishing, or that she had done nothing wrong. "Mrs Hunter — or is it Mrs Calvert?" She smiled at that. "I am arresting you for procuring a Crown servant to commit offences under the Official Secrets Act. Anything you say will be given in evidence."

For a moment she appeared stunned.

Then, as the full impact of Gaffney's pronouncement struck home, she stood up.

"This is ridiculous," she said. "I have done nothing to interest you. All I have done is to gather information that might be of use to me in my business. Anyway, it concerns Pakistan and India. It's nothing to do with this country."

"I doubt if an Old Bailey jury will see it that way," said Gaffney quietly. "Of course, you may not be tried in this country."

"Oh?"

"There is the question of the murder of Harry Rossman in New York, ten years ago, to be resolved," continued Gaffney. "In your apartment in Manhattan, when you were calling yourself Mia Neidhart."

"What on earth are you talking about? I know nobody called Rossman or . . . what was it? Neidhart?"

"A diplomat who specialised in the Indian sub-continent, Mrs Hunter, and who was shot with a three-two pistol. You had an affair with him too, didn't you?"

She laughed. It was the laugh of a

woman completely bemused. Baffled that the police should fabricate such wicked stories. And frustrated that they would not believe her protestations of innocence. "This is all utterly preposterous," she said.

"You have been identified by the porter at the apartment block," said Gaffney, "from photographs which we took of you during the last few weeks." Gaffney knew that that would never stand up in court, but it was worth a try.

She looked at the two detectives. "Are you raving mad?" she asked. "I've never been to New York in my life."

Gaffney shrugged. "Then why did you tell the German police that you had?" That produced no reaction: the woman was either an accomplished actress, or she was innocent. Certainly much of the evidence that the police had assembled was circumstantial. Perhaps her association with Foster and Bartlett was purely sexual and, to be honest, the identification by the superintendent at the apartment block in Manhattan wasn't worth two-penn'orth of cold tea. But there again, there was the computer upstairs with Bartlett's name on it.

"Be that as it may," he said, "the United States government has said that it intends to apply for your extradition." Gaffney knew that that wouldn't stand up either.

"I wish to see my solicitor," she said. "And I want the embassy informed."

"I don't know whether you have the Pakistani Embassy in mind," said Gaffney, "or the West German one, or even the American, but I would remind you that you are a British subject."

"I do not need reminding of that," she said.

Don Sullivan, the head of Sussex CID, had put a room at Gaffney's disposal at John Street Police Station and it was there that he and Tipper, together with Jack Mant, the local SB DCI, and Dave Wakeford, now gathered to plan the next part of their operation.

"Shouldn't we have co-ordinated all this?" asked Tipper. "I mean, it would have been rather good to have scurfed up Bartlett at the same time."

"Sure," said Gaffney, "but until we

had a look at Gisela Hunter's computer, we didn't have any evidence. A lot of suspicion, but that was all. Supposing that we had pulled them both in without these . . . " He tapped the box of disks they had brought from Gisela Hunter's house. "They would both probably have admitted to having an affair — which they undoubtedly did anyway — and we wouldn't have had a cat-in-hell's chance of proving it was anything else. All we would have done is to warn them, and they'd have walked away from it. We'd never have got them after that."

"Incidentally, sir," said Wakeford, pointing at the box of disks, "our expert, Cane, suggests that the disk with all the evidence on it should be copied as soon as possible. I understand that some electrical freak could wipe it clean, then we'd be back to square one."

"Yes," said Gaffney, "I think he's probably right."

"Leave it to me, guv," said Tipper. "I'll get someone to do it."

"Right, then," continued Gaffney. "The next move is to bring Bartlett in." He glanced at Wakeford. "We took surveillance off him, didn't we, Dave?"

Wakeford nodded. "Had to, sir. Hadn't got the manpower. It was the old story, the familiar cry: never enough men. It tended to determine priorities very sharply."

"Address in Petersfield, yes?"

"Yes, sir. Unless he's still at his club."

"Right," said Gaffney. "Find him and let me know where he is." He looked across at Tipper. "You'll be at Brighton magistrates in the morning, Harry, for a week's lie-down, but once that hits the Press, Bartlett will take it on his toes. Therefore, gentlemen, it's essential that we find Mr Bartlett before ten o'clock tomorrow morning."

It was easier than they had hoped. Julian Bartlett was at home in the village where he lived near Petersfield, on the edge of the Meon Valley. His wife Cynthia was there too, and she answered the door.

There was no easy way to do it, and neither Gaffney nor Tipper saw why there should be. But they always felt sorry for the wife, who in most espionage cases was completely ignorant of her husband's treachery.

"Julian Bartlett, I have a warrant for your arrest on charges of giving information to another which you acquired as a holder of an office under the Crown."

Bartlett surveyed them superciliously. "Oh?" He lifted his chin slightly. "And who is this person that I'm supposed to have given information to?"

"Gisela Hunter, an agent of a foreign power," said Gaffney.

"And who the hell's Gisela Hunter?" Cynthia Bartlett swayed in the doorway of the sitting room, clutching at the doorpost for support. A shapeless green frock, too long and dipping at the back of the hem, hung to her thin body, and it was clear that she had been drinking.

Bartlett smiled confidently. "It's all a mistake, my dear," he said. "I don't know what they're talking about."

"Is she another of your fancy women, eh, *eh*?" Bartlett's wife lurched at him, grabbing at the front of his jacket. "How many times did you lay her, then, eh?"

"It was nothing like that," said Bartlett

calmly, taking hold of his wife's painfully thin wrists and pushing them downwards.

"I know what it was like," said Cynthia. "Just like all the others . . . like . . . like . . . " She burst into a hysterical sobbing, and tearing her hands away from Bartlett's grasp, started hitting his chest in a frenzy of weak blows.

Bartlett took hold of her once more, trying to control her outburst. "It was nothing like that," he said again.

But Cynthia Bartlett was in no mood to be placated by mere words. She started screaming. "What's going to happen to me . . . when you go to prison? What am I going to live on? And what am I going to tell the children? Did you think of that, when you were screwing this woman . . . whoever she is? Who is she? Who?"

"I'm not going to prison," said Bartlett quietly. "I told you, it's all a mistake. I'm sorry," he added. "There is an explanation, I assure you."

"Like all your other explanations, your other excuses, I suppose," said Cynthia. Suddenly, like a roused tigress, she clawed at Bartlett's face, tearing her nails down the skin and drawing blood.

Fortunately, Gaffney and Tipper had had the foresight to bring WDC Marilyn Lester with them, and she now stepped between Bartlett and his wife. Seizing Cynthia roughly by the shoulders, and wrenching her arms down to her sides, she struck her two sharp blows across the face with her open hand. For a brief second Cynthia Bartlett looked stunned at the ferocity of the policewoman's action, then she crumbled, dropping into an armchair and sobbing uncontrollably.

Bartlett looked at Gaffney, anger showing in his face for the first time. "I hope you know what you're doing," he said. "I shall take this up with the highest authority." He glanced at his wife before looking back at Gaffney. "You have absolutely no proof . . . you can't possibly have. I'm not guilty of any transgressions." He was very controlled, and Gaffney could only assume that he had absolute faith in Gisela Hunter's integrity not to expose him. He had no idea, of course, that she would have been so foolhardy as to list his name on her computer as her star informant. "I suppose you want to take me to the police station?" The question was almost contemptuous.

They drove him to London, to Rochester Row Police Station, within walking distance of Scotland Yard.

Gisela Hunter had been remanded to Brixton Prison for a week, but not without a bit of a struggle. Lay magistrates are always touchy about anything they see as encroaching on their judicial independence, and when a detective chief inspector like Tipper steps into the witness box and casually asks for a remand in custody at a prison miles away, they tend to bristle. But after withdrawing to consult their clerk, the only legally qualified person among them, they acquiesced. They may have been persuaded by the fact that the Attorney-General was always involved in Official Secrets Act cases, and as a member of the government might have some influence in the matter of honours. He most certainly did not, but they didn't know that and weren't prepared to take the chance.

Gaffney was not particularly interested

in Gisela Hunter, which was why he had directed Harry Tipper to seek a remand to Brixton instead of into police custody. She had virtually convicted herself in his view, and there was nothing further to be said. It was quite probable though that the Security Service, if not MI6, would want to talk to her just to see if any damage had been done to British interests. As for the Americans, Gaffney made a brief telephone call to Joe Daly, telling him of the woman's arrest. Daly promised to send an urgent telegram to the States, asking them if they still wished to pursue the matter of her extradition, but both he and Gaffney agreed that the evidence was not strong enough, neither would the British Government be likely to surrender her when she was facing charges of spying in this country.

Bartlett, however, was a different matter. Technically the only evidence against him so far was the attribution which Gisela Hunter had carelessly recorded on her computer, and the uncorroborated evidence of one co-conspirator against another was not usually sufficient to secure a conviction.

But apart from that, there was the little matter of the murder of Peter Kerr in Islamabad.

When they brought Bartlett into the interview room at Rochester Row, he seemed to have lost none of his bounce and confidence. He just sat down and smiled urbanely at his interrogators. "I do not intend to say anything without my solicitor being present," he said, and leaned back in his chair as though that was an end of the matter.

Gaffney had anticipated that Bartlett would react in this way, but as they wanted to talk to him about the murder of Peter Kerr anyway, he had decided that Tipper would conduct the interview.

"We haven't asked you to say anything," said Tipper. He didn't like the Julian Bartletts of this world. In his view, they stood for everything he despised, were — by and large — a bit thick, and only held the positions they did because of a privileged upbringing, a public school, and the inevitable Oxbridge degree. But what they lacked, and Tipper knew they lacked it, was what he called pavement cunning. And that was to his professional advantage. Harry Tipper had come up the hard way. His father had drunk himself to death, and had been unemployed for most of his life, too besotted with alcohol to take any interest in his son's progress at the big central school in Enfield where he had received what passed for an education. After a few years discovering that he was not cut out to be a garage mechanic, Tipper had joined the police, taking the view that it would do for a few years until he found a proper job. But his senior officers recognised, early on, that he had an aptitude for criminal investigation and he became a member of the CID. Clawing his way up to the rank of detective chief inspector, he had been transferred to the élite Special Branch as a direct result of his handling of the murder of Penelope Lambert by a diplomat, just like the supercilious snob who sat opposite him now. It was no wonder that he had little time for Julian Bartlett.

Bartlett gazed at Tipper, a half-smile on his face.

"I'm going to tell you something now," said Tipper, "about the murder of Peter

Kerr." Bartlett's expression remained unchanged. "Kerr, as you know, was the resident SIS man in Islamabad. His job was to acquire intelligence for the benefit of the British Government. But that wasn't all. He had to be alert to anyone who was acquiring information from the British for someone else's benefit. And I suggest to you that he caught you at it, and you murdered him." Still Bartlett remained unmoved. It did not escape Tipper's notice. "I see that that comes as no surprise to you."

Bartlett shrugged. "You don't expect me to admit to that fiction, surely?"

"You see," Tipper went on, "the spread of shot in Kerr's body was too wide to have been fired by the shotgun from where it was when we found it. When Kerr was killed the shotgun was much farther away. As a matter of fact it was a pretty amateur job all round." But that was all he said. He made it a practice never to furnish suspects with any more information for their defence than the law obliged him to. Bartlett went to say something, but Tipper carried on. "Your wife was so drunk that night that two other women took her to her bed, senseless. We have statements to back that up. So you didn't go to bed with her yourself Mr Bartlett . . . at least, not at the same time."

"I didn't say that I did," said Bartlett peevishly.

"And you decided that it would be an opportune moment to do a bit of ferreting about for more information. You see, Mr Bartlett, your spymistress" — Tipper smiled as he said that — "Gisela Hunter, was putting pressure on you constantly, and she was prepared to throw you to the wolves at any time, because you were committed . . . and expendable. You'd supplied information because she'd settled your gambling debts in Germany, added to which she was having an affair with you, and she could have blown the whistle on you whenever she liked. Either to the authorities, or your wife, or both. And provided she was out of this country when she did it, she'd have walked out of it scot-free. Unfortunately for you — and her — she's currently locked up in Brixton Prison awaiting trial." That was varnishing the truth just a little. Tipper knew that Gisela Hunter could not be sent for trial without the Attorney-General's fiat. But Bartlett probably didn't know that. Even so, it seemed to have little effect on him. He was one of those self-confident individuals who could not conceive of someone as rough as Tipper being able to put him behind bars. So supremely full of his own importance was he, that he was convinced that once his solicitor arrived there would be just a few formalities before he was released with fulsome apologies. He just smiled.

"But Peter Kerr caught you at it and you murdered him. And that, mister, is what I'm going to charge you with." Tipper leaned back with an air of finality and drummed his fingers on the arm of his chair, a rhythmic little tattoo that seemed to convey that it was all as good as settled. But then he leaned forward. "I have to caution you," he said with heavy formality, "that anything you say will be put in writing and may be given in evidence."

Human emotions are peculiarly perverse and rarely, under such circumstances, does a prisoner crumble. But his face will often mirror the machinations of his brain as it goes into top gear to deal with a hitherto unforeseen twist of fate. The urgent determination to survive will make the mind operate like a highly tuned computer as it shoots like lightning down avenues of escape and, as it finds each one blocked, will as quickly re-route itself until it finds what it believes to be a solution. And far from displaying panic, this mental activity will manifest itself in an unnatural calm. Tipper knew all this, because Tipper was an expert interrogator.

"If I tell you what happened, will it count in my favour with the other business?" Bartlett kept commendable control in his voice.

Very slowly, Tipper shook his head. "I'm a policeman, Mr Bartlett, not a trader, and I should tell you that this 'other business', as you call it, is probably worth about twenty years."

Bartlett didn't know just how much Tipper knew, but at last it was dawning on him that he was in trouble. Serious trouble.

Tipper let him off the hook at just the right moment and with just the right words. "However, your co-operation, if it's forthcoming, will be drawn to the attention of the Director of Public Prosecutions." What he did not say yet was that the Director-General of the Security Service had told Gaffney that he might be prepared to recommend waiving prosecution altogether if Bartlett was willing to assist in exposing the full extent of Gisela Hunter's activities — if there was a fuller extent — and had repeated the views of the Foreign Office that they could well do without another scandal. There had been enough of those in the past.

"I can tell you what happened that night," said Bartlett, his shoulders drooping slightly in resignation. "I know who killed Kerr. That person guessed that I had been passing information to the Pakistanis, had caught me one night going through papers that I was not entitled to see. I was blackmailed into helping . . . threatened with exposure. I got Peter Kerr's body into the armoury — the keys were in his pocket — and arranged it to look like suicide. I got the Ambassador's Purdey out of the cabinet, muffled it with a blanket and fired it into a cushion — "

"So it wasn't the Ambassador's Purdey that killed him?"

Bartlett smiled, pleased at knowing something that Tipper did not. "No," he said.

"What then?"

"Then I went to bed."

"In that case," said Tipper, "there's only one other piece of information I need. A name."

Bartlett leaned forward, although there was no need for confidentiality, and spoke, his voice barely above a whisper.

Tipper grinned and leaned back. "Well, well, well," he said. "And what was that all about?"

18

THE wheels of the Boeing touched the tarmac of Islamabad Airport with the familiar but disconcerting yelp of screeching rubber, and almost immediately the engines went into reverse thrust. Gaffney gripped the arms of the seat until his knuckles showed white, waiting until the aircraft had slowed sufficiently for him to be assured that he would arrive alive and uninjured.

The stooped, patrician figure of Henry Forbes stared towards the exit from the Customs Hall, searching for the two policemen and haughtily sniffing the curious, indefinable odour of Pakistan; he had never grown accustomed to the unique but not unpleasant smell of the country. Porters rushed about with baggage, and native merchants, regarding the airport as an extension of the bazaar, vied with one another as they shouted their wares in high-pitched screams — at European travellers for the most part — until shooed away by airport policemen who would not think twice before inflicting painful blows with their *lathis*. People stared openly at Forbes whose tall figure radiated an unmistakable and innate authority; it was not often that the airport saw Her Britannic Majesty's Ambassador, nor he it.

He had been disconcerted by the secret telegram that Gaffney had sent via the Diplomatic Wireless Service, and determined that he would discuss matters with him as soon as possible.

"Ah, Mr Gaffney, Mr Tipper." Forbes stuck out a bony hand which each of the detectives grasped in turn, briefly. "This way." He spoke rapidly in Urdu to a couple of licensed porters who grabbed the policemen's grips and bore them away through the crowd.

Outside the terminal building stood the Ambassadorial Rolls-Royce, a Union Flag hanging limply from the jack-staff which had replaced the famous flying lady.

Policemen saluted, and one held up the traffic to allow the stately vehicle to emerge from the airport in safety. Britain and the British were still held in high regard despite Pakistan's severance from the Commonwealth.

Forbes hit the button on the armrest, a little more violently than was necessary, and sent the dividing screen purring upwards. "I understand from your signal, Mr Gaffney, that you have someone in mind for the murder of Peter Kerr." He spoke in his usual dry, diplomatic voice much as he might when explaining cricket to the American ambassador.

"It's a little more than that, sir. We have an admission from Julian Bartlett. This is a copy of his statement." Gaffney took the sheaf of typescript from Harry Tipper and handed it to Forbes.

The Ambassador, no stranger to paper, slipped on a pair of horn-rimmed half glasses which he took from his inside pocket, and rapidly scanned Bartlett's statement. From time to time he tutted, probably when he had reached something for which he personally could be criticised, and occasionally shook his head, slowly and in apparent disbelief With one final shake of the head, he handed the statement back. "It's beyond belief," he said.

"It may be beyond your belief sir," said Tipper, "but I'm afraid it's very familiar territory to us."

Forbes looked at the Chief Inspector for a while, giving his words careful consideration. "I suppose so," he said eventually, as if Tipper had made a profound utterance. "I'd never really thought of that." For a whole minute he stared out of the window, at one point looking back sharply at a cart that had lost a wheel, and whose driver was laying into the bullock which led it as though it were the animal's fault. "Is that sufficient evidence?" he asked turning again and gesturing at Tipper's brief-case which now contained Bartlett's statement.

"It's probably enough," said Gaffney, "but I'd rather have more. I should like your authority to search the flat, if I may. The Bow Street Magistrate didn't seem to think that his warrant would be much good here." Gaffney smiled.

Forbes didn't see the humour of that. "Of course, of course," he murmured.

There was another longish pause and then: "When would you want to do that?"

"Preferably while the occupant is at work," said Gaffney. "And I'd feel happier if you or a senior member of your staff were there when we did it."

"I'll willingly be there, but why?"

"Some people are not above suggesting that the police plant evidence," said Gaffney drily.

"Anyway," said Tipper chirpily, "you'll be glad to know that it wasn't your shotgun that was used."

"Thank God for that," said Forbes earnestly, and Gaffney got the distinct impression that the use of his gun had disturbed him more than anything else.

They crossed the compound with its tired patch of browning grass in the centre and mounted the steps to the verandah on the first floor of the end block. There were half-a-dozen flats off it, each with a front door and French windows, and an air-conditioning unit set over them. Forbes opened the front door with a master key and led the way into the tiny hall. Doors led off a narrow hallway, at the end of which, facing them, was a cupboard. But Gaffney and Tipper moved first into the sitting room. Forbes followed, the expression on his face implying guilt at being in someone else's flat without their knowledge.

The room was furnished to the standard determined by the government for the occupant's grade: a sofa, a couple of armchairs and a combined bookcase and cocktail cabinet which stood against the wall opposite the door. There was a bureau in one corner, open, with papers spread about on the flap, and in the opposite corner, against the wall, a table on which were a couple of photographs in wooden frames. One was of an old married couple, the man with his arm round his wife's shoulders, and in another a small girl with a large dog. The photographs, the papers in the bureau, and the books in the glass-fronted cabinet over the drinks cupboard, were the only imprint of the occupant's personality.

Tipper picked up one of the photographs and stared closely at it. Then he replaced it and picked up a small wooden shield, about three inches high, on which was an engraved metal plate. "Interesting," he said, handing it to Gaffney. "Awarded at a clay-pigeon competition in Norfolk, five years ago." He grinned. "It would appear that our suspect is handy with a shotgun."

Gaffney put the tiny shield back on the table and turned to the Ambassador. "Did you know about that, sir?"

"No," said Forbes thoughtfully. "It's never been mentioned. Funny that. I tried to organise some clay-pigeon shooting last year but no one showed any interest . . . including the winner of that." He pointed at the trophy.

"I think I'll have a look round," said Tipper, rubbing his hands. Gaffney smiled. He could always tell when Tipper had the scent of the hunt in his nostrils.

It was all there. Pitted into the back of the sofa were a number of stray shotgun pellets which Tipper carefully removed and placed in a plastic bag. "If they don't match the pellets taken from Kerr's body, I'm a Dutchman," he said.

They found the shotgun in the

cupboard at the end of the hall, half-hidden by an old coat. In the pocket of the coat was a box of cartridges. And under the bed, wrapped in a blanket, was a cushion impregnated with shotgun pellets.

"That explains why there were only three," said Tipper with obvious satisfaction.

"What does?" asked Gaffney.

"There were only three cushions in the sitting room," said Tipper. "One in each armchair, but only one on the sofa. There's usually two."

"You will see, Ambassador," said Gaffney drily, "that my assistant is a bit of an armchair detective."

Forbes stood in the centre of the room, gazing round and shaking his head. "Who would have thought it?" he said.

"There's nothing to it," said Tipper. "You just have to read *Homes and Gardens* every month."

Kerr's office was still unoccupied, SIS having yet to appoint his replacement. It was not only the most convenient room in which to conduct the interview, it was still the only one available. But Gaffney and Tipper were conscious nevertheless of the irony of the situation.

Gaffney had seated himself behind Kerr's desk and waited. Thoughtfully, he took the photograph of the dead SIS man's wife and children and placed it in a drawer, face down. Then he straightened the blotter and the inkstand, pausing to wonder why Her Majesty's Government still issued them. Almost everyone used a ball-point pen nowadays.

The door opened and Tipper stood to one side. "Won't you sit down." He closed the door and stood briefly with his back to it, waiting.

"Diana Gibson," said Gaffney, "I am arresting you for the wilful murder of Peter Kerr. You are not obliged to say anything, but anything you do say will be put in writing and may be given in evidence." The sonorous prose of the Judges' Rules caution was followed by a silence that seemed interminable.

Then Diana Gibson sighed, a deep unremitting sigh. "I'm glad it's all over," she said. For a few moments she gazed at the toe of her shoe, then looked up. "D'you mind if I smoke?"

Gaffney signalled to Tipper to sit down, and waited. He was sure that Diana Gibson was about to relate the whole sorry tale. The evidence was strong: he had Bartlett's statement, and he had the tangible evidence of the shotgun, the cartridges, the cushion and the blanket . . . and the pellets that Tipper had taken from the back of the settee. Consequently, he was only really entitled to put questions that would remove ambiguity, enable him to recover stolen property, or safeguard another who might be in danger. So far, none of those conditions applied.

"We were lovers," said Diana. It was a bleak statement, and she said it with a conviction that seemed to imply that it was sufficient explanation.

"Not chess, then?"

"Oh yes. That's how it started. But I'm afraid it didn't stop there. Couldn't really, if you think about it. He was a married man, a normal healthy male with normal healthy appetites, and I must admit I egged him on. We had some wonderful nights . . . " There was a wistful faraway look in her eyes and she seemed now, oblivious of the two detectives, almost as if she were thinking aloud. "But it couldn't last, I suppose. I thought — hoped — he would leave his wife and we could get married. I don't know why I thought that, really. He never actually said it, but he sort of implied it." She looked earnestly at Gaffney, willing him to understand her predicament. "We had been lovers for about seven or eight months, I suppose." She stopped then, and for a while Gaffney thought that she was going to say nothing else. But then she went on. "It was the night of the dinner party . . . the one that HE gave for you. That's bloody ironic, isn't it? I had to pick the night there were two Scotland Yard officers here, didn't I?" She laughed scornfully at her own ineptitude. "It was after the dinner party. He didn't really want to go, but HE said he had to be there because you were. I waited up for him, and he came across as soon as he could get away. It must have been about half-past midnight . . . " She looked down at her feet again. "He didn't want anyone to see him. We could hardly have said that we were going to play chess at that time of night, could we?" A stillborn quip about Fool's Mate crossed Gaffney's mind. "It was his own fault, really: he'd started to take me for granted. That night he walked in, looked me up and down, and said something coarse like 'You've still got your clothes on.' I'm afraid that caught me on the raw and I said that I wasn't going to jump into bed before I got an answer to a question . . . not any more. He said that that sounded serious. He was being very sarcastic, and of course he'd been drinking. I could always tell. Then he flopped down in the centre of my settee, grabbed me by the wrist and tried to drag me down next to him. I was very annoyed by then, and I pulled my arm away and asked him outright if he intended to marry me. That's what did it. He laughed. He sat there laughing and laughing. He asked me if I'd gone mad, and said that I ought to grow up. All single girls on foreign stations went to bed with married men, and I should know that. He was very sarcastic and said that he had no intention of leaving his wife. I felt sick. I'd given him everything he wanted, and then he just spurned me. That wouldn't have been so bad, but he laughed, and I couldn't stand that. I got the shotgun out of the cupboard and loaded it. I was really angry. I went back and stood in the doorway of the sitting room and pointed it at him. Then he laughed again and said I wouldn't have the guts to use it." She stopped talking and Gaffney could see the anger in her face, and he thought, yet again, how brilliantly perceptive Congreve had been when he wrote "Nor hell a fury like a woman scorned". "So I shot him," she said.

"Deliberately?" It was the first question Gaffney had posed since she started, and he was half-hoping that she would say no.

"Absolutely. It was no accident, if that's what you're suggesting. I shot him and I intended to kill him." Diana Gibson's green eyes held Gaffney's. Blazing, and daring him to argue. She seemed to relax again, almost immediately, and reverted to the level tone of voice in which she had been telling the story. "I got hold of Julian." She smiled, as though she was telling a girl friend that she had just acquired a new tennis partner. "I knew he was across at the residence, and I'd seen Angela Conrad and Margaret Booth bringing Cynthia home. Smashed again." She laughed bitterly at that. "And I knew he'd be coming over soon." She lit another cigarette with the butt of the first. "He wasn't too keen to help, actually, but he hadn't much choice. He's a spy, you know. At least, I'm pretty sure he is. I found him one night, quite late, going through some files and photographing them with one of those tiny cameras . . . "

That was a revelation. "What did you do about it?" asked Gaffney.

"I told Peter."

"When was this?"

"About a week before I killed him." Again there was the blaze of anger in Diana Gibson's eyes.

"What did he do, d'you know?"

She shrugged. "No idea," she said dismissively. "But it turned out to be useful." She laughed savagely. "He's a wimp . . . Julian. I think he'd have helped anyway. Just in case."

"Just in case what?"

"Just in case I changed my mind and let him have me." Again she spoke in matter-of-fact tones that made the dispensing of her sexual favours sound very clinical. Which it probably was, thought Gaffney, but he pondered the paradox of a man wanting to go to bed with a girl who minutes previously had murdered her last lover. "He had asked me, but I refused. I'm afraid Julian Bartlett didn't turn me on at all." For a moment she watched the spiralling smoke of her cigarette. "He got the body down to the armoury and set it all up."

"Whose idea was that?"

"Mine. Julian could never have worked that out. But I suppose he ballsed it up. I heard about your investigations."

Gaffney guessed that that might be the case. Guessed also that if Diana Gibson had risked going to the armoury with Bartlett, the errors which had led to her arrest might not have been made. "Hell of a risk, wasn't it . . . with people

410

drifting back from the dinner party?"

"Yes, I suppose it was." She laughed . . . a little too long. "Peter had the keys of the armoury on him. He always carried them. I told Julian to get another shotgun . . . I knew HE had a pair of new Purdeys." She chuckled at that. "I'll bet that upset him."

"It did," said Gaffney.

"What happens now?" Diana Gibson leaned forward and stubbed out her half-smoked cigarette, breaking it in two in the process and tutting with annoyance.

"You go back to England . . . with us, and you'll appear before the Bow Street magistrates. If they find you've a case to answer, then there'll be a trial . . . probably at the Old Bailey." But Gaffney was by no means sure. Instinct, and years of experience, told him that this was not a well woman.

"I'd better pack, then," she said, and stood up.

James Marchant smiled. "Hello, John. You've solved your nasty little domestic murder, then."

Gaffney sat down in one of the chairs

in the SIS man's office. "Yes. And your nasty little domestic espionage job, too."

"Oh, I knew about that." Marchant grinned and waved pipe-smoke out of his line of vision.

Gaffney's eyes narrowed. "How? Did Kerr get a message to you?"

Marchant nodded and fussed with his pipe. "Yes, but it was only a case of further and better particulars, as the lawyers say."

"But Kerr was killed shortly afterwards. What did you do for information then?"

"My other man was on top of it." Marchant struck a match and got his pipe going again.

"What other man? Or aren't you going to tell me?"

"Oh, it's no secret, not now. Brooks."

"Brooks?"

"Yes," said Marchant. "Manna from heaven, he was. We'd had our eye on Gisela Hunter née Toller ever since that business in Germany with . . . " He paused and flicked his fingers.

"Dieter Muller."

"That's the fellow. Well after that, she went off to America, to New York.

That's when she started screwing with Harry Rossman . . . and screwing him for information." Marchant smirked at his little joke. "He was in the State Department . . . Indian section, you know."

"Yes, I do know," said Gaffney heavily. "But the State Department appeared not to."

Marchant struck another match and spent a few seconds drawing on his pipe. "Perhaps not," he said, "but the CIA did."

"She murdered Rossman, you know."

"So I believe," said Marchant as though he'd just been told that England had lost the Ashes yet again.

"The FBI are talking about extradition," said Gaffney. He knew there was little chance, but was piqued by Marchant's superiority . . . not for the first time in their long association.

Marchant scoffed. "No chance of that," he said. "That'd mean opening up a can of worms. And they don't want to do that with a ten-year-old can. Often find the contents have gone bad," he added enigmatically. "They'd rather forget all about it. Anyway, some time after that the lovely Gisela came to England and renewed an old friendship."

"Julian Bartlett?"

"Exactly so. A rather stupid man."

"That's putting it mildly," said Gaffney quietly.

"Bartlett wasn't averse to picking up the threads again. Bloody fool thought that he was in love with this gorgeous rich German girl, probably because she'd very obligingly got him off the hook when he was in Germany by settling his gambling debts. He also thought that was the last of it . . . but spymasters never let go, and Gisela Hunter's got talons like a damned eagle. Even so, she laid low in this country for a while, but once we found that she'd resumed operations, we started to take an interest in her activities. It was then we discovered that Detective Sergeant Brooks was getting his leg over the lovely Gisela. Couldn't believe it. Marvellous. What's more, I don't think there was anything in it but sex, unless she thought that a policeman might be a useful addition to her collection." He shot a sideways glance at Tipper and grinned. "Your lot obligingly punished him, and he resigned the moment he'd got his pensionable time in. I think that's the way it was." He looked enquiringly at Gaffney who nodded. "We took him on straightaway. Fixed for him to go to Islamabad in some lowly security post, one where he could legitimately be anywhere and everywhere. Once he'd told Gisela Hunter where he was going she recruited him, told him about Bartlett . . . the whole lot. But then again, I suppose she thought that because he'd been reduced in rank by the police, he'd have an axe to grind with the government. Bit of a dangerous assumption, really, but there we are. She's not very bright as spies go."

"No," said Gaffney, "not if her computer records are anything to go by."

"So Brooks kept an eye on everything for us. Jolly useful."

"What prompted it all?"

"Undoubtedly the murder of her husband. She was convinced that he had been killed by the Indians because he was pro-Pakistani, and a successful business man to boot. It was at the time of the

Indo-Pakistani war of course, and from then on she threw herself wholeheartedly into working for the Pakistani Secret Service. Funnily enough, I don't think it was an Indian who killed Hunter. Story is that it was just a robbery that went too far."

"Well, thanks for telling me all that," said Gaffney sarcastically.

Marchant smiled and smoothed his hand across the top of his desk. "No reason why you should have known before, John," he said.

"Only that I went out there to investigate a case of espionage involving that bloody woman, that's all."

"Really?" Marchant looked up, a twinkle in his eye. "I thought you'd gone out to arrange the security for the Prime Minister's visit."

"My dear Ambassador, how good of you to come." Sir John Laker, the Head of the Foreign Office, shook hands and then sat down behind his huge desk.

The Pakistan Ambassador had not had much option. He nodded and sat down in the gilt armchair nearby.

416

"A minor problem has arisen concerning a member of your staff, one which I think can be resolved informally as I am sure you would wish it to be." Laker smiled thinly.

"I am sorry to hear that, Sir John." The Ambassador put his head on one side, waiting, but said nothing further.

"You will be aware that a woman . . ." Laker's eyes dropped briefly to the note that lay on the broad expanse of his otherwise clear desk-top " . . . a Mrs Gisela Hunter, was arrested by the police and found to be in possession of information which . . ." Laker silently washed his hands and then opened them. "Shall we say information embarrassing to your government when coupled with the fact that she was seen to meet and have lunch with a certain member of your diplomatic staff?" Laker smiled again.

It was all a bit of a charade. The Ambassador had been fully briefed in advance so that he would know what was coming. He and Sir John Laker were just playing out the diplomatic niceties.

"Most regrettable, Sir John," said the Ambassador, "but I am advised that the diplomat in question was the trade attache." He smiled. "You will be aware that Mrs Hunter — a British lady, I believe?" Laker nodded reluctantly. "You will be aware that Mrs Hunter has interests in Karachi, commercial interests, inherited from her late husband, also British, who was unfortunately murdered there. I am told that Mrs Hunter visited my embassy on several occasions to discuss questions of import and export."

"Oh, I see," murmured. Laker.

The Ambassador spread out his hands. "It is most regrettable that an erroneous construction has been put on such meetings. And of course, Sir John, you will realise that I cannot be responsible for the sort of information that this Mrs Hunter happens to collect . . . for whatever reason. Particularly as she is British," he said once again.

Laker smiled. "I knew there would be a satisfactory explanation, Ambassador," he said. "Better to iron out these little problems face to face, don't you think?"

"Of course, Sir John," said the Ambassador, rising.

"Good, good," said Laker. "And we shall be seeing you on Friday, shan't we? Lady Laker is so looking forward to meeting you again."

Julian Bartlett did not stand trial. In exchange for his full co-operation, the Director of Public Prosecutions authorised an immunity, but the Foreign Office decided that it would be wiser to dispense with his services. The last that Gaffney heard of him, he was selling insurance . . . not very successfully.

Gisela Hunter was sentenced to five years' imprisonment for an offence which the judge described as 'gravely damaging to the British Intelligence effort', a statement that baffled the Prosecution as much as it did the Defence. At the start of her sentence in Holloway Prison she made the acquaintance of a cultured Indian woman who was serving eight years for drug-smuggling, and they became firm friends. Gisela Hunter taught the Indian woman German, and the Indian woman taught Gisela Hunter Hindi. The Americans never raised the question of extradition again.

Roy Foster's wife Daphne divorced him just after his arrival in Pakistan which enabled him to regularise his new relationship with one of the secretaries at the embassy, a rather plain girl called Jill Pardoe. Oddly enough, she was very like Daphne Foster both in looks and manner.

Diana Gibson was remanded in custody to Holloway Prison pending her trial, but while there she attempted to strangle a woman prison officer. That, added to a rapid deterioration in her mental health, resulted in her being deemed unfit to plead. Three months after the death of Peter Kerr, she was ordered to be detained at Her Majesty's Pleasure in an institution for the criminally insane.

Other titles in the
Ulverscroft Large Print Series:

TO FIGHT THE WILD
Rod Ansell and Rachel Percy

Lost in uncharted Australian bush, Rod Ansell survived by hunting and trapping wild animals, improvising shelter and using all the bushman's skills he knew.

COROMANDEL
Pat Barr

India in the 1830s is a hot, uncomfortable place, where the East India Company still rules. Amelia and her new husband find themselves caught up in the animosities which seethe between the old order and the new.

THE SMALL PARTY
Lillian Beckwith

A frightening journey to safety begins for Ruth and her small party as their island is caught up in the dangers of armed insurrection.

THE WILDERNESS WALK
Sheila Bishop

Stifling unpleasant memories of a misbegotten romance in Cleave with Lord Francis Aubrey, Lavinia goes on holiday there with her sister. The two women are thrust into a romantic intrigue involving none other than Lord Francis.

THE RELUCTANT GUEST
Rosalind Brett

Ann Calvert went to spend a month on a South African farm with Theo Borland and his sister. They both proved to be different from her first idea of them, and there was Storr Peterson — the most disturbing man she had ever met.

ONE ENCHANTED SUMMER
Anne Tedlock Brooks

A tale of mystery and romance and a girl who found both during one enchanted summer.

CLOUD OVER MALVERTON
Nancy Buckingham

Dulcie soon realises that something is seriously wrong at Malverton, and when violence strikes she is horrified to find herself under suspicion of murder.

AFTER THOUGHTS
Max Bygraves

The Cockney entertainer tells stories of his East End childhood, of his RAF days, and his post-war showbusiness successes and friendships with fellow comedians.

MOONLIGHT
AND MARCH ROSES
D. Y. Cameron

Lynn's search to trace a missing girl takes her to Spain, where she meets Clive Hendon. While untangling the situation, she untangles her emotions and decides on her own future.

NURSE ALICE IN LOVE
Theresa Charles

Accepting the post of nurse to little Fernie Sherrod, Alice Everton could not guess at the romance, suspense and danger which lay ahead at the Sherrod's isolated estate.

POIROT INVESTIGATES
Agatha Christie

Two things bind these eleven stories together — the brilliance and uncanny skill of the diminutive Belgian detective, and the stupidity of his Watson-like partner, Captain Hastings.

LET LOOSE THE TIGERS
Josephine Cox

Queenie promised to find the long-lost son of the frail, elderly murderess, Hannah Jason. But her enquiries threatened to unlock the cage where crucial secrets had long been held captive.

THE TWILIGHT MAN
Frank Gruber

Jim Rand lives alone in the California desert awaiting death. Into his hermit existence comes a teenage girl who blows both his past and his brief future wide open.

DOG IN THE DARK
Gerald Hammond

Jim Cunningham breeds and trains gun dogs, and his antagonism towards the devotees of show spaniels earns him many enemies. So when one of them is found murdered, the police are on his doorstep within hours.

THE RED KNIGHT
Geoffrey Moxon

When he finds himself a pawn on the chessboard of international espionage with his family in constant danger, Guy Trent becomes embroiled in moves and countermoves which may mean life or death for Western scientists.

TIGER TIGER
Frank Ryan

A young man involved in drugs is found murdered. This is the first event which will draw Detective Inspector Sandy Woodings into a whirlpool of murder and deceit.

CAROLINE MINUSCULE
Andrew Taylor

Caroline Minuscule, a medieval script, is the first clue to the whereabouts of a cache of diamonds. The search becomes a deadly kind of fairy story in which several murders have an other-worldly quality.

LONG CHAIN OF DEATH
Sarah Wolf

During the Second World War four American teenagers from the same town join the Army together. Forty-two years later, the son of one of the soldiers realises that someone is systematically wiping out the families of the four men.